# Acknowledgments

TO the talent of El Carmen's Third Street Writers, specifically: Gerald Citrin and the telegram to Madrid, Janet Gregory for her continued faith in this book, Karen Sandler for the questions that made me probe deeper, Tim Haley for his belief in Candelaria, and the deepest heartfelt gratitude to novelists Katherine V. Forrest and Jeffrey N. McMahan for sitting with me through the final prune.

Thank you.

Laurence Heath Taylor for your patience and companionship.

With unending love and gratitude to you, Gillis, without whom this project would never have started.

With love and appreciation to my oldest friend, writer Norine Dresser who introduced this novel to W. W. Norton & Company.

My thanks also to my editor Amy Cherry for reading the novel I wrote.

# First Confession

# 1

## 1947—A small Mexican town across the Texas border

ONE particular photograph best shows the difference between Victor and myself. Taken at his fourth or fifth birthday party, Victor is surrounded by every kind of toy imaginable, facing the camera, about to cry. I am next to him, claiming as many toys as possible and grimacing arrogantly.

The only two people as different as Victor and me were our fathers. In those days, Father was a beautiful wild man, powerful, lawless; his lawlessness was internal, natural. I was his true daughter.

Victor's father, Dr. Hugo Escalante, was a fine-boned man who laughed with his eyes. His quietness gave him a mysterious aura which would have kept people away except that his eyes were too filled with amusement. Victor was like that. I loved him.

Polio was a big word in those days. That summer, Victor's parents went to New York so that my uncle could study its treatment; Victor and Alicia, his maid, came to live with us in our home. Our mothers had carefully designed the summer for us.

Victor and I were to be tutored in the mornings—we had flunked the third grade. I had been unable to pass the reading test and Victor had refused to speak English to the nuns at the Ursuline Academy, the beautiful spacious Catholic school we attended on the American side. No matter how much our fathers donated to the school, the sisters wouldn't pass us until we could do the work.

To me, school was a word; Father was the world. For the first nine years of my life, he took complete control. Mother would beg Father, "Hector, Andrea must go to school." He would reply, "She's learning more from me." As a result, I was barely able to read, write, braid my hair, or tie my shoes. Mother had been able to read since she was three.

After tutoring in the mornings, our afternoons were to be dedicated to catechism classes. Our First Holy Communion was to be a big social affair at the end of the summer when his parents returned from New York.

That was the plan.

Victor was teary the day he arrived at my house and clung to his nursemaid, Alicia, who seemed as frightened as he was. He had never been separated from his parents. She had only worked in the Escalante home.

"Look, Victor, you'll sleep here, in Andrea's room," explained Mother in her broken Spanish. She was a tall, thin, blonde American—the tallest mother in town. Her name was Diane.

Victor said nothing.

Mother turned to Alicia. "The two bottom drawers are empty. You can put his clothes in there. There's plenty of space in the closet for his other things."

Mother was trying to be sweet and all Victor and Alicia did was stare at her. "Andrea, maybe it's my Spanish. Talk to Alicia."

I shrugged.

Finally Mother pried Victor's suitcase from Alicia's grasp,

laid it on the bed, opened it and started to put his clothes away. When Mother was nearly finished, Alicia stepped in and unhappily completed the task.

"There!" sighed Mother with relief. "Now Petra will show you where to put your things."

Alicia seemed shocked. "Can't I sleep here, with Victor and Andrea?"

Mother was embarrassed. "Three beds won't fit in here. Petra sleeps in the other room with the baby, and my husband and I are in our room . . ."

Alicia pleaded, "I'll sleep on the floor."

Victor blurted out, "Please, Auntie!"

Mother knelt down and held him to her chest. "You'll be fine. Your uncle and I will be up here with you. Alicia is just downstairs. You can see her anytime you want." Turning to Alicia, she explained, "There isn't any room upstairs and you'll be much more comfortable with Alma and Rosa. They're young girls like you."

Alma and Rosa were sisters who did the washing, ironing, sewing and cleaning. Petra was in charge of everything else— me, my eighteen-month-old sister, Cristina, our meals, our baths and even my parents.

Alma and Rosa were much younger than Petra. They had dark, smooth skin and flat noses; Alicia had clear, green eyes and a thin nose and her skin was almost as light as Mother's.

Petra came upstairs to take Alicia to her sleeping quarters. Slowly, reluctantly, Alicia followed, not before begging Victor, "Come with me."

The servants' room was downstairs and separate from the main house. We entered as a group, Petra, Alicia, Victor and I standing in the doorway. Instinctively, Alma and Rosa moved next to each other.

Petra said to Alma and Rosa, "This is Alicia from the Es-calante family."

The sisters moved closer together.

"She'll be staying with you while the family is away," Petra explained.

"Señor said this was our room," said Rosa.

Petra spoke sternly. "You're sharing it with Alicia for a few weeks."

No one spoke. The sisters were practically on top of each other by now. Victor and Alicia were united—arms around each other's waist. They stared at the dark-faced sisters. I drew closer to Petra.

I whispered to Petra, "Tell me what's happening."

"Go upstairs. Take Victor with you," Petra said.

Victor tugged at Alicia's hand. "Come with me."

"Go with Andrea, Victor," Petra said. She ushered us out of the room. Victor waved goodbye to Alicia.

This was the first time we had been alone since he arrived. I waited for him to talk first. He wasn't about to open his mouth. Tears were gathering in the corners of his eyes.

Later Petra came upstairs and went into Mother's room. We could hear them talking.

"Señora, maybe Alicia should stay with Victor in Andrea's room. I'll make up a pallet. There may be trouble."

"Nonsense," said Mother in a shrill voice. "It's just for a few weeks. I won't have them dictate what goes on in this house."

"Señora, remember Alicia is different. She's not from the river. Those girls don't like her."

"They just met. They'll get used to each other."

Petra insisted, "Can we ask the señor?"

"No!" Mother shouted. "This is my house too!"

I knew Mother was wrong. We all did. We also knew that she couldn't understand some things in our town. Things that were never explained—they were just known—felt.

Mother was an American. She had met Father when she was an art student in Mexico City. When they married, she

abandoned her studies, her home in Los Angeles, and, for what seemed the rest of her life, she tried to learn Spanish. Her accent, her height, caused me great shame in those early days. I was the one with the different mother, and I resented her. I was more embarrassed about her than I was about being nine years old and still stuck in the third grade.

She kept her easel, paints and sketch pad upstairs in a special room that Father had built for her. It was a bright room with many windows, but I never saw her do anything but read. She loved poetry.

"Andrea, come, listen to this," she would say in English.

"*No quiero*," I would always answer.

"But this poem is about a tiger. You'll like it," she would coax.

I first learned the feel of sadness from her. My pity was to come later.

On the day Victor came to stay with us, I felt only resentment for Mother, resentment for not listening to Petra. Next to Father, I acknowledged only Petra.

Petra was a kind, strong woman who never became impatient with Mother or me. Petra's face had thousands of smallpox scars all over it. I don't know how old she was, but she had worked for Father and his family even before my parents were married. She could read and write, do numbers and speak some English. She tried to teach Mother how things were done in our town.

Petra tried to explain to Mother why Alma and Rosa could not sleep in the same room with Alicia. Alicia was more like us. She was lighter—lighter than me—and Victor's family dressed her in clothes bought from the American side, clothes like those of the people who had maids—not like those of the people who were maids.

Alicia was tiny, her face narrow, her hands thin; Alma and Rosa dressed in clothes they had made, and their hands were

also small, but they were thick, square and their faces were broad. Alma and Rosa were from the river.

Mother saw those differences, but didn't read them. Yes, we all knew mother was wrong and there was nothing we could do. Victor would sleep without Alicia.

Alone with him in my room, we heard Petra fail to convince Mother. I looked at him and finally he released his tears.

## 2

WE lived in a town thriving with postwar prosperity. Father was one of those businessmen who made money because of the United States' involvement in the war. In some sections of town, milk and ice were still delivered in horse-drawn carts. Our family was one of the few on the Mexican side of the border that had a refrigerator.

Mother crossed the border several times a week to buy groceries from the American side. She believed they were better; our kitchen had a different smell from the rest of the families'. I guess you could say we were rich. Our friends were too.

I have no memory of meeting Victor. We were spoiled, celebrated children. Until this particular summer, our parents were pretty people who laughed daily and had big dreams of moving to Mexico City when they had made their fortune in our small border town. Our parents did everything together: dinner, parties, and always the important bullfighting circuit.

I saw the great Manolete fight in Monterrey—and according to Father, this was the most important part of my life. I learned the difference between a *paso natural*, a *verónica*, an *afarolado*, bullfighting passes Father taught me to recognize because it was important that I know them.

Victor was prettier than I. He had soft, curly hair, long dark lashes and deep-set eyes with a slight downward slant, giving him a sad, thoughtful look. He was quiet around everyone but me.

FATHER taught Victor how we played in our house. In the mornings, before shaving, he would come into the bedroom and rub his stubble across our cheeks, growling and tickling us. I loved it, was used to it, but Victor wasn't and his laugh was broken by short insecure "ows," the kind that hide fear. Afterward we would have breakfast with Father, Mother, and Cristina.

Breakfast was the noisiest part of the day as Father would talk to everyone at the same time. Cristina, the baby, would be in her high chair and he fed her directly from his plate—Mother always objected and was always ignored.

The third day of summer vacation Father asked, "What are you two up to today?"

Mother answered for us. "They're going to the tutor's."

"We've been twice this week," I said.

"Doesn't seem fair, does it? asked Father. "You're supposed to be on vacation."

"Yeah," said Victor, "we're supposed to be on vacation."

Mother stopped eating. "Hector, don't start. I promised Milita they would make up their lessons. They lost so much school last year."

"They won't learn during the summer, not when all their friends are out playing. Would you?"

"I wouldn't know. I never failed." Mother was getting tense.

Father laughed. "Well, I did. Easiest thing in the world, right?" he asked Victor and me.

"Right," we piped. We were happier by the minute. We knew what was going to happen.

Father took Mother's hand. "Seriously, Diane, this summer's going to be one of the worst. We'll send them to school in August when it gets too hot for them to be outside anyway. Besides, that will be right before school starts and it will get their heads going in that direction. Whatever they learn now they'll forget by September."

"Hector, you can't make that decision about Victor. He's not your son. We promised his parents he would go to school."

Father kissed Mother's hand, leaned over and gave her a long kiss on the mouth. Victor put his head down. I saw Father put his tongue inside Mother's mouth.

"Tell you what. I'll call Hugo today and ask his permission. That fair?" Father winked at Victor.

"If you're going to call New York, talk to Milita, not Hugo."

"Men do business with men," Father said. "Wait for me in the car, kids."

"Now what are you doing?" asked Mother.

"I'll place the call from the office. That way Victor can talk to his dad, right?" Victor got another wink.

Mother was very upset. I wasn't worried. Victor was. He kept looking at her, waiting for permission from her to leave the table and go wait in the car as Father ordered. I nudged him roughly and he followed me outside.

Father had the fastest and newest car in town. A convertible coupe—an Olds—with white interior and a white top. Everything was automatic. You pushed buttons and the windows went up. It was bright banana yellow and could be seen from very far away. Riding with Father was special; if people stopped and waved to us, he would honk one of his two horns.

One was loud, like a truck's, and the other was a whistle that chimed "Pop Goes the Weasel." Mother thought our car was vulgar, but the newspapers took a picture of me and Father in it.

We waited in the front seat for Father to come out. Victor was still nervous about leaving the table. "Is Auntie mad at me?"

"She's mad at Father. She wants us to go to school."

The screen door opened. They stood in the doorway and kissed for a long time. They did that every day—unless they had had a real fight. We saw him press hard against Mother. She always looked around to see if anyone was watching; he laughed because she worried about people seeing them. Some-times he would pull her out to his car and kiss her once again when he was in the driver's seat; it didn't matter if they were out in the street; he would do it, then speed away and we would hear "Pop Goes the Weasel" for blocks and blocks.

Sometimes our house seemed to sigh with a mixture of relief and sadness after he left.

That morning Father pressed and pressed against Mother until she laughed and pushed him away.

We went to his office and called New York. While waiting for the call to go through, Victor and I wandered through the warehouse and climbed on top of Father's trucks. In a few hours we were back home. We not only got out of summer school, we got out of having to go to catechism as well. We were free for the summer.


DON't go near the river was Father's only rule. Petra called out these words to Victor and me as we left in the mornings to roam through the town, the club, or the playground. *Don't go near the river* was such an established law that I never considered wanting to break it. There was no need to; we had

absolute license to do as we pleased because the Durcals, my father's family, were an important part of the town's history.

During the Revolution of the late twenties my grandfather, General Durcal, had brought the railroad to the town and, as I heard constantly, "made it part of the Republic." As a result of my ancestor's achievements, we were never punished for our destructive sprees. The bills were quietly passed on to my father.

Those first days of that summer Victor and I were particularly destructive. Sometimes our goal would be to do fifty bad things before lunch. We were obsessed with mischief and keeping track of our sins; we knew whatever wrongs we committed would magically disappear when we made our First Confession. The sisters at school had told us Jesus would forgive the greatest sinner if he confessed and did his penance. We felt safe.

The club our families belonged to offered the greatest opportunity. Stealing glasses from the bar and then breaking them in the parking lot, leaving faucets running in the bathroom, stuffing toilets with wash towels, stealing Lucky Strikes and getting sick trying to smoke them were pranks we considered sinful acts of bravery. We didn't do them for long; we became bored quickly, and besides, after a while, they didn't even seem bad.

Standing by the side of the road yelling obscenities to people who drove by was thrilling.

"Son of a bitch!"

"Shit eater!"

"Dogshit eater!"

"Thief!"

"Liar!"

"Killer!"

This came to a quick end. Mexico and Texas share the same summer sun and the baking heat drove us inside. Besides, we

didn't know enough profanity to make it worthwhile. We avoided the playground. It was full of friends who had passed on to the fourth grade. Our schoolmates didn't care who our parents were, nor were they interested in the number of bull-fights we had attended with our fathers. They thought we were dumb and told us so.

Indoors or outdoors, life was becoming dull until the morning Victor asked me, "Andrea, do you know how to spy?" The look on his face told me something wonderful was beginning.

He taught me how to watch people without their knowing. There was a trick to it. He could spy on anyone—Mother, Petra, anyone—and they would never turn around. I had trouble at first until he told me, "Don't think of the people when you're watching them." Sure enough, it worked. And we saw a lot about my house.

We learned that Rosa blew her nose on her apron, then looked at it for a long time. We laughed about that. We learned that Father combed his hair to cover his bald spot and then put on his hat so that his hair would stick out. Father also smiled and winked at the mirror. Victor thought that was funny. Petra plucked hairs off her chin with Mother's tweezers. We never caught Mother doing anything in secret.

Alicia, Victor's nursemaid, had become so quiet since she came to live with us that she seldom spoke even to Victor. One morning we hid under the stairway and watched as she gathered the morning dishes. We saw her stuff her mouth with all the leftovers: eggs, bread, coffee, milk, sausage. It took three, four minutes at most. She chewed fast and never took her eyes off the kitchen entrance.

After the family ate, it was customary for the maids to prepare a leisurely breakfast for themselves before they started the day's work. Petra asked Alicia to join them and she said, "No thank you. I'm not hungry." Then with a look of triumph on her face, she went upstairs to make the beds.

"Alicia's lying," I whispered to Victor.

"That's not a lie," he answered hotly. "She's not hungry. You saw her eat, didn't you?"

"Then she's a thief. She stole food from the plates."

"No one wanted it."

"Why won't she eat with them?" I was displeased that his maid wouldn't eat with mine.

"I don't know. This makes me sad. I don't want to spy here anymore. Let's go."

NEAR the house was Popeye's, a store that sold paper goods, magazines, material, crayons, ropes, mops, anything anyone could want. The shelves were stacked with canned foods; the aisles were cluttered with sacks of pinto beans, rice, garbanzo beans, peas.

Popeye's was divided into two sections. Armida, a fleshy woman who always wore bright flowered dresses, ran the front counter. The rear of the store had a pool table and bar run by her husband, Don Pancho, a dark, thick, smelly man who would let us go in and pick up cigarette butts off the floor so we could practice smoking.

He demanded that people call him *Don* Pancho and everyone did—even his wife. After his noon meal, he would go to a side section of the bar and sleep until evening. The bar stayed open long after the store was closed. While Don Pancho napped, Armida worked both sections of the store.

"You're going to turn into midgets," she would warn whenever she caught us smoking and order us out of the bar section. We would run out the side exit, then sneak back into the front to steal whatever we could while she was busy serving beer to the men playing pool. We loved stealing, especially from Popeye's.

One day while Don Pancho slept and Armida worked the

bar, we discovered some stairs which led to a loft above the store. The floor was made of rough wooden planks, with enough space between to allow us clear view of everything beneath.

The loft was dusty, full of cobwebs, but that didn't matter. From then on, we would lie on the floor and spy on people for hours. We thrilled to the dirty words of the men in the bar. We were drunk with power. We watched Armida and learned her secrets.

One afternoon during the hottest and sleepiest part of the day, three high school boys came into the store and stood around pretending to buy something. They waited until the store was empty and then, one by one, they went with Armida behind a curtain. She let them reach up her dress and go into her pants.

While they touched her she raised her head and smiled and we could see her front teeth, all of which were framed in gold. While the boys touched, squeezed, and tasted her breasts, she would flutter her fingers up and down the zipper of their pants. Once alone, she stuffed her money in a nylon stocking hidden in the center of a large coil of rope. Minutes later, she was back in the bar. Watching Armida sell touches became our favorite thing to do.

The game changed when a different type of boy came into the store. He was the same age as the rest, but he was dressed in clothes that weren't as nice. I figured he was probably from the river. He fidgeted a lot. I had the feeling I'd seen him somewhere before.

"He's scared," Victor whispered.

When Armida was alone in the store with him she asked, "Well? What do you want?" She too could tell he was not from our side of town. When he didn't answer, she added, "I haven't got all day."

He reached into his front pockets and held out money to

her. She eyed him suspiciously, shrugged, scooped up the money, and took him behind the curtain. He stood there and did nothing. Impatiently, she lifted her own dress, took his hands, and guided them into her pants. The boy pinned her against the wall and unzipped his pants. His *thing* popped out and he held it in his hands pressing between her legs. She fought, but he was strong.

Suddenly the bell in the bar rang for her. He continued jerking up and down against her until he made a grunting noise. He leaned back, out of breath, and closed his pants. She shoved him away. He pulled her by the arm and tried to kiss her. When she turned her head away, he reached up her dress and violently plunged his hand into her pants. Then he let go of her, smiled, and walked out of the store, smelling his hand.

Trembling, Armida stayed behind the curtain for a few moments. Again the bell nagged. "I'm busy!" she yelled. Her voice startled me. It was rough and husky. For some reason I felt terribly close to her. I wanted her to hurry back to the bar, but she stood there brushing some invisible stain off her dress. She put away her money and finally answered the bell.

"Andrea, let's go home," Victor said hoarsely.

"I can't move." My legs were shaking, my throat was dry, stiff, from wanting to scream.

"Hold my hand." Although his pale face was covered with sweat and his curls were stuck to his head, his eyes were shining, and that made me trust him. I followed him down the narrow stairs—both of us holding our breath until we were outside in the hot brilliant sun.

The searing heat comforted me. The brightness of the sun bleached out what we had witnessed between Armida and the boy. It was like going to see a scary movie in the afternoon and just when you start believing that the darkness of the theater and the action of the film are endless, and true, the lights come on, and outside the sun is brighter than the lights

in the movie house and the terror goes away and becomes fun.

We walked in silence. I was starting to feel giddy.

"We have to confess this," Victor said solemnly. The shine in his eyes was gone.

"Why? We didn't know what was going to happen. It's only a sin if we go back to watch."

"This is worse than stealing. This is the biggest sin we've ever done." He kept nodding his head.

"Let's go to church right now. We'll promise God we'll never go back there. Right now, let's go to church and swear." I pushed him toward the direction of the church.

He stepped away from me. "It's no good, Andrea. We have to confess this."

"Why?" I was truly scared. I knew I could never tell Padre Lozano what I had seen. He and my father were friends. Padre Lozano had baptized Cristina and me and Victor. He had blessed our house. He thought I was funny. No, I could never tell Padre Lozano about Armida and that boy.

"We should have left," continued Victor. "As soon as he opened his pants we should have run out."

"They would have seen us," I argued.

"Don't be stupid. They were behind the curtain."

"I wanted to leave."

"Don't lie, Andrea. You liked it. We both did. We were scared, but we liked it."

I screamed, "I didn't like it. I swear I didn't."

He screamed back, "Don't swear on a lie, Andrea. You'll have to confess that too."

He was right. I had liked it. I remembered the glow in his eyes and wondered if I had had such a shine. Shit, so what, I thought to myself, I still won't confess.

"We'd better ask someone else about this," I suggested.

"That's worse than telling Padre Lozano. He can't tell any-one what he hears in confession. Even if a killer tells him, he

can't tell. If he does, God would kill him in a minute, with lightning."

That gave me some consolation. Nevertheless, I was not convinced that seeing was as bad as doing. "We'll ask the maids, Alma and Rosa." Victor frowned. I ignored him and continued, "They go to church more than anyone I know. We'll ask them in a way that won't really be asking. I know how to do that."

When we got home, Petra gave us a cool tamarind drink. "You're hot," she said, placing her hands over our heads. "Have you been playing in the sun?"

I quickly answered, "We've been at the playground, in the shade."

Victor scowled at me. I could tell that he was keeping track of another lie I would have to tell Padre Lozano. A break had opened between us; I distrusted him now that he was so damn insistent on confessing everything. We stayed in the kitchen and drank our ades until Petra left. Once we were alone, I motioned Victor to follow me. Silently we tiptoed out of the kitchen and headed for Alma and Rosa's room. I wasn't allowed to bother them when they were in their room—Mother said they were entitled to their privacy. But I knew the real reason was she didn't want me near them. They were from the river and they told me stories that later gave me nightmares.

Alma was sewing and Rosa sat on the bed leafing through one of Mother's American magazines. The radio was playing and the sisters were speaking quietly to each other when we walked in. They sat up straight—as if on guard.

"Hello!" My voice was cheery but counterfeit. "Can we listen to the radio with you?"

I sat next to Rosa. Victor stood in the doorway and looked down at the floor. He was being shy, and he was making me madder and madder by the minute. I motioned him to sit next to me. I had the feeling that he was going to ruin things. I

wanted him to be friendly like me; I feared his loyalty to Alicia would keep him from talking to our maids with any kind of sincerity. Alicia was still terribly unhappy about staying with us and avoided Alma and Rosa as much as possible by staying upstairs cleaning rooms that weren't dirty.

"Come here, Victor," I insisted and patted the bed. "Come on," I urged. Reluctantly he sat next to me. It was obvious Rosa didn't want to share her bedspace with us. Still, she moved over. She had no choice.

"Will you take us to church next time you go?" I spoke to Alma, the more talkative of the two.

"Why?"

"We're getting ready to make our First Holy Communion."

"Not till *his* parents get back," snapped Alma, not bothering to mention Victor by name.

"We want to pray and light candles." I could hear my phoniness.

The sisters gave each other sidelong glances. Victor looked at me and I realized I wasn't doing very well.

Victor took over. "We don't know what to confess." He spoke with his eyes cast down.

"You confess *all* your sins. When you receive Christ there can't be the tiniest sin on your soul, and you can't eat any-thing, not even water. That morning tell Petra to tape your mouth when she gives you a bath so that no water creeps into you before Jesus enters your body." Alma stared intensely at me.

The image of the boy rubbing himself against Armida's body flashed into my mind. I shook my head violently.

"We already know about fasting," said Victor. "The sisters taught us all about that." He sighed impatiently and whispered, "Andrea, let's go."

Alma heard him. "Well then, ask your teachers. Why bother us?" Her face puffed out.

I wasn't about to be sent out of the room, not by them, not yet, not while there was the slightest chance they might tell us we wouldn't have to confess what we had seen at Armida's.

"We're not sure if we have to tell if we *see* sins happening," Victor said.

Rosa turned off the radio; Alma put down her sewing. We weren't prepared for such attention.

"What sins?" Alma questioned Victor directly. "What sins have you seen happening?"

Victor stammered. "Just some sins, lies, at school. If people lie and we know they're lying, do we have to confess that too? Does their sin come off on us?"

I wanted to kill him. He might as well have told them the whole thing. I glared at him but he didn't look up. All three of us stared at him as he sat there, digging his nails into the palms of his hands and rubbing his feet against each other. He looked so damn guilty.

The silence made me nervous. I tried turning the radio back on, but Alma stopped me and whispered tightly to us, "When people see bad things and don't confess, their eyes dry up. First they won't be able to cry, then one morning, they won't be able to see. Their eyes will just dry up and get as hard as beans. When people go around hearing bad things and don't confess them, their ears close up. The sides of their heads get as flat as tortillas. And if you ever hit your mother, your hand will dry up and wither away until it finally falls off."

We exploded into a chorus of tears. I didn't know about Victor, but I knew I had done all those things. I had even hit my mother. Although I was only four at the time, Mother had seen to it that I knew.

A strong firm voice ordered, "Get upstairs. Immediately!" Petra stood in the doorway. We ran without looking back. Petra slammed the door shut; I could hear her scolding Alma and Rosa. Victor and I didn't dare stop; we ran up to my room

and flung ourselves on our beds. Victor cried miserably into his pillow.

LATER, I said to Victor, "All right, we'll confess. Don't be mad at me, okay?" I was lying, but all I wanted was for us to be together again. He was tired and nodded.

He sighed sadly. "I want my parents."

He went looking for Alicia and brought her back into my room. Their arms wrapped tightly around each other, they both looked terribly unhappy.

For the rest of the afternoon the three of us sat there looking at the beautiful pictures in my Little Golden Books. Victor and I couldn't read much; Alicia couldn't read English, but the pictures helped us. A sort of bond grew between us that afternoon. We were a strange lot: two nine-year-old outcasts on their way to hell—blind from seeing evil, and deaf from hearing it—and a pretty, fair-skinned maid—shunned by the dark sisters downstairs. My thoughts filled with Armida.

Near dinnertime Mother came home. Petra, urgency written across her face, met Mother outside. They went upstairs to Mother's room and spoke in whispers for a long time. Then Petra went to Alma and Rosa's room. Victor and I watched from the stairway, the same place where we had spied on Alicia only a few days ago.

Petra came back into the living room and sat down. She looked tense and uncomfortable. Eventually Alma and Rosa showed up, carrying their belongings in two hemp bags. Petra took money from her apron and handed it to Alma. No one said a word, even after Petra searched their bags and took out the radio, some of Mother's nylon underwear, the crucifix that had hung in their room, and a clock. Petra opened the front door and the sisters left.

Confused, we went searching for Mother; she was in her

studio, reading. My sister was with her. Mother held her arms out to us. "My babies, are you all right?"

It sounded dumb because I knew she had already been told; I went into her arms anyway. She always felt so cool, even on hot days.

"Did Alma and Rosa frighten you?" she asked.

"Yes, Auntie," Victor said.

I nodded in agreement.

"Everything's all right now," she reassured us.

"Where did they go?" I asked.

"They left."

"It's because of us," I said, feeling guilty.

"And other reasons."

"What other reasons?" I insisted.

"Don't start, Andrea. Everything is fine. Listen, how would you two like to have your dinner upstairs? I'll read you a story."

"First tell me where Alma and Rosa went," I demanded.

Her voice was beginning to shrill. "Home. They went home."

I didn't want to hear that. I didn't want to know that because of me, Alma and Rosa would have to sleep at the river, the place where people from our side of town went to get servants.

The first day Alma and Rosa came to work for us Father had promised, "Girls, you'll never live at the river again."

Petra bathed me; Alicia bathed Victor. In the evening Mother came in carrying milk and peanut butter and jelly sandwiches. She always removed the crust and then cut them into quarters. Victor loved the tiny white squares—squares made of bread that came from the American side.

Mother put the tray down on the floor and the three of us sat in the center of the room to have dinner. Mother told us a story which was enough for me to forget Alma, Rosa, and Armida.

She told us a tale of revenge, a story of a young, handsome prince who had to solve the murder of his father. Convincingly, Mother acted out the parts of the uncle who had murdered his brother, the king, and then married the queen. She also played the part of the ghost of the dead king, and of the prince's sweetheart who drowned. The father of the prince was murdered by his brother, who poured poison in his ear while he slept.

It was a wonderful, terrible story. The prince solved the murder, but was himself killed in a duel. As the prince died, Victor was again brought to tears for a second time that day. Ecstatic with the success of her performance, Mother tucked us in and blessed us with good wishes: "May flights of angels sing thee to thy rest."

For a long time we twisted and turned, trying to figure out a way to sleep so that poison couldn't be poured in our ears. No matter how we moved, one ear remained exposed. I feared being alone and awake, so every time Victor started falling asleep, I poked my finger in his ear to remind him that he was in danger. Finally, he whispered angrily, "Leave me alone! No matter what you say, we still have to confess everything."

I discovered that I was too tired to argue and gave myself over to sleep, not caring about my ears, my soul, Alma and Rosa, Armida and the River boy who had pressed her against the wall. Yes, it was my fault that Alma and Rosa were back at the river, and if they wanted to pour poison in my ear, I deserved it.

# 3

THEY'RE poor," he seethed. He walked into the bathroom and slammed the door so hard the windows rattled.

No one had to tell us twice to get dressed that morning. Mother came in my room. She was embarrassed with Victor. "Your uncle is upset this morning. He's not mad at you, or at you, Andrea. Come down for breakfast. Put away your pajamas. We all have to help Petra and Alicia now that the other two girls are gone." She spoke in rushed, quiet tones.

I shook—heavy with guilt. I knew everything had happened because I had insisted on talking to Alma and Rosa about confession. I remained silent.

With a long, sad face, Petra served us breakfast. I hugged her and she pressed my head to her stomach and kissed me. "I hate it when he yells at you," I whispered.

"Shhh. It's all right," she said, giving Victor an affectionate pat on the back. She saw Father coming downstairs and hurried to the kitchen.

Mother stayed upstairs with my sister that

morning, so it was just Father, Victor and me at the table. I could smell liquor from the night before on Father's breath. It was a familiar smell.

Maybe twice a week he would come home with that smell and sometimes Mother and Petra would have to help him up the stairs, undress him, and put him to bed. On those occasions his arrivals were very noisy. One night he parked the car on the neighbors' lawn.

My parents had had a big fight about that. Mother threatened to return to Los Angeles. But Father always found a way to make her laugh and forgive him; this was a power she did not have. When Mother was really angry at him, Father would arrive at dawn with mariachis, and serenade Mother from the street. Then Petra and Mother would have to cook breakfast for the nine or eleven mariachis.

Father's noisy nights were usually followed by silent mornings. Father would barely speak during breakfast and if he did, he would ask very precise questions like "Why is the clock in the kitchen five minutes fast?"

This was such a morning; Father spoke to no one. Though we were finished with breakfast, we were afraid to leave and attract attention to ourselves. We sat there, pushing cold eggs back and forth, until he finished eating and shouted, "Petra! Come in here!" He didn't wait for her to come to him. He threw his chair back against the wall and stormed into the kitchen. "Go find them. Bring them back. They're staying here until we find another family for them to work for."

We ran upstairs and hid in my room. Even though we didn't read, we sat with books on our laps. It seemed like a respectable thing to do. We could hear him speaking brusquely to Mother as he prepared to leave for work. Doors slammed upstairs, then downstairs, then we heard his yellow car roar off.

After he left, the house went through its usual settling pe-

riod. Mother and Petra had another of their secret conferences; then Petra left the house shortly thereafter.

"I bet she's going to the river," whispered Victor.

"Let's follow her."

"You're crazy, Andrea. Your father would whip us. He'd tell my dad and he'd whip me too."

"If we followed Petra we really wouldn't be going alone," I argued. "It's our only chance to see what's there. Besides, there's nothing else to do around here. We can't go to the playground or to Popeye's." He was giving in. "It would be like spying, and we're only going this one time."

In less then five minutes we were watching Petra as she stood on the corner waiting for the bus whose route ended at the border bridge that separated Mexico from the United States. At the border Petra would have to walk upstream through shanties that line the river. We made sure she got on the bus, then started walking north, past Popeye's, past the club, past the main highway, and then across several muddy lots and finally, we arrived.


THE banks of the Río Bravo were lined with tiny shacks inhabited by people from the interior of Mexico who came hoping for a better life on the American side. They had no other place to live; the Mexican side of the river could not employ the hundreds who left their homes for the border. They made it to the river and got stuck there.

The river spawned disease and violence, and Victor and I and other children from our side of town had been warned to stay away. I never thought of disobeying Father until Alma and Rosa were sent back because of me. I had to see where they had gone.

When Alma and Rosa first came to work for us, they told me that people sometimes threw unwanted babies into the

river. One spring, when the river flooded its banks, people drowned in their sleep. In the morning their corpses floated down the current. According to Alma and Rosa, the river ripped their clothes right off their bodies. People could see them dead and naked.

Alma told me of a man whose family was starving after the flood. He went out to the river and lassoed a dead cow that was floating by and slit its belly open. He fed the meat to his wife and children and all night the family screamed with pain and by morning they were all dead, including the baby who had not eaten any meat but had taken milk from the mother. Both Alma and Rosa had sworn everything was true; reluctantly Petra confirmed it.

We arrived before Petra. From a block away, we spotted the American hat Mother had given her. The river people were washing and eating; never had we seen so many people in such a small place. We watched Petra weave in and out of the shanties, probably asking for Alma and Rosa's whereabouts; we moved parallel to her, carefully staying out of her vision. Before long, we lost interest in Petra's mission and became immersed in the river world.

"It smells like shit," said Victor, cupping his hand over his nose.

Mounds of garbage, empty cans of food, fruit peelings, old shoes, scraps of clothing, and yellowed newspapers separated the shacks. The piles were nearly as tall as we were and people were pouring kerosene over them, trying to set them afire. Some lit, some didn't. Wherever there was a bonfire, there were dozens of children standing around watching the flames, looking for something to throw into the blaze. Mesmerized by the flames, we loitered with the river children.

All of them were barefoot. Many of the boys wore only a shirt; all the girls were dressed. I had never seen naked boys my age, Victor was so private, and I kept trying to peek beneath

their shirts to see what they looked like. Theirs was smaller, bouncier, compared to the one we had seen at Armida's.

"I know what you're thinking," said Victor. "You're think-ing of that boy, Smelly Hands."

I laughed. Victor always gave people the best names. "Yes, aren't you?"

"Not like you. I don't have to. I'm a boy," he sneered.

That made me mad. "Shut up, Victor. You don't fuck yet."

His older cousins had taught us the word at Easter when we saw two stuck dogs crying outside the movie house. Still, he was shocked to hear me use the word. I was too. I had never used it out loud before. Somehow being at the river made it all right, and it felt good to say it. "Shit" was usually the worst word. That day I discovered "fuck" had a power "shit" didn't have.

We moved farther along the river, and I realized we had lost sight of Petra. I panicked.

"Look," Victor said, pointing toward the bridge which sep-arated Mexico and the United States. "We just walk back there, and then go down that way."

I followed his gaze toward the bridge and saw that the American riverbanks were clean, smooth, their sides cemented. Victor's ability to calm me made me feel close to him again. He said the river smelled like shit, but it really smelled like dogs, wet, dirty dogs. They were everywhere—many of them were pregnant, swollen, their ribs protruding against their sides; black teats hung down from their bellies. The bitches nosed through the garbage. If they stayed around too long someone would grunt angrily at them and the dogs quickly dodged away.

We continued walking along the banks of the river, still trying to find Petra. She had disappeared.

"We've gone too far," I said. "Let's start back."

"Not yet, look!" he yelled, pointing to a valley of colors.

Ceramic cats, dogs, bulls, matadors, horsemen, Spanish dancers, and guitars of silver, green, bright pink, red, gold, blue, and white all crowded together on carts. Until that moment, all we had seen was women, children, and dogs. Now we saw men, the vendors who hoped to peddle their wares to American tourists who visited Mexico, gathered around the burning piles. Although it promised to be a boiling day, the men held their hands out to the fire, as their children had done earlier. Some drank from brown clay cups; others ate beans and tortillas.

I had seen these men follow cars and people—energetically trying to sell piggy banks in all sizes and designs. The men looked different at the river. They were quiet, serious, and spat a lot. We watched them carefully take goods out of boxes. They dusted the dark clay cups, fluffed the feathers of birds, and arranged piggy banks according to size. Later that day these men would be in the town plaza in their corner stands; their voices would be cheerful, playful, musical.

We watched them for a while, then walked on and on until we came to a very different part of the river. No women or children were here. There were only lone men with stubble, dressed in ragged clothing. This end of the river was silent. The fires barely came up to their knees. They fed small pieces of driftwood into the flames; they had no garbage to burn. The men stood with their arms folded tightly around themselves. It didn't make sense. It was still early; I was already feeling the heat of the day, yet these men seemed cold.

I looked at Victor and made the sign which meant these men were drunks. It was a gesture we had learned from the maids whenever our fathers came home drunk. The little finger and thumb were extended and the rest of the fingers were curled down into the palm; then they moved their hand to their mouth to simulate a bottle being drained down the throat.

I singled out one of the men to Victor. He was Rancho Grande, the most famous bum in town. He was a lot taller

than the rest; his coloring was light; his hair was white with blond. No one shared Rancho Grande's fire. Squatting, he stared into the flames; his eyes were blue and his broad, wild beard was striped with gray strands. He stroked it with long, thin fingers.

Rancho Grande worked the streets near my house. On Thursdays when the maids took out the trash, he would come by, a long hemp bag strung over his shoulders, and go through our bins, methodically inspecting every item; he neatly put back everything he didn't want. He never left a mess. This was one of the reasons Mother and Petra never shooed him away.

Another reason was his fair skin and thin, delicate hands, hands Mother insisted were those of an artist "defeated by life."

"Defeated by the bottle is more like it," Father would say. Yet if he was home on the evenings Rancho Grande came by, Father would go out to give him money. I would go with him; it was thrilling to get close to Rancho Grande, but I was puzzled by his lack of gratitude. Although he accepted money, food, and clothing, he never said thank you. The maids said that he was really very rich and had a treasure buried somewhere in his shack by the river.

Rancho Grande saw me pointing him out to Victor. He stood up and started walking toward us. As he got closer, he made the same hissing sound river people made at stray dogs who dug through garbage. "Sssstt! Sssstt!" We failed to move and he started throwing small pebbles at us; they landed at our feet. He got closer. "Sssstt! Sssstt!" The stones continued to fall around us.

"Don't you know me?" I yelled and pointed to my face. His blue eyes gave no sign that he knew me, but when he got closer to us he whispered, "Canales, Canales," and threw a few more rocks near us. Canales was the street I lived on.

We ran back the way we had come and slowed down only when we got back to the vendors. The scene was familiar, only now there was more activity along the river. The noise had increased; more children were awake; more men were standing around drinking hot liquid from clay cups.

Peddlers were parceling out their items to boys barely older than we were. We had seen these boys, these young salesmen, when we came out of the movies. "*Mire, mire*," they would cry, shaking puppets and Cantinflas dolls at me. I never noticed what they were selling, but I often felt strange being called "child" by boys barely older than me.

We kept walking and I looked for Petra, who was nowhere to be seen. I saw women wash clothes by beating them against the rocks clustered around the banks of the river. The dog smell was heavier.

Finally we arrived to where we had first waited for Petra. We saw streams of children running toward a particular shack. We followed them. A man about the size of my father was holding a puppy by its front legs and shaking it up and down. The puppy was yelping.

With his free hand, the man was twisting the puppy's head back and forth. The man could make the puppy cry as loudly as he wanted just by shaking it up and down, and he could control its tone just by moving its head. Playing with the radio, Victor and I had often achieved the same effect by moving the station dials horizontally while at the same time raising and lowering the volume.

The children watched and responded to the sound of the puppy's cries. They laughed as the man was laughing. How could that little baby—barely ten inches long—make those terrible sounds?

I reached out to grab Victor, but was shoved away by a boy I had never seen. I looked around and realized I was surrounded by children who were laughing or just staring at the man. Victor had disappeared.

Whatever pity I felt for the dog was nothing compared to the fear I felt at finding myself alone. Frantically, I pushed my way through the crowd, away from the sounds, away from the river, through the muddy lots which I hoped led back to town. Halfway across the lots, I could still hear the animal's screams. I ran faster. I saw the highway, crossed it, and I was finally free from the smells and sounds of the river.

The lots were dry on this side of the highway. I could see the town, the well-formed letters on top of its buildings, and I was grateful for the cement on the streets. I saw the big sign of the club, the club that we had so quickly outgrown those first two weeks of summer, and knew Victor would be there.

He was sitting on the seesaw that was in the children's area in back of the club. His face had a sad, thoughtful look, a look I had come to recognize as being particularly his but which I did not understand. I walked up to him and sat on the same side of the seesaw. When he looked like that, I usually waited for him to talk first because if I pressed him, he would close up for a long time. That day I didn't care.

"You left me," I accused.

He stared down at his shoes; they were full of vomit, mud and dog shit. He was wearing short pants and dry puke caked his legs from the calves on down. His socks, laces and shoes were stiff, encrusted with a dry layer of breakfast. Only when I sat down beside him did the fumes reach me.

I jumped away from him. "You stink!"

"Look at your feet. They're full of it too!" he yelled.

He was right. My shoes were so thick with mud and dog excrement that there was no division between my heel and the rest of my sole.

"Well, at least I didn't vomit," I said.

"We both stink."

Other children were standing around staring at us, waiting to use the seesaw. Victor glared at them, then got up. I wiped my shoes on the wooden section of the board where they would

have to sit if they wanted to use the seesaw. He did the same.

We entered the restaurant and bar section of the club, looking for Tony, the waiter who always waited on our families. I trusted him, maybe because like Petra, he had countless smallpox scars on every section of his face. He was smoking a cigarette and talking idly to the bartender. He saw us, waved, and walked over.

"Where have you two devils been?" he asked cheerfully.

"Hi, Tony."

His smile faded when he saw our feet. "You're a mess," he said. "You can't stay in the dining room."

Taking us by the hand, he led us to the rear of the restaurant and called to one of the busboys, "Rodrigo, get me a knife from the kitchen." He turned to us. "Where have you two been?"

"Playing," said Victor, looking miserable.

"Where? In the water? What water? Have you been at the river?"

"No," we answered.

"Only the river has any mud this time of year." He stared at us as if expecting some sort of explanation. We said nothing.

The busboy arrived carrying a big knife. Tony ordered him, "Cut that mess off their shoes. I'll get a bucket of water and wash off their legs."

I looked toward the busboy. An involuntary gasp escaped from me. Standing next to us, dressed in black pants and a white shirt, was Smelly Hands. When Victor looked up, he too gasped. That confirmed it; it was the boy we had seen with Armida the day before.

"Raise your leg," he told Victor.

Victor looked up to Smelly Hands and the knife. "I don't want to," he mumbled, casting a glance at me.

"I don't want to clean that mess either, but I have to," said Smelly Hands. Without waiting, he leaned over, raised Vic-

tor's leg and began slicing off the mud. Victor hopped on one leg, making it nearly impossible for Smelly Hands to do the job well. "Better give me your shoes, you too," he snapped at me.

Obediently we gave him our shoes and stood in silence as he cleaned them.

Tony returned carrying towels and a pail of water. "Stand over there," he said. Carefully he washed our legs down. He and Smelly Hands finished at the same time.

"Thank you, Tony," Victor said.

"Thank you, Tony," I echoed.

"Thank Rodrigo too," said Tony, frowning at us.

"Thanks," we stammered reluctantly.

I didn't enjoy being rude to Smelly Hands. It was just that I didn't like him to touch anything that belonged to me, even if it was a pair of dirty shoes. I knew the kind he was. I knew where he put his hands. The two men stood over us watching as we put on our shoes.

"I don't know how to tie my shoes," I confessed.

"I'll do it," Smelly Hands said to Tony, and bent down beside me. His fingers were stubby, and strong. I could smell the brilliantine on his hair. He tied my laces a lot tighter than Petra.

"Now you can go into the dining room," said Tony, handing towels, pail, and knife to Smelly Hands. "Come on, you two, cheer up." Tony picked us up and carried us inside. Victor and I smiled for the first time in hours. We wrapped our arms around Tony's neck. We must have been a heavy load; his neck muscles were sticking out and his face was red, but he took us all the way to a clean table.

"Now, what'll it be?"

"Two 7-Ups," I said.

"With lots of cherries," added Victor.

"Coming right up."

"I hope he brings them to us—not Smelly Hands," whispered Victor, even though Tony was out of sight.

"Me too," I said, holding my nose and making a gagging sound. We laughed.

"When I saw him at Armida's yesterday, I knew I'd seen him before."

"You didn't see him here," argued Victor. "I'd have recognized him too."

"Where else would I have seen him?"

"I don't know. We'll ask Tony."

"Ask Tony what?"

Victor became impatient with me. "Ask him how long Smelly Hands has worked here."

"You ask him. I know I saw him *here*," I stated.

Our 7-Ups arrived, two very tall glasses crowned with red cherries.

"Tony, Victor wants to ask you something," I said.

"Tony, Andrea wants to ask you something," Victor said, imitating my voice.

"No, he does," I said.

"She does."

"He—"

"Stop!" shouted Tony. "What's the matter with you today? I've got work to do. Ask me whatever you want."

We looked at each other and I began talking slowly. "We want to know . . ." That was as far as I was willing to go. I looked at Victor.

". . . if the boy who . . ." He looked at me.

". . . cleaned our shoes . . ." His turn.

". . . is new," Victor finished.

"That's it?"

"Yes."

"Two days. Rodrigo has been with us two days. Any more big questions?" We shook our heads. "Now, who's going to sign the check?"

"I will," Victor offered. Tony placed the tab in front of him. In very, very tiny writing he wrote, "Victor Escalante."

"Thank you, sir," Tony said politely. "And don't go where you shouldn't," he added emphatically.

We put our mouths over our straws and didn't look up until he was gone. "He knows we went to the river," I said. "What if he tells?"

"He won't," said Victor. "Andrea, you lied again, didn't you?"

"About Smelly Hands?" I asked, knowing full well what he meant.

"Yes. You lied. You said you'd seen him before and you haven't. You just lie and lie." He had a look of superiority on his face.

"Victor, I have seen him before. Maybe not here, but I have seen that boy somewhere. Look, I swear to you." I made the sign of the cross, saying, "I swear by Jesus Christ that I have seen Smelly Hands before."

He pointed an accusing finger. "You're going to have more than me to confess. That's for sure."

Meaning every word, I said, "Victor, sometimes I hate you so much."

He shrugged. "Sometimes I double hate you."

We sipped our 7-Ups in silence. Once in a while Smelly Hands would pass by our table. He never looked at us; he carried water and stuff to various tables. Always we were careful not to look at him.

"Let's go," said Victor finally. "I don't like being near him. We'll go to your house."

I agreed, knowing full well there was no other place for us to go to. Secretly, I wanted to return to the river. I wasn't finished looking at everything, but I knew that Victor wouldn't go back—at least not yet. And I knew why.

Victor's family loved dogs. The previous year his father had stayed home from the hospital three days to save their dog,

Dinosauro, who had been hit by a taxi. Victor was allowed to stay home from school and, so that I could be with him, Father had let me stay home too. My parents fought a lot over my missing school, Mother insisting that I couldn't afford to miss another day, Father contending that my place was with my friend.

For three days Victor and I watched his father hover over Dinosauro. The Escalante living room had been turned into a hospital with two nurses taking care of their pet day and night. Later on, Mother talked about newspaper articles which had criticized my uncle for making such a big deal about a dog. Dinosauro lived, at least until Victor's birthday party, when a bee stung him on the nose and killed him.

We left the club and slowly walked home. As we passed Popeye's, I had the urge to go in to check how things were going. I didn't dare mention it for fear of setting Victor off about confessing all over again.

"She's the richest woman in town," he said, aiming his thumb toward the store.

"What about Rancho Grande?"

"He's not richer than *her*," he said with assurance.

"The maids say he's the richest man in town," I countered, remembering how many times I had seen Father go out to give him folding money. "My father gives him lots of money."

"So what?" he asked angrily. "More boys go touch Armida than people give money to Rancho Grande. Anyway, my father gives him money too."

I had seen many boys touch Armida, but had only seen Victor's father and mine give money to Rancho Grande, so maybe Victor was right. Still, I added, "Alma and Rosa say he has a huge treasure."

"They're liars," he said. "Like you."

"Victor, remember you're easy to beat up," I warned. That ended that argument.

WE entered my house through the back door. Alicia was washing the kitchen walls. She would not acknowledge either our entrance or our greeting. She looked upset about something. We walked through the house into the living room. Alma and Rosa were sitting on the couch, which was usually reserved for company. Something was wrong.

Mother was on the phone talking in English; Petra sat on a chair, my baby sister asleep in her arms. We joined them, trying to be as inconspicuous as possible. I looked at Petra and she put her index finger across her mouth asking for silence. I smiled at Alma and Rosa; they looked past me, their eyes dead.

". . . I already called them. They don't need anybody either. . . . No, they won't work separately. . . . Call me if you hear of any openings." Mother hung up and sighed loudly. She saw us. "Where have you two been?"

"At the club with Tony."

"All this time?"

"Call him. I swear to God." I was swearing again; I could feel Victor's stare.

Mother dialed another number from her phone book. "Hello, Tina, this is Diane Durcal. . . . Fine, just fine. Listen, Tina, by chance you aren't in need of two girls, are you? They're very good. . . . Sure, I understand. Maybe we'll see each other Saturday. Yes, it should be fun."

In midafternoon Petra fed us in the kitchen. We ate alone. Mother didn't eat, tied to the telephone—neither did Alma and Rosa, rooted to the couch. After lunch, we stayed around the house—I didn't want to stray too far because I could feel something was going to happen.

Mother was on the phone all afternoon, telling people how

wonderful Alma and Rosa were. They could be trusted with everything; they came from a nice family. Well yes, they were from the river, but they could read, sew, cook, iron. She just had to find a good home for these girls. "A good home like yours," I heard her add as the day progressed.

In a way it was all true, but in a way it was all lies. I had seen them do all those things Mother said they did. Yet Mother never mentioned why they had been fired, nor that they had been caught stealing underwear, a crucifix, a radio, and a clock.

I wondered how they felt listening to Mother talk about them. I saw them lower their heads. They reminded me of a bull that had been weakened by the lance of a picador. Like the injured bull, the two women stood fast—braced for the next attack.

I blurted out, "Why don't we just keep them?"

Mother exploded at me. "Get upstairs now!"

When Father came home near suppertime, his mood was better. He had honked "Pop Goes the Weasel" for several blocks. Victor and I greeted him at the door.

For the second time that day Victor and I were lifted off our feet. Father bit us under the chin and tousled Victor's hair and pulled playfully at my braids, using the ends to tickle my nose. The laughter was short-lived. We were put down as soon as he assessed the situation. He nodded politely to the maids; Mother seemed to wilt under his glare.

"Hector," she said weakly in English, "I've called all day—called the Mexican and American sides. I can place one, but not two, and they refuse to be separated."

"I'll make some calls after dinner," he said. "Girls, take your things and go wait in your old room for now."

They picked up their hemp bags and left. Their faces were dark masks. Why had I insisted that they talk to us about confession?

That night we ate in three shifts. Petra and Alicia served

the family. No one spoke about Alma and Rosa, who remained in their old room. Then Petra and Alicia ate. Then, when everyone was finished, and maybe for the first time that day, Alma and Rosa were fed.

Mother, Alicia and Petra busied themselves with Cristina, Victor and me, making sure that we bathed and got ready for bed. Victor tried talking to Alicia, but she was unreachable. The young maid moved like an automaton doing only what was expected from her and offering nothing more. I watched Victor try to hold her hand. She pulled it back. He tried several times; always she resisted.

That night Mother told us a story about some young lovers whose parents hated each other. We weren't paying attention. All of us were straining to hear whatever bits of conversation drifted in from downstairs. It was obvious that Father was failing as Mother had failed that afternoon.

Father came in. His face was sweaty. "No luck. I'll try again in the morning."

Quickly Mother brought the story to a bloody end and kissed us good night. Then we heard my parents arguing because Father had told Alma and Rosa they could stay in the house overnight. At one point, Petra was called into their bedroom and Father talked to her. Petra must have said the wrong thing, because suddenly Father was screaming at her too. Father got his way. Alma and Rosa were to sleep in the living room and the house was finally quiet.

It was a strange silence. The feel of my house was not quite right. A dark invisible movement was somewhere, but the memories of the river overshadowed any other concern I might have had.

When we were alone I confessed to Victor, "I want to go back to the river."

"The river's a bad place. I wish I'd never gone."

"You're afraid because of the dog, aren't you?"

"And the smell and the people."

"They don't hurt puppies every day. If they did, would people be running up to see it?" I knew I had him.

"I guess not."

"Remember how fun it was spying on people around here?" He laughed and I pressed further. "Imagine all we'd see at the river."

"No, Andrea, it's dirty."

"Just at first," I insisted. "I want to see it again, slower this time. I want to spy. No one's afraid of anything down there. They just do things."

"They do things we shouldn't know about. They're dirty."

"The women wash clothes."

"They're dirty in other ways," he said with finality.

I wasn't about to give up. "What about Rancho Grande? Let's spy on him. Maybe we could steal his treasure."

"He has no treasure, Andrea. Besides, he threw rocks at us." He paused for a moment. His voice gathered strength as he added, "I'd rather take Armida's money. We know where she keeps it."

Lying there in the darkness, I thought that if I opened my eyes wide enough, I would be able to see his face. I wanted so badly to see his face at that moment.

"Victor, what a great idea! If we had our own money we could do anything—go to the plaza and buy toys from those men we saw at the river today."

"No, Andrea. Someone would ask where we got them and then we'd have to lie."

"So what? We'll confess that at the end of summer. What's the difference?"

"We'd have to keep lying every time we came home with something new. They'd catch us."

"You mean you don't want to steal Armida's money?"

"I do. We know it's there. Besides," he added slowly, "it's sin money. It's not really hers."

"It is too! It's more hers than Rancho Grande's. His would be better to steal—more exciting." I wanted to argue that going down to the river would be better than stealing Armida's money out of the coil of rope; I didn't. While he was talking about how we would spend our money, I fell asleep.

# 4

IT was early morning when we heard Petra scream over and over from inside my parents' room, "*Venga, señor, Dios mío, Dios mío!*" I ran into the hallway.

My parents' bedroom door flew open and Father raced down.

"Diane, stay here," he ordered Mother.

She didn't and neither did Victor and I, even though she tried to push us back into my room. Mother, Victor, and I rushed through the living room. It was a shambles. But we didn't stop, for the uproar was in the back—in the maids' quarters.

Father looked in and cried loudly, "*Dios mío, no! Por qué?*" He covered his eyes. He grabbed Mother to stop her from looking in. She screamed and Father threw his arms around her and buried her head into his shoulder and carried her back into the house. Victor and I saw Alicia lying in bed with a big hole in her throat. Blood soaked the sheets and blankets. Her mouth was wide open.

I felt a strong pull on my arm. Petra was fiercely dragging us out of the room.

"Is she dead?" I asked.

"Is she dead?" Victor echoed. "Is she? *Tell me*, is she dead?"

He struggled against Petra and threw himself onto the kitchen floor in a wild effort to return to Alicia's room.

"Come with me," she begged him.

Tears streamed down Petra's face. I could feel her pain and helped her to restrain Victor. He kicked violently, his foot catching her across the face. I threw myself on him. With strength I never knew he had, he hurled me off.

Then Father was there, pinning down Victor's shoulders. Father ordered Petra and me to Mother's room. He then shook Victor. "Stop that, Victor! I need you."

Her eyes swollen shut from crying, her mouth quivering in nervous spasms, Mother tried to calm down the shrieking Cristina, who had absorbed the hysteria in the house. Petra wrested the baby from her.

Mother turned to me. "Are you all right, Andrea?" Her trembling hands touched me all over.

"Yes." I held down her hands; their shaking scared me.

"*Cálmese, señora. Las niñas*," said Petra.

Mother took hold of herself. "Where's your daddy?"

"Downstairs with Victor. He wants to go back in there."

"Victor? Did he? Did you see?"

I nodded.

"Oh Andrea, you didn't go in, did you?"

"Just a little." Mother hugged me. I asked, "Is she really dead?"

"Yes, my baby," she whispered. "Poor Victor. We have to put a call through to New York. What will his parents say? What will I say?" She trembled again.

I looked toward Petra, and she took charge. "You must dress, señora." She took Mother's hand and guided her to the bathroom. "Help me, Andrea. Dress yourself."

"I'll dress Cristina too," I offered.

"No, dress yourself and wait for me in your room." She kissed me. "I'll braid your hair later."

I crossed the hall and cautiously peeked downstairs. There were no signs of Father or Victor. I did as I was told. I got dressed and waited. I wondered if Alicia had had time to scream. Maybe she had been screaming all the while they were cutting her. Was that why her mouth was open? Had they used a kitchen knife? I hoped Mother would throw them all away. Alicia was small and thin; she must have died quickly. I felt bad for her—but not bad enough—not as bad as everyone else in the house. I felt sorrier for bulls. They bled a long time. I decided to make a pity list.

Victor was first on my pity list. I remembered how sick he had been seeing the man with the puppy. What would he do about Alicia? I wished his parents were home so that they could comfort him. Sadly I wondered if our plans to steal treasure—anyone's—would be abandoned.

After serious reflection I put myself next on the list. If Victor's parents didn't come home he would get a lot of attention from everyone and I would be left out.

Next on my pity list was Father, because he had made Petra bring Alma and Rosa back, and then had insisted that they sleep in the house. I put Mother after Father on the list. I knew she would be sick and trembling for a while, but Father would be real nice to her and take her places and buy her all kinds of new things. And last was Petra, whom I loved more than anyone. She was the strongest so that made her the one I felt least sorry for.

The sound of screeching brakes, then male voices interrupted my thoughts. I opened my door and saw Dr. Salas, the other doctor in town, following Petra upstairs. She knocked lightly on Mother's door before entering.

I tiptoed down the stairway. Father was in the living room with strangers—men in uniform and other men—no sign of

Victor anywhere. They spoke in low, hurried voices. Two men walked through with a stretcher carrying Alicia. She was covered with a sheet. All I could see was a few strands of hair.

I remembered her light eyes.

I ran back upstairs, through Mother's studio and then out to the balcony that faced the street. I had a clear view of everything.

The men pushed through the crowd which had gathered in front of the house. "Move back," said one. A neighbor tried to lift up the sheet and was roughly pushed away. They slid Alicia's body into the van and slammed its back doors.

"*Quién és?*" asked members of the crowd curious to know who it was.

An old woman who didn't even live on our street chased the ambulance driver to ask him, "*És la americana?*" He didn't answer her. How could he let anyone think *that* was my mother? Stupid man!

"*No es mi mamá! No es mi mamá!*" I hollered. I yelled at the crowd with all my strength, but they ignored me. The van slowly inched through the crowd, and drove away.

Furious, ignoring Petra's plea to wait for her, I rushed downstairs to the living room calling for Father. He found me immediately.

"The people outside think Mother's dead!"

"What?"

"I heard them from the balcony. They asked, '*Es la americana?*'"

"I'll talk to them." His voice was hoarse.

A policeman stepped forward. "I'll talk to them, Señor Durcal," he offered. Father nodded gratefully.

"Listen, everyone," the policeman shouted from the front steps. "There's nothing here to see. The family is all right. *All* the family is all right. The maids had a fight. One girl is dead. We are investigating. Go home."

"Where's Victor?" I asked.

"Resting in my study."

"Can I see him?"

I had to wait until Father finished talking to the police. He led me into his study, a room that was usually kept closed. Still in his pajamas, Victor was lying on the couch.

"Did they take her away?" he asked.

Father nodded.

"Where did they take her?" His voice broke and Father took him into his arms and held him. "I'll never see her again."

"She's with God now," said Father. "We'll have a special Mass said for her."

"I bet she's mad," I said. "I bet she's mad at all of us." Father gestured for me to leave. I ignored him.

I looked at the litter on the floor of Father's study. Pictures of me that had hung on the walls had been taken out of their frames and torn into tiny pieces. I saw myself strewn over the tile—parts of my mouth, my head; parts of me were everywhere in the room. I could feel Alma and Rosa's hatred over my body.

"Get dressed," Father said to Victor. "You're coming with me."

"Where?"

"We have work to do. I need you to help."

"I'm coming too," I said. I didn't want to be in the house.

"No, Andrea. We won't be long. Come on, Victor, let's get going." Victor left the room filled with self-importance.

Once Father and I were alone, I demanded, "Where are you taking him?"

"Don't get that way, Andrea. I'm just taking him with me to the office. I have to call his parents."

"Call from here."

He didn't answer. Dr. Salas joined us.

"Thanks for coming so quickly," said Father.

"Hector, I'm sorry." He shook Father's hand slowly. "I've

given Diane a shot. She's upset, but I don't think all this will affect the baby."

"You sure?"

"I'll know more in a few days."

Father walked with him to the door and then went back upstairs. Feeling terribly abandoned, I stayed in his study. Everyone was worried about everyone but me. Father and Victor left without saying goodbye.

I went into the living room and looked at the damage for the first time. The paintings which Mother loved had been knifed. They had slashed a portrait of my parents. Stuffing from the couch and chairs was strewn across the floor. The dining-room drawers had been emptied of all silver.

I felt afraid, vulnerable.

My room was the only place I felt safe. I crawled into bed and fell asleep. The next thing I knew Victor was shaking me, urging, "Come see, Andrea. Hurry!"

From the top of the stairs we watched Father directing his warehouse workmen to carry out everything that was cut or broken and load it onto the two trucks. The men worked rapidly, in silence, until my house was empty.


FOR the next few days Father kept us out of the house as much as possible. In the morning we crossed the border to the American side, where we had breakfast, shopped, lunched, and shopped some more.

Every time we crossed the bridge Victor and I looked down at the river shacks. We saw women washing clothes and saw people standing around fires. I wondered if Alma and Rosa were down there hiding and laughing. I wished them dead.

While Mother and Petra chose bright-colored furniture for the house, Victor and I took care of ourselves and Cristina. We felt needed and important. In the evenings we met Father

at the club for dinner, and then went home to the smell of wet paint. Father had ordered the entire downstairs painted.

Shopping with Mother had been a special treat in the past, because if I behaved, I got a present. That no longer mattered. We bought and bought; we bought without joy. There was a heaviness in Mother that I had never felt before, and that weight spilled over into the house and into our lives.

Our house was refurnished with many beautiful things, but no matter how much we bought, it never felt the same. And in the evening when we came home, Mother would try to be excited about the day's shopping but then she would stammer, her eyes would tear, and Father would take her in his arms, and whisper, "I love you . . . I'm sorry." Then they would go upstairs and Petra would feed us dinner in the kitchen.

On such nights Victor and I avoided talking about Alicia's death or her funeral, the first we had ever attended. Alicia's mother and brothers and sisters had cried loudly all during Mass and graveside services. Later the family thanked Father for giving Alicia such a fine burial.

Mother had been too sick to attend. Petra made us get dressed up and we went with her and Father. I expected Victor to mourn loudly like the rest of Alicia's family and friends. He didn't; he stood quietly between Petra and me. Later he swore to me that he felt Alicia's soul at the funeral. He was against swearing, so in a way I believed him. I figured he wouldn't swear on such a big lie.

Then Victor took matters further; in the evenings he would tell me what she was feeling in heaven. "She's very happy and she's dressed in white. There's no blood on her anywhere. Two angels are her friends and they go everywhere with her."

Sometimes he reported that Alicia was singing; once he said she was going to be his guardian angel. After that I stopped believing him. I never told him; it made him happy. I never really understood why he was calm after Alicia's death. I know

if Alma and Rosa had killed Petra I would have wanted to chase them down myself and kill them. Mother seemed more upset than Victor.

Sometimes, to make Mother feel better, we would ask her to come tell us a story. She didn't tell the stories from memory anymore. She read them out of books and they weren't exciting. No one died; no one cried or used poison; they were plain stories of animals or giants.

There were nights when Alicia's death really hovered over the house, and we could hear Mother sobbing, "That poor girl." Those nights we would go back to talking about what we were going to do with Armida's treasure.

# 5

"Uncle, will Alma and Rosa come back?"

We were having breakfast in our freshly painted pale yellow dining room when Victor asked what perhaps had been haunting all of us since Alicia's murder.

Father reached for Mother's hand. "No, they won't," he answered.

"Did the police find them yet?"

"Not yet."

"Then how do you know they won't come back?"

Father was uncomfortable. "Because they're not in town or at the river. They have run away—they're probably miles from here. The police are still looking for them. They'll find them."

"I doubt it," I said.

"Have you two been afraid?" Mother asked.

"Yes," we answered, admitting it to each other for the first time.

"Why didn't you tell me?" Mother asked Victor.

He toyed with his food a while before answering, "Because you cry so much."

It sounded mean, but it wasn't meant to be. My parents seemed to understand; they looked at each other briefly and exchanged smiles. Father squeezed Mother's hand.

"I haven't been acting very grown-up lately, have I?" Mother leaned over and kissed us. "I'm embarrassed. You're brave children."

"You certainly are," Father agreed. "Don't feel afraid anymore. I've hired a night watchman to guard the house until Alma and Rosa are found."

"Is he a policeman?" I asked.

"No," said father almost apologetically, "but he's a good man. He watches the warehouse for me."

My mind raced ahead of the conversation. I remembered where I had seen Smelly Hands before.

"Why haven't we seen him?" asked Victor.

"Because you're asleep. He rides a bicycle and patrols our street and the blocks near us."

Sometimes Mother visited Father at the office, and Don Tomás, the watchman, would wave her car through the security gate. A boy would often be at his side; the boy was Smelly Hands. Now it all made sense. That was why he had been so helpful to us at the club. His father worked for mine.

"Does he have a gun?" continued Victor.

"A brand-new one, and a whistle too. He blows it several times a night to let us know that everything is all right."

I announced loudly, "I know who he is!" I smiled triumphantly at Victor.

"You've seen him at the warehouse, I'm sure," said Father.

"His son works at the club, doesn't he?"

"Right! Very good, Andrea," said Father. He seemed impressed with my ability to recognize the same person in two places. "I got Rodrigo a job at the club. He's a young man now."

I didn't know if having the father of Smelly Hands as our protector made Victor feel any safer. It didn't me. All I was

happy about was that in this instance Victor knew I hadn't been lying. He ate the rest of his breakfast in silence.


IT was my idea to go to the plaza, the square in the center of town, to watch the vendors and shoeshine boys. They had always been there. I had passed them so many times that I had stopped seeing them. Before I had gone to the river I had seen only the toys and not the men selling them. Now I only saw the men and not the toys. The plaza had changed for me.

We sat on a bench to watch them. "Tell your mother you want this," they said, holding piggy banks or puppets up to our faces.

I wished I could buy something from them. I knew where they lived; I had seen their faces that morning by the river before they came to the plaza.

As the morning went by, tourists, Americans, came across the border and the vendors whistled at cars, especially those with children in them, and playfully waved their curios at them. When a car stopped at a light they would crowd around it like ants over a crumb. Sometimes they sold something; most of the time the drivers wouldn't look at them—staring straight ahead until the peddlers went away. The farther they walked away from the tourists, the more their smiles faded. Then a new batch of cars would arrive and the smiles came back, wide, big, stretched.

"They don't really smile, do they?"

"They pretend," said Victor. "They go 'Whee!' when they see a car." He made a high shrill sound and laughed. "And then they go 'Whooooo' when the car pulls away." He brought his voice way down and turned his grin into an exaggerated frown. It was funny.

I tried it alone the next time vendors swarmed around a car. "Wheeeee!" I shrieked as the salesmen ran toward the car;

then as the car pulled away and their grins shrank, I made a
low-pitched "Whoooo!"

Then Victor and I did it together in perfect timing. We
played that game until the noonday sun seared our heads.

"I'm glad I'm not them," said Victor about the vendors.
"They have to stay here, or else they won't have money for
food or anything."

"I wish I had money to buy their stuff, don't you?" I asked.
If we were ever going to steal anyone's treasure, I had to make
Victor want money.

"It would make them happy."

"I know," he said. "But I don't want their stuff—it's junk."

"We could give it to someone, to the river kids. They don't
have toys."

"Andrea, you're trying to sound so good." He laughed at
me.

"So what? If we got toys for the river kids that would be
charity. Sister Cecilia said we had to do charity."

He laughed again. "Don't be stupid. Those things come from
the river, remember?" They don't want them."

I remembered that none of the river kids had been playing
with those toys, or any other kind. "How do you know they
don't want them?"

"I just know, that's all," he said. "They want cars and dolls
with hair like the ones you have. They don't want piggy banks
and shit like that."

I was happy when he said "shit." That meant he felt more
as he had at the beginning of summer. I checked to make sure.

"Yeah, it's all shit." He didn't even look up. Confident, I
asked, "Do you still want to take Armida's money?"

He thought for a long time before asking, "If you do a bad
thing to do a good thing, is the bad thing still bad?"

My heart was beating fast, but I controlled myself. If I acted
too excited he might not want to go through with it.

"If we took Armida's money to buy toys for the river kids, would it be a sin?"

"No, not if it's bad money. You said it was bad money," I reminded him.

"Letting people touch you for money is bad," he said. "That makes the money bad too."

It was settled. If we used Armida's touch money to buy toys for the river kids, we would just be turning bad money into good money.

AFTER lunch we rushed to Popeye's. We had to be up in the loft before Armida's afternoon trade started. With eighty-five centavos in change we bought a few marbles and some ribbon. I let Victor do the buying. I was sure Armida would hear my mind and catch us. We waited until she was busy with other customers, then sneaked up to the loft.

Eventually, Don Pancho took off his apron and in a gruff voice ordered, "*Armida, cuida la tienda. Cuidado con el cambio.*" Take care of the store. Careful with the change. Don Pancho went back to their living quarters to nap.

We lay in silence. My breathing never seemed so loud. I closed my eyes and dozed for a while. Victor nudged me. I heard the familiar rattle of Armida's curtain. I peeked through the space between the boards and saw her with a brown-haired boy. He did the usual thing—lifted up her dress and touched her. Then he went out and another followed. A third boy went in; he did her breasts and her pants. She stuffed their money into her bosom.

Then Armida went back to the bar section to serve beer to the grown men. Another customer came into the store, and she left the bar, waited on her client, rung up the sale and waited for the store to be empty. When she was sure she was alone, she walked to the coiled rope, took the money out of

her bosom and stuck it in the nylon stocking. By the time she was back in the bar, we were halfway down the stairs and heading toward her money.

I got there first. I reached into the center of the coiled rope, pulled out the nylon stocking and fled. I ran down the block as fast as I could. I never looked back. I reached the empty lot in back of Popeye's and sat on the stocking. I was shaking all over and had bitten the inside of my mouth so badly that I could taste the salt of my blood. I strained to hear Victor's footsteps. After one hundred years, he arrived.

"There's more!" he said, throwing a stocking full of money at me.

"More what?"

"More money!" he yelled. He picked up the stocking and hit me in the face. I snatched it away from him and sat on it too.

"More than this?"

He nodded breathlessly. "Lots more."

"Let's get it," I said, and made him guard the money we had already taken out. I ran back to Popeye's—held my breath as I tiptoed toward the coiled rope and pulled out another stocking and raced back to Victor.

My head was pounding. I could feel my blood heating at the top of my skull. I threw the stocking at Victor; he caught it and hid it. By now he was atop a fat cushion of money.

"Is there any more?" he asked.

"I didn't look."

"What do you mean, you didn't look?" he barked.

"I'm not going back," I said, exhausted.

"Well, I am. Wait." He hurried off.

I sat on the stockings fully expecting my parents, the police, Padre Lozano and Petra to arrive at any moment. Victor came back, his eyes on fire; he was carrying two more stockings full of money.

"I got it all!" He beamed. He dropped the money and sat on it.

We warmed it for a long time. Our breathing slowed; we were tired. It was hot, and our lips were white from thirst. My legs were sopping wet from sitting on the money. I was afraid to stand for fear that someone would pass by and see the bills.

"Now what?" I asked.

"We gotta hide this quick!" said Victor. "We gotta hide it where no one will look."

"Where? Think of something, Victor."

That part was not up to me, I thought. After all, he was the one who had wanted to take Armida's money. I had wanted to search for Rancho Grande's treasure at the river.

Finally, he said, "We'll hide it in the room where Alicia died. It's empty now."

"Mother's looking for a new maid, remember? Besides, it's probably haunted in there."

"Don't be stupid."

"What about the trunk in my closet? It's huge. My Communion dress is in it."

I didn't know if it was a good idea. I did know that I wanted to get us and the money out of that lot. The thrill of stealing had worn off—replaced by painful questions. How were we going to get five stockings filled with money back to my house? What if we were caught? We couldn't hide that much money on our bodies. I wasn't sorry we had stolen the money. I wished we had planned the escape better.

We took off our baseball caps and stuffed them; not half a stocking was emptied. We took off our shoes and stuffed them too. Bad idea. We could hardly walk. The first stocking was still half full and we had four more of them to get home. I wanted to cry.

Suddenly Victor took money out of one of them and dashed

back to Armida's. He didn't tell me what he was doing; he just went. He came back with two hemp bags and then poured the bills into them.

IT was quiet in the house when we finally got home. Mother was showing her new furniture to a friend; Petra was not home—she usually went to the market in the afternoon. Had the living room been empty, we might have been able to get the money to my trunk safely. It wasn't, and the risk of getting caught was too great. We had no choice; we went to the room where Alicia had had her throat cut.

We hadn't been there since that morning when Petra found her. The mattress was gone; all that was left was a wire bed frame, a dresser, an ironing board, and new blankets, which were folded over the back of a chair.

After stuffing our pockets with as many bills as would fit, we moved the dresser away and put the two bags behind it. We didn't stop to count it—besides, we couldn't count very well. We pushed back the dresser, made sure the bags weren't visible, and hurried back to the plaza and the vendors.

We found a perfect bench in the center of the plaza. From it we could see everything. Victor called over a shoeshine boy, a boy about our age, and asked him for a shine. He was a brown-skinned boy with dark dye embedded deeply into the crevices of his fingers. We watched as he meticulously dusted the loose dirt off Victor's shoes, applied the wax with his fingertips, waited for it to dry, and then with a flourish buffed the shoes to a high gloss.

Victor paid with a five. "Keep it," he said. The boy snatched up the bill and gave us a wide speechless smile.

Victor looked at me and gave a loud, "Wheeeeeeeee!"

We spent the rest of the afternoon making grown men and little girls go "Wheeeee!" We felt happy. Powerful. We bought

toys—any kind—paid for them in bills and never asked for change.

Our pockets were emptying fast. We tried slowing down our spending, but it was impossible. Word had gotten out that we had money, and we were courted, cajoled, taunted, teased into buying all that was put before us.

Victor called a hat vendor over and we tried on straw hats. They were shaped like baseball caps rather than sombreros and they had *Mexico* woven in colored yarn across the front.

"Choose your favorite one," Victor said. "We'll keep these forever."

I chose one with bright green lettering; Victor's had bright purple lettering. The hats had been woven with fresh straw— strands of pale green ran through intricate patterns. I put my nose to the hat and smelled the alfalfa.

"Yes," I promised. "I'll keep mine forever."

Our arms were full of toys we didn't want, toys we couldn't take home because we couldn't explain their purchase. The vendors pressed around us, sensing there was more to be gained. We must have been a dream come true for them.

Unable to carry or eat one more item, we found some American children and dumped our goods on them. Confused, they nevertheless accepted piggy banks, clay cups, plaster cats, matadors, Cantinflas puppets. Their parents called us back; we ignored them. Then in a burst of a newfound zeal, we dashed around the plaza until we had spent every cent and given away every toy. But we kept our hats.

Exhausted, elated, penniless, we went home—for more money.

# 6

WE hurried back to Alicia's old quarters, where we had hidden our treasure behind the dresser. Mother, Petra and an old woman were in there.

We stood in the doorway—dead still. Mother introduced us to the old woman. "Candelaria, this is Victor, my nephew. He's staying with us for the summer. And this is my daughter, Andrea."

We mumbled something and Candelaria did the same. Apparently she was more concerned with placing her belongings in the dresser. The drawers were stuck and every time she wiggled one loose I thought I could see our bags fall to the floor.

Mother asked, "Where did you get those silly hats?"

Victor quickly answered, "I bought them for us, Auntie. From an Indian boy for a few centavos."

Mother nodded absently. To Candelaria she said, "The blankets are new. We took out the other bed, so you'll have plenty of space."

Candelaria grunted.

Mother continued, "Let us know if there's anything you need."

Candelaria grunted again.

Mother's voice grew nervous. "Petra will help you with the rest of your things." To us she said, "Let's go in the house."

I begged, "Can't we stay?"

Mother placed her hands on the back of our heads and firmly guided us toward the house. Terror coursed through me when I looked back and saw old Candelaria effortlessly move the bed from one wall to another.

In the house, Mother sat down on a sofa in the living room. Everything was new, fancy, nice. But it felt borrowed, sad. I knew we were going to get some sort of talk. Mother always got her face to look patient when she had explaining to do.

"Candelaria is from Veracruz," she started, "and people from Veracruz have different customs. They talk differently, too. She has worked with many of the families in town. She cooks, sews, irons, washes and cleans."

"She's pretty old," I said.

"That's true, but she can still do the work of two maids."

"Can she talk?" asked Victor.

"Of course she can. She just has peculiar habits. She won't wear shoes. You mustn't upset her, understand?"

Mother told us more, even though her patience was gone now and she looked tired. She told us that newspapers had written many things about Alicia's death and that was why she couldn't find people to work for us. "Not even new river people will come. Candelaria came because she wanted to. She smokes a pipe. Don't stare. Petra says she likes to talk a lot. Be polite to her. Let her do her work."

Victor asked, "We can be friends with her, can't we?"

"So long as you don't bother her."

"My father says that when someone new comes to work for us, we should welcome them and make them feel like they're part of the family," said Victor.

"He's right," sighed Mother. "But let's give her a while to get used to us. Now go play till dinner."

We waited until Mother was out of sight, then raced back to what had now become Candelaria's room. Petra was still there.

Candelaria had moved the bed, along with the big crucifix, the ironing board—but miraculously, she had not moved the dresser. At least not yet. We stalled around the backyard not daring to speak of the money for fear of being overheard. When Petra left, we casually drifted in to talk to Candelaria.

She was sitting on the bed smoking her pipe. Her skin was dark, a sweet soft brown; deep lines framed her eyes and mouth. She had white lashes and eyebrows and two white braids that wrapped around and around her head. She wore a bright red satin blouse and a long cotton skirt which fell past her ankles, down to her brown, bare feet. Her feet were as wide as they were long, and she had them propped up on the bed, so they were the first thing we saw of her as we walked in.

The heels of her feet were cracked, creviced, and instead of toenails she had what looked like masses of hardened clay. She smelled like Father's warehouse men.

We tiptoed in. She drew on her pipe, aware that we were there but not acknowledging us. I had never seen anyone like her. In my own home, I found myself feeling shy before this old maid. Nevertheless, I wanted to get closer to her.

She slowly turned her head toward us. She looked at Victor and blew out a long column of thick, smelly smoke. We coughed, drew back, fanned ourselves free of her cloud. But we stayed in the room; Victor and I stayed close to each other.

She studied us, then she singled out Victor. In a fast melodic voice she said, "I remember when your father first came to town. He was the new doctor then. He was strong." She laughed to herself, then added, "He's skinny now."

Victor flushed. "My father's not skinny."

Candelaria laughed again. "Yes he is. He's skinny and his hair is falling out."

I agreed with Victor, but I didn't say anything. My uncle was small, but not skinny. Victor looked at me if expecting me to answer her. I didn't because I had the feeling that I was next. She pointed to me with her pipe. "Your father's a *big* man in town—know why?" She looked deep into my eyes, deep into me. "Your grandfather brought the railroad into town, that's why. Your grandfather was really a *big* man. I was here then. I saw him on his horse working his men. They put down the track. Then they rode the train into town. Your grandfather was a Revolution man. He changed things."

None of what she said was uttered with anger or derision of any kind. The woman sucked calmly on her pipe and told us about our fathers and said things which probably were true. And yet I felt invaded by her, and Victor must have too, because he stood there, his body tense, as if waiting for some dark truth to come hurling down on him about his father or about himself. Candelaria seemed to look at him more than she did me.

I felt defenseless. The old woman didn't have a tooth in her mouth, and she sucked on that pipe as I had seen my baby sister pull on Mother and later draw on a bottle. She stared at us, blind to our status. Obviously she didn't care what she said to us, nor did she expect us to talk to her. I wondered if she knew she worked for me. I didn't dare say anything to suggest it.

Painfully, I struggled to think of some way to get her out of her room long enough for us to get our money from behind the dresser. I couldn't think of anything to move this woman.

"You're living in a haunted room!" blurted Victor in a high screechy voice.

He amazed me. I looked to Candelaria, expecting her to ask why.

She slowly pulled on her pipe and looked at him. "You're

lying," she said. "My father was a priest. I have the light of God in me."

Mentally I blessed myself. I blessed myself twice, once for Victor and another time for me. Had Candelaria been sent by God to punish us for stealing Armida's money? Did she know everything about us?

Slowly we backed out of her room. Once we were safely in the house we hurried to my bedroom. "She knows," I said after shutting the door.

"Shhh!" ordered Victor. "How can she?"

"I don't know. I feel it. Maybe she already found the money."

He thought for a while, then shook his head no. "Where's the trunk you said you had?"

"In here." Together we went to the back of my closet and took out a large trunk which my father had bought when he was young. It was made of metal and wood; we strained to open it. Inside were my Catholic school uniforms, my Holy Communion dress and some clothing Mother thought too good to give to the poor. We saw with relief that there was plenty of room for our money.

"Victor," I confessed, "I'm afraid to go back to Candelaria's room. How will we get the bags out?"

"Tonight when she and Petra are eating, she'll have to be out of the room. We'll get it then."

I didn't trust his plan. "What if they catch us?"

"I'll guard and you move the money," he said.

"No. You move the money," I said.

"Okay. I'll move the money and you talk to them in the kitchen until I've taken the bags out."

That didn't sound right to me. "No, I don't want to talk to her again. You talk and I'll move the money."

WE heard Father's familiar "Pop Goes the Weasel" and went out to meet him. He was home early and Mother seemed par-

ticularly happy to see him. The living room, which earlier that day had seemed so foreign to me, was now full of joyful, familiar sounds. Father was playing with us, and he was making Mother laugh with news that old friends of theirs were in town.

"When did they arrive?" Mother asked. "Will I have time to get ready?"

"They're staying at the Río Bravo. Carlos has to fly to Mexico City tomorrow and Betty's staying with her parents in Dallas till he returns. I made reservations for the four of us at the club tonight."

"Hector, why didn't you call me earlier? I have to get ready! I haven't seen Betty in years. My hair's a mess!"

"Who are they?" I asked.

"I went to college with Betty at Art Center," said Mother. "Carlos is a friend of your father's. We introduced them and they got married. They've been married almost as long as we have." Her voice had taken on a low, soft tone.

"Do they have any children?" I asked.

"Not yet," Father cut in. "But they will. Carlos will get his way."

Mother then told Father about Candelaria's arrival and he went into the kitchen to meet her. Full of bravado, I followed.

Candelaria was standing barefoot beside the stove cooking and barely looked up when Mother introduced her to Father. The woman who had appeared so threatening and all-knowing was now, as I stood next to my father, an old Indian maid without shoes or teeth.

"What are you cooking?" Father asked her.

"Your dinner," she answered.

"Smells good," he said.

"We'll see."

Father shrugged and returned to the living room. Until Petra served dinner, he talked and joked with Mother, giving her every moment of his attention. She brought down evening

dresses, asking him to choose the one she should wear that evening. Father liked them all. Victor and I took part in the judging.

"The blue one!"

"The pink one!"

The pall that had descended on our home since the night of Alicia's murder was, for that evening, lifted. We sat down to dinner and for the first time in weeks no one spoke about the police, Alma and Rosa, the need for a new maid or the newspapers.

That evening Father spoke of Manolete, the greatest bull-fighter. "That new guy, Domínguín, keeps challenging him. It may make him careless," declared Father.

"Manolete wouldn't endanger his life for a few sarcastic comments," Mother said.

"Rumor has it that he will retire at the end of this season," Father continued.

"That means I'll never see him fight again," I said.

"That means the world will miss the purest of them all," said Father solemnly. "I hope he lasts the season."

Mother took the conversation elsewhere. She spoke of our upcoming Holy Communion and the ever-increasing guest list, and the arrival of my "American grandmother," who would be coming from California to meet me.

After dinner my parents went dancing at the club. They looked good together; Father seemed to have pulled out of the sadness brought on by the thought of anything harmful happening to his idol, Manolete. After kisses and hugs and our promises to go to bed early and not cause trouble, they left to meet their friends. Victor and I joined Petra, my baby sister, and Candelaria in the kitchen, and stood around listening to them talk. Petra saw us, but that didn't stop her from telling Candelaria in secret adult language about my father's late hours and his wild drinking sprees.

"About twice a week," she said, making the familiar drink-ing gesture.

And no matter what Petra said, Candelaria would always answer, "I know, I've heard."

We went in and out of the kitchen until the maids got used to seeing us. The time had come to move the money upstairs. We had decided finally that *both* of us would move the money. We waited until Petra and Candelaria sat down to eat. When they looked comfortable, we strolled casually to the backyard.

We raced to Candelaria's room and moved the dresser to pull out the bags. I took them and crept around the side of the house to the front. According to our plan, Victor was to go through the kitchen and unlock the front door for me.

I did my part. Then, with two hemp bags filled with money, I waited and waited at my front door. Where the hell was he? I didn't dare ring the front door. Petra would have to answer it. We weren't allowed to open the door.

I was sure I was going to get caught—alone. Darkness set-tled, increased. Cars drove by, their headlights catching me outside. Two neighbors walked by and said hello. My knees buckled.

Too afraid to go back the way I came, I looked around the front yard for a hiding place. My house had two small rose gardens, one in front, the other along the side of the house. It was a tight squeeze, but I crawled through the rose bushes, fighting back tears as the thorns tore my shirt and dug into my back. I dragged the bags behind me, then crawled out, amid more punctures, more silent tears.

I stood in front of the rose garden checking to see if the stash was visible. It wasn't. The sun had set. With murder in my heart, I went hunting for Victor.

Legs crossed, he was sitting in the kitchen talking to Petra and Candelaria.

"Do it again," he chirped. "Let Andrea see." His voice scaled higher the minute he saw me walk in.

Candelaria looked at me. "Andrea doesn't want to see any-thing," she said.

"Yes she does," insisted Victor. "Don't you, Andrea?" Now his voice was almost pleading.

I glared at him. I yelled, "What? See what?"

"You want to see her chew meat? Look, she can do it with-out teeth."

I watched as the old woman dropped some fried meat into her toothless mouth. She chewed and chewed, swallowed and opened her jaws wide enough for me to look in.

"All gone," she said.

Petra and Victor clapped and laughed with her. Mimicking them, my sister clapped and laughed too. Candelaria repeated her trick for me a few more times. She wasn't funny; she was horrible.

The response I had secretly been waiting for finally came when Petra exclaimed, "Look at your back! What did you do?"

Almost brusquely, she turned me around and demanded to know, "Where did this happen?"

I wasn't afraid. I knew she was angry *and* worried, so I had no reason to feel threatened. Now came my time to get even.

"Victor pushed me. He pushed me into the rose bushes and ran away and left me."

Immediately Petra led me upstairs to the bathroom. "Take your shirt off." She inspected my back, mumbling impatiently, then took off the rest of my clothes and dotted my scratches and punctures with alcohol. "A doctor's son doing this to a girl. I can't tell your mother about it, poor woman."

I was put to bed two hours earlier than usual. Victor came upstairs and Petra looked at him and shook her head in disbelief.

"It was an accident," Victor lied feebly.

Petra stroked my head and left the room. I refused to speak to Victor and went into Cristina's room. She was nearly asleep,

and I knew Victor couldn't yell at me for fear of waking her; if he didn't, Petra might forget he was a guest and really scold him. I knew Victor was afraid to have anyone else angry at him. He followed me with his head down.

"It was Candelaria," he whispered. "It really wasn't my fault."

"You broke the plan."

"No," he said. "Listen to me. Candelaria said, 'Hey, doctor boy, can people eat meat without teeth?' And I said, 'No,' then she said, 'Watch me,' and I did and she chewed her meat without teeth." He looked at me expectantly, then added, "It was funny."

"It wasn't. You got scared, that's all. You got me to do the hard work and then you left me out there because you got scared."

"I wasn't scared. I stayed to watch and she kept making me look at her. I had to stay."

I let him suffer for a while. Finally I left Cristina's room and returned to mine so we could talk.

"Where's the money?" he asked.

I wasn't finished with him yet. "You're a coward. It was your idea to steal the money and then you left me out there to take the blame."

"You're getting mad for something that didn't happen," he argued.

"But you didn't know for sure it wouldn't happen. You never went to see if I was all right. Now you want to know where the money is. Look what happened." I lifted my pajama top and dramatically pointed to my neck and back wounds.

He looked very sorry. "Andrea, I didn't leave you," he insisted.

Tears were gathering in his eyes. I waited for more. His nose was starting to run and I watched his sorrow; the greater his pain, the less my rancor. He wept silently, wiping his nose with his hand, something he would never do under normal

circumstances. I watched him cry silently penitent tears, tears he feared someone would hear.

He whimpered, "I'm sorry, Andrea. I didn't leave you. It was an accident."

When he cried he reminded me of Father and his apologizing to Mother for making Alma and Rosa sleep in the living room; I felt weak and sorry for him. I told him where the money was.

"I'm not going back to get it, Victor." Once again I showed him my wounds. "I don't give a damn who finds it."

"I'll get it. I'll go tonight—alone." His face had that determined look I knew well and partly feared.

"When?" I taunted. "You can't go out the front. It's locked. Petra will be upstairs in Cristina's room."

"Don't worry. I can do it tonight—sometime tonight. Maybe after your parents are home from the club. I promise, by tomorrow morning the money will be in the closet." He set his chin. I believed him.

WE played quietly for the rest of the evening. I don't remember when he went to sleep. I don't even know whether Petra made him take a bath.

Sometime later that night, Victor shook me awake and motioned for me to follow him downstairs. I waited as he unlocked the front door and watched as he headed toward the rose bushes. The evening air was warm in my nostrils. I crouched by the door fighting sleep, but knowing I had to wait for Victor and Armida's money.

He was taking a long time. Against my will I ventured out only to see a uniformed man on a bicycle pedal by with a gun on his hip and a whistle in his mouth. I darted back into the doorway lest I be caught by the very man who was supposed to guard our house.

Quickly I closed the door, abandoning Victor out in front.

A few dogs barked and then once again there was silence. I opened the door again and I heard familiar noises, the rustle of hemp bags dragging across the dirt. I opened the screen door to let him in. He had both bags with him; he walked past me in silence. Quietly, I locked the front door and followed. By the time I caught up with him, half the money was emptied into the trunk and all I could do was help him finish. We worked rapidly, soundlessly. Once the bags were empty and hidden under my mattress, he managed a weak "Good night."

I waited for him to say more; his breathing became heavy and I knew nothing would follow.

# 7

"ANDREA, we can't spend this money until we bless the trunk with holy water."

WE walked to church, each of us carrying two brandy snifters. Morning Mass was over and in a small town like ours, few stayed after services.

"Only old Indians, old widows and old virgins stay all day," I had heard Father say.

Victor and I dipped our glasses into the salty water at the marble fonts near the church entrance, filling our containers. By the time we got home, half the water had spilled out.

With one of Father's handkerchiefs, Victor gravely tried to wash every inch of the trunk with holy water. The last few inches were barely covered. Victor made us go back for a refill. This time we took highball glasses.

I took over. Rather than wash down the trunk, I sprinkled it with water in the form of a cross.

Convinced that our stash was properly

cleansed, Victor announced, "Now we can buy toys for the river kids, dolls and cars. How much are they?"

Neither of us knew the cost of anything other than gum, candy, and comic books—the few things we were allowed to buy without our parents.

"Let's separate the money into different colors and take some of each."

For the next hour we sorted fives, tens, twenties and fifties. Armida must have been touching a long time—so much paper! So many walks behind the curtain! And now we had it all. I felt sad.

Had she discovered it was gone? I figured she hadn't, since those boys only came in the afternoon. I felt a strong impulse to tell Victor that there was still time to return it.

"Victor . . ." I started.

He didn't look up; he was very busy—methodically, precisely straightening out the rows of bills, making sure that all the faces were looking up and corners squared. It was too late.

I forced myself to stop thinking about Armida as a person, a woman whose money we had stolen; I concentrated on the good we were going to do with our money. We were going to give to the poor.

"Give to the poor." Those words helped me to forget my shame, and to ignore the word "thief." We took bills from each stack and left.

Getting out of the house was easy that morning. Mother was still glowing from seeing her friend Betty the night before. They were to see each other again that day. She fretted over where to take Betty. Mother wore a yellow-and-white loose-fitting dress. Her hair was curled—bouncy—and I remember thinking as I saw her talking to Petra that morning that I had a pretty mother.

I had not met Betty, but someone who could come to our town and make my mother so happy must surely be a special

person. I had my own concerns that morning, concerns which have since paled, but now, in the retelling of that summer, I find my mother's radiance on that particular day a memorable image of that part of my life.

WE went to the store where our parents bought our toys and picked out ten cars and ten dolls. The storekeeper told us we didn't have enough money, so we settled for three dolls and ten cars. We had a few pesos left over.

The sun was high; the day's summer heat was already uncomfortable, but nothing could interrupt our mission. We were doing what we'd said we would do: spend Armida's money to help the poor.

The packages were individually wrapped for us by the storekeeper, and it was difficult to keep them from falling. At first Victor insisted on carrying all the cars himself, but after three blocks in the heat, he let me carry three. We moved toward the river.

Usually, on the way to the river we would have to go by Armida's. That day we took the long way around—a precaution. The extra walk made us thirsty and we stopped by the club for 7-Ups. The place was empty.

Tony was there, and so was Smelly Hands. I couldn't help but wonder how much of his money was in my trunk.

Tony looked at our packages. "Where are you going today?"

"We're taking toys to the poor," said Victor importantly.

"Yes," I added. "To poor children." It felt good to say that.

I could tell Tony was surprised. He raised his eyebrows and looked down at us. "Where are these children?"

Both of us were silent. Tony knew as well as we did that people from our side of town never went to the river. I also knew that my parents saw him regularly, as he was their special waiter at the club. I knew that if he knew where we were

going, he would have to tell them. I bore Tony no resentment.

"Where are these children?" he repeated.

"Padre Lozano told us where to go." Completely in control of himself, Victor reached into his front pocket and slipped Tony a bill. Again Tony was surprised; we never paid cash for anything at the club.

"Keep it," said Victor, in a manner very much like his father.

While Tony was still staring at him, Victor picked up the cars and motioned me to the door.

I looked back one more time and saw that he was still watching us; standing next to him was Smelly Hands. They were talking about us.

"Victor," I said, "look at them. We have to go back. Tony will call the house if we cross the highway."

He saw that I was right. "Shit," he said.

We turned around and headed for home; we circled the club by several blocks. The packages were getting heavier, the sun hotter. My throat was dry, and we weren't any closer to the river. We stopped to rest.

"Let's do it tomorrow," I argued. "I'm tired. I want to eat. Petra will be mad at us. It's hot. My head hurts."

"We have to do it now, Andrea," he said.

In a tired and sweaty silence, we walked for what seemed an eternity before we crossed the highway and the muddy lots. The river shacks appeared in the distance; a few wisps of smoke trailed across the blue sky.

The closer we came, the less tired we were. Suddenly, we were almost running. The smell of the river was sharper than the first time. The smells of dog, garbage and waste didn't bother me. Few fires burned. It was quiet; the vendors were working the plaza.

Women laundered, small children trailed behind, dogs trailed after the children. Holding on to our hats, we walked parallel to the river. People looked at us. We said hello, Victor

tipped his hat. The adults ignored us, but I could see curious children staring at us. The packages grew heavy.

"When do we do it?" I asked. We were approaching the part of the river where we had seen Rancho Grande and the other bums.

"I don't know," he said.

"Let's just give it to them." Victor looked at the throng of children following us. "We don't have enough for all of them."

"Then let's leave the toys on the ground and run."

He was adamant. "No. We have to hand them out, other-wise it's no good."

I figured he was right and followed him farther down the riverbank—our gifts to the poor in hand—trying to figure out how to do charity and cleanse ourselves.

I came to a solution. Having won several prizes in school by racing against classmates, I proposed that we hold a contest.

"But," said Victor, "the boys will have to race against the boys and the girls against the girls."

He motioned them over to us and waited until they all stood quietly before us. Slowly, dramatically, Victor unwrapped the prizes and lined them up before the children. He announced, "You can win a car if you win a race, and if you're a boy. The girls will win dolls. There are only three dolls."

At last something was happening. The kids came closer; they seemed interested. Victor asserted himself and quickly took control.

He then pointed to a boulder sticking out of the riverbank. "Run from here to that big rock and back again." The kids looked at the distance; it was about a block long. "Who wants to be in the first race?" Victor asked.

Everyone raised a hand.

Unexpectedly Victor yelled, "Go!"

They were as surprised as I was, but they took off. They sprinted toward the rock and back again. A tall boy reached

us first, arm extended, hand stretched open; he snatched the car before Victor could give it to him.

The boy waited until all the other contestants were back, then said loudly to Victor, "You didn't do it right. The little ones will never win. And you're supposed to say, 'On your mark, get set, go!'"

"I forgot," said Victor. "Do you want to do a girl race?" he asked, quickly turning to me.

I could tell he was embarrassed by the boy's scolding and was trying to divert some of the group's attention to me. I looked around and noticed that there were more boys than girls; this was good, because we had only three dolls. But even among the girls some were much bigger than others.

Not wanting to bungle my race as Victor had his, I asked, "How many of you are ten?" Most of them raised their hands, even though it was obvious some were much older and others were much younger.

"Do it big, medium, and small," said the tall boy who had won the first car. I figured him to be about twelve.

Without waiting for our approval, he organized the girls into three groups. "You're in this group, stupid," he called to a big girl who was standing with the medium one. He ordered around a few more, and from the bantering that went back and forth between them, I learned that his name was Beto.

Some of the girls talked back to him and he laughed at them; it was clear they they were used to taking orders from him. When he was satisfied, he held up his hand and called, "On your mark, get set, go!"

The tall girls took off, the rest of the kids cheering them on, each calling out the name of a friend.

Victor and I watched the race in silence. I was mad. It was supposed to be my race. We both knew what was wrong: Beto. Beto had stolen our game from us and there was not a thing we could do about it.

When the winner, a girl with long, thick braids, raced up to claim her prize, Beto told me to give her a doll. I obeyed. There was no glory in my action. I felt nothing. That exhilaration that had run through my body when we first arrived at the river was gone, vanished, replaced by humiliation.

Beto organized the next two races for boys, and sullenly Victor gave out the cars. It was time for a girls' race again, Beto decided.

"This doll will go to whoever sings the best song," I said, attempting to regain some control. Victor seemed pleased with me.

"You can't do that," snapped Beto.

"Yes, I can. They're my dolls. I can do whatever I want." My voice betrayed me; a tremor ran through it.

Beto spoke with finality. "They're not going to sing. You said they had to race and that's what they're going to do."

I started to argue with Beto, but Victor begged tiredly, "Andrea, let them race."

So the medium girls raced, and I gave out the doll to the winner. It went on like that until the toys were gone. Beto controlled the contests and we gave out the prizes. The adventure had lost its luster. The winners said "Thank you," but they said it to Beto.

"Bring more tomorrow," ordered Beto as we were leaving.

"We can't come tomorrow," answered Victor.

Beto shrugged and walked away; the rest of the kids followed him.

"We were dumb to come. I'm *never* coming back," said Victor bitterly.

"That boy Beto ruined it all. You shouldn't have let him boss us around."

"Shut up, Andrea. You didn't say anything. He was too big."

I was mad at Victor, the river kids, Beto and myself. I was

hungry and worried that we would be discovered. My stomach told me that we were long overdue at the house.

"Now what are we going to do with the money?" I asked.

"Stick it in the church," he said simply.

That sounded awful to me. I wanted to recapture the feeling I had first had when we arrived at the river, our arms full of gifts, our hearts eager to do good. That had been a most wonderful feeling.

Now Victor wanted to give the money away—just like that. It seemed terribly unfair, even if it was to go to a church. I thought of the trouble we had gone through to steal it, get it home, smuggle it in the house, bless it, buy the toys, walk and walk to the river. So much work! We couldn't give it up. No sir, not without witnesses to see us do charity.

We were tromping through the muddy lots, and I was about to fight Victor about the money when out of nowhere, Beto reappeared. He was with two other boys about his size. They stood before us, blocking our way.

I knew we were going to get hurt.

"Why can't you come back tomorrow?" Beto demanded of Victor.

"I can't. I won't ever come back." Victor's voice was close to breaking.

"Leave him alone," I said. "We came to give you gifts. We did it to be nice."

"Why didn't you bring more?" Again, Beto spoke only to Victor.

"That's all we could buy," said Victor, desperately trying to keep his head up while talking.

"You bought that stuff with *your own money?*" He narrowed his eyes.

"Yes."

"How much money do you have?"

"I don't have any more."

"You used *all* your money to bring *us* toys?"

"Yes."

"I don't believe you."

Beto walked up to Victor and started searching him. We both must have remembered the extra bills at the same time, because suddenly both of us shoved Beto away. He fell back—but only for a split second.

Beto's fist caught Victor across the nose, then he spun around and faced me, his fist raised to strike again. For a split second he hesitated. If the hesitation was because I was a girl, it didn't last long. Down came his fist across my mouth. The blow pushed my lips against my lower teeth and blood spurted down my chin.

"Let me see!" Beto ordered Victor, pulling violently at his pants.

Victor cupped his hands over his face while Beto searched in his front pockets and pulled out some crumpled bills. He tossed them back to his companions. All three lunged at us.

They hit, kicked, pushed until we fell. I yelled and pulled down on my hat. Victor took more blows. They stood over us; I could hear their breathing. We lay crying in the mud for a long time. I didn't dare move. Then, slowly, they pulled away.

Perhaps it was fear that prevented me from feeling any specific pain. Somewhere my back ached; my scalp did too. I remembered them yanking at my braids several times and reached to make sure my hat was still on. It was.

I looked up; they were gone. Victor's nose was bleeding, and there were cuts across his lips and eyes. A big gash sep-arated his ear from his head. His ear was purple—a ripe fig hanging from a tree.

I inched over to him; he couldn't see. One of his eyes was totally closed; the other was a slit. Victor turned his head toward me and tried to say my name. His sobs were interrupted

by shrieks of pain as he struggled to his feet. I leaned over to help him, but anywhere I touched him was the place that hurt most.

I looked down and saw that his hat was crushed into the mud. "Victor, your hat is in the mud."

"I don't want it. Help me."

I stood absolutely still, letting him find the way to lean on me. He draped one arm around my shoulders and, with me holding him by the waist, we wormed our way toward town. After a few yards, I realized that I was incapable of holding him any longer.

"Victor, I can't walk any more."

He muttered, "Tony."

What the hell does he want with Tony, I wondered. Parts of my body were beginning to send out painful signals.

"Tony," repeated Victor.

My lips throbbed. I eased Victor to the ground. "Do you want me to go for Tony?" I asked. "I'll go for him. Stay here."

He wailed, "No!" and his hands grabbed my ankle and gripped it like a vise.

I tried to pry him loose. "Victor, let go. I have to go for help. I can't walk with you any more."

He sobbed. "Don't leave me."

"I'm not leaving you. I'm going for help. Let go of my foot!" I pleaded, close to anger.

I think I smelled him coming before I saw him. Tall, thin, clad in mismatched pants, shirt, and coat, wearing shoes but no socks, he loomed over us, his blue eyes clear and knowing: Rancho Grande, our town's most mysterious bum.

Gently, the man took up Victor in his arms and cradled him. Then he took my hand and motioned me to take hold of his coat. He walked slow enough for me to keep up. I heard Victor sob, and softly Rancho Grande said, "Shhh. Shhh." Occasionally, Rancho Grande's long fingers stroked Victor's matted curls.

Tony was showing Smelly Hands how to hose down the parking lot when Rancho Grande arrived at the club with me holding on to his coat tails and Victor in his arms.

"Canales, Canales," the name of our street, was all Rancho Grande said to Tony as he transferred Victor over to him.

"Call an ambulance," Tony said to Smelly Hands. "What happened?" Tony asked me. He looked at Victor's ear and winced.

I burst into tears. "Some river boys beat us up. Rancho Grande found us." Crying kept me from saying too much.

"Were you *there*?" Tony asked angrily.

I was trapped. Weakly I mumbled, "We went to see the river—just to see it."

Rancho Grande was standing by, watching me talk to Tony. I sensed he knew I was lying. Tony opened the screen to the main dining room and I hobbled in; when I turned around to look for Rancho Grande, he was gone.

Somewhere, I heard, "Give them water with sugar. It will calm them." They put me in a chair; Victor was stretched out on a big table. Our lips were too swollen to drink the sugared water. Smelly Hands brought straws for us. In the background I kept hearing the name of my father mentioned by one waiter or another and then Mother appeared, demanding to know, "Who did this?"

"Rancho Grande found them by the river and brought them here," Tony quickly explained. "I don't know the details."

Victor was no help. He looked so horrible no one asked him anything. Bruised, battered and cut though I was, I feigned more. I couldn't have said anything to Mother, other than the truth, and that was impossible. Taking my cue from Victor, I whimpered instead of talked. It worked, mainly because everyone was so worried about us.

I could have brought all that crazy confusion to an end if only I had told the whole story. Victor and I were being treated like heroes, but the truth was that we were thieves who only

now had learned about the river and why we had been forbidden to go there.

THE ambulance arrived while Mother and Tony were trying
to clean blood and mud from our hands, faces and legs. It was
impossible for them to remove the mud without our cuts re-
opening. I remember Mother's frantic requests to Tony to call
Father to meet us at the hospital.

During the hysteria, I remember noticing too that Mother's
friend Betty was not with her, and that Mother had lost that
special look she had had earlier that morning—that open, expectant look. Once again she had regained the pained American
expression I had always associated with her.

But what bothered me the most—admission of this is particularly difficult—was that despite my fear of getting scolded
for being at the river, and despite the possibility of someone
discovering that we had stolen Armida's money, for whatever
reasons, Victor was getting most of the attention.

Mother was able to see that I would live, but she was unable
to diagnose the extent of Victor's injuries. Frightened, she
banged her fists on the club tables wanting to know who had
hurt Victor.

I was jealous. Even after she broke down and once again
ordered Tony to find Father.

Jealousy scorched me again after the ambulance arrived and
Mother jumped into the van for the race to the hospital.

The ride could have been exciting. But the thrill was lost
by Mother's tenderness with Victor. "Are you all right? . . .
Can you feel my hand?"

Father was waiting. He looked awful. They rushed Victor
in first; then a nurse came out and looked at me. She was in
no hurry to take me anywhere. Holding Father's hand, I waited
my turn, resentful that Victor had snatched everyone's
attention.

# 8

FATHER brought me home from the hospital that same day and laid me down in his and Mother's bed. I slept through the evening and awoke in the middle of the night.

Father lay next to me. The light was on. We looked at each other for a long, loving moment. Then the day's events rushed back.

"They hit us," I murmured. I didn't know what he knew, but I was sure he would find out more than I wanted him to. I wondered if Victor had told Mother about the money.

"You're here with me," he soothed. "Sleep."

"My mouth hurts."

"It will for a few days." He stroked my head; I didn't tell him that my scalp hurt.

"Where's Mother?"

"With Victor at the hospital."

"Is he going to die?"

"No." He smiled. "Dr. Salas wants him to rest there for the night."

"Mother's sleeping at the hospital?" Jealousy returned; I kept it out of my voice.

"Just for tonight. They'll be home tomorrow."

Outside, the four-note whistle of the night watchman wailed in the hot darkness. Father had hired him to keep us safe, had hired the father of Smelly Hands to keep our house safe from Alma and Rosa, and who else? I thought of Armida's money in the trunk. Smelly Hands' money was in that trunk. I felt sorry for myself.

"It's late, isn't it?"

"Yes."

"Daddy, are you mad at me?"

His eyes watered. "Yes, but I love you. I love you more than anything else in the world." He took my hands and kissed them. My heart broke.

I woke up alone in the big bed and went to the bathroom to see myself in the mirror. I didn't look like me. I had stitches inside my lower lip, and some over my right eye. Half my face was swollen. Lifting my nightgown, I saw that my legs were budding with bruises. I touched my back, and pain told me that I was bruised there too.

The house was quiet except for Father talking on the phone. Then, when I heard him tell Petra that Victor's mother would be arriving that evening, and that she should pack his belong-ings, I realized Father had been talking to Victor's parents.

Daylight came and I was afraid. I ran back to bed at once when I heard Father coming upstairs. He was frowning; his face lost its sternness once he saw my battered face. I was grateful for the bruises.

He sat next to me, again kissing my hands. His eyes were sad.

"Listen to me, Andrea. Listen to me very hard." He was breathing rapidly.

I didn't dare speak.

"You and Victor did a dangerous thing. You could have been killed." So he knew we had been to the river. "I talked to Victor's parents. They don't trust me anymore."

"Can't you tell them it was an accident?" I pleaded. "I swear, we were only looking."

Would I never stop lying?

"Accidents like this happen when parents are disobeyed. I promised Victor's father I would take care of his son and . . . I didn't. I broke a promise to my dearest friend and now he doesn't trust me." He swallowed hard. "Can you understand that? Can you see what your disobedience has caused?"

"I'm sorry."

"It's too late. Petra will help you dress. There's medicine for your eye. Stay home today." His lips brushed my head and he hurried from the room. Later on, I heard his car speed away.

I felt tears on my face. The tears were for him and for me and for what I could never let him know about me. It hurt to see him in pain; I was sorry for that. I was also ready to let Father bear his share of the sorrow.

WHEN Mother arrived, I was standing on the balcony, the same place I stood the night they took Alicia away. I noticed Mother was still wearing the same yellow-and-white dress she had had on the day before. She looked tired, almost ugly, and her blonde hair was now a darker color. Yet she carried Victor easily into the house, not unlike the way Rancho Grande had carried him to the club. Physical strength was something I had never associated with Mother.

I went downstairs to meet them. Mother blew me a kiss while carrying Victor, whose bandaged head shocked me almost as much as her strength. He was dressed in a hospital gown.

"Petra!" I yelled.

"No, baby, it's all right. I can do this."

She laid Victor down on my bed while Petra changed his sheets. I looked at him and he placed his index finger across his lips. I'd never loved him so much. He hadn't told.

Mother helped Victor to his newly made bed, then she held me and kissed me and asked if Father had spoken with me. I said, "Yes," and tried to look contrite. Then she left to buy chocolate and strawberry ice cream for us. Petra asked her if she shouldn't first bathe and rest. Mother shook her head.

"Father knows we were at the river," I whispered to Victor once I was sure we were alone.

"You told?"

"No! I swear! He must have talked to Tony. Did you say anything?"

He squirmed and lowered his voice even more. "I cried a lot for my mother. That's all."

"She's coming home today."

He smiled, a weird smile, crooked, swollen, blue. "I know."

"Father's mad at me. He said it's because of us that he broke a promise to your dad. He said he promised to take care of you."

"Yeah," he said, pointing to his wrapped head. "And Alicia's dead."

He hit a nerve. Mine. "Victor, it's all our fault. We did everything. Don't blame him."

"Not everything," he emphasized. "It's not our fault Alicia's dead. *He* let those maids stay here. Not even your mother wanted them to stay. Everybody knew there was going to be trouble. Petra said so. She knows."

I hated Victor. "If we hadn't gone in to talk to them about confession, they would still be working for us. Mother didn't want them to scare us. Besides, you're the one who wanted to confess everything we saw at Armida's, remember?"

I was happy he had been hurt more than me. Cloaking my anger, I investigated the bandage around his head and asked, "Is your ear still there?"

"Why?" His fingers groped over the contours of his bandages.

"Just wondering. The last time I saw it, it was hanging, just hanging. I thought it was going to fall off. Did it?"

"I don't know!" he cried, frantically pulling at the gauze and tape around his head.

I had wanted to upset him, but not that much. Petra might hear him and I would really get in trouble. Still, I wanted to pay him back for what he had said about Father. *His* father never did anything wrong, so it seemed. When people talked, and in our town people always did, they talked about Father and "his ways." Victor's father saved people, except for the time he had stayed home to care for his dog.

I let Victor tug fearfully at his bandages awhile longer before assuring him, "It's still there."

He didn't believe me and he pulled so violently at the side of his head that he frightened me.

"I was teasing. Your ear is still there. Stop crying." He wouldn't. "Give me your hand," I demanded. I took his index finger and traced the outline of his ear over and over until he was convinced.

"Feel the bump?" I asked.

He nodded.

"That's your ear." After he calmed down I asked, "What are we going to do with the money? I won't leave it at the church. I want to see the good we do with it."

"I'm never going back to the river—ever. I hate the poor."

"You shouldn't say that, Victor. Jesus was poor."

"I don't care. He never beat up anybody. People beat Him up. There's good and bad poor. Beto and his friends are bad poor."

An idea came to me. "I know! We'll give it to the good poor! The beggars outside the church!"

His bruised face contorted into a smile. God, he looked ugly. "They wouldn't hit us near the church."

"We could see their faces when we give them money. Every-one gives them change. We have bills. Won't they be surprised?"

"When's Sunday?"

We counted back and figured it was three days away. We talked and I listened to Victor's plans to pay Beto back.

It seemed like a wonderful idea. I most certainly would have loved to beat up Beto and his friends as they had me, but I couldn't believe that wish would come true. Some things never happen, no matter how much you wish or dream. I don't remember ever being taught that; no particular incident in my life brought me to that realization; it was something I had always known about life. I guess I sensed it and that was something people like Victor and Mother would never understand.

We stayed in the room the rest of the day. I listened to him talk of his mother's arrival, something we both knew would be the only highlight of our day. I was saddened at the idea. I knew I would lose Victor to her. I asked if he wanted to take some of the money home, and he said no. We napped until the sound of Father's "Pop Goes the Weasel" woke us up.

SUDDENLY everyone was in my room. Victor's mother, Tía Milita, burst out crying the moment she saw her son. He did the same. My parents and I watched; I could tell they were embarrassed. Victor was sobbing and blurting out about Alicia and Beto and the river all at once. He made sense only to me, and I was grateful for that. Tía Milita kissed and held him.

When she saw me, she had new tears. "They hurt you too, my precious." Moved to self-pity, I joined in the weeping, hugging and kissing until Father interrupted.

"It's just cuts and bruises, Milita," he said, trying to calm

her down. "They need rest. Dr. Salas said they'll be fine in a few days."

My aunt looked at Father with a scowl. The room grew dead quiet. The adults looked at each other; Father and my aunt seemed about to burst with the unsaid.

Finally Mother spoke. "I think we're all overwrought. Let's go downstairs. Dinner is almost ready."

My aunt would have none of that. "I want to take my son home."

"Of course you do," said Mother. "But stay for dinner. You're tired. Your house has been closed since June. It will be easier for you—and us. Please stay."

"I can get what I need," my aunt insisted. She looked for Victor's clothing; Petra had it ready. "Get dressed, darling," she said to Victor.

My family stood by in self-conscious silence while my aunt stood between us and her son to shield him from our view.

When she saw his back and legs, she turned and glared at Father.

"Don't blame him," I pleaded. "It was my idea to go to the river, wasn't it, Victor? Tell her, Victor," I coaxed. He said nothing. "Tell her!" My voice shook out of control.

"It's not Uncle's fault," he mumbled.

"And?" I demanded.

"He told us to stay away," he said, staring at the floor.

Father spun around and left the room. He slammed his bed-room door so violently that the noise startled my baby sister, who began to scream. Our mothers shrieked at each other at the same time, and I was in the middle of the chaos urging Victor to tell my aunt not to be mad at Father. Then Petra came in asking when she should serve dinner. It was crazy.

My aunt rushed out. She allowed Mother to give her ice cream for Victor, but she refused to accept dinner for herself. My parents and I sat down to eat. We tried to speak of some-

thing other than Victor and his mother, but the conversation always came back to them. I asked to be excused and left without waiting for an answer. They didn't notice.

From upstairs I heard them talking, then arguing, then finally shouting about whose fault everything was. I wanted to tell them everything. I wanted to tell them about Armida and the boys who touched her, and the money and Smelly Hands.

I wanted to help them understand how Victor and I had caused all this—but the truth was that although I was sorry for them, especially for Father, I felt I had, by my silence, a strange power over them, a power I was not about to relinquish.

I had secrets now, secrets of my own, secrets they would never know about, and I treasured them, clung possessively to them, knowing full well that secrets told lose their power.

I remained upstairs listening to my parents yelling, tearing at each other. I stayed in my room after Father, having had enough of fighting, got into his car and roared off. I sat still and listened to Mother's lonely crying.

# 9

NEXT morning Mother and I went to Victor's house. Mother took some groceries and stayed with us while my aunt ran errands. Later Tía Milita returned with a new maid, Rosario—a woman about Petra's age.

"She's a widow," my aunt whispered, "looking for a quiet place—no more than one child. I hope it works out."

"I'm sure it will," said Mother.

My aunt didn't respond.

Victor wasn't allowed outside, so we played in the house—always within my aunt's line of vision. It wasn't much fun. The women talked, tried to be friendly and natural in their conversation. It didn't work.

When Mother asked about New York, Tía Milita gave little information. Then when my aunt asked about Alicia's death, Mother paid her back and also said as little as possible.

I wanted to leave and looked expectantly at Mother, who ignored me. Little was being said, yet for reasons unclear to me, Mother stayed. It was obvious her help was not needed.

Finally my aunt said, "I have so much to do, Diane, do you mind?" She stood up and led the way to the front door.

Mother did not move from the couch. "Milita, let me help you," she insisted and added, "There must be something I can do."

"Really, thank you," my aunt said stiffly. "There's Rosario."

"I'll stop by tomorrow," offered Mother.

"No need to," said my aunt.

We returned the next day. The women were still distant with each other. However, this time my aunt gave Victor permission to play out in front. She opened the windows and peered out frequently to make sure we didn't stray. She had brought back some unusual toys for Victor and we played with them, particularly the Erector set. It wasn't much fun.

We didn't talk about the river or the money; we played the way children are supposed to play. Every time my aunt looked out and saw we were still there, I felt proud that we were doing what was expected of us.

I saw him when he was a block away from us. "Victor, look!"

It was Rancho Grande. In silence we watched him do what we had seen him do many other times: search through people's trash cans, take out what he wanted, put it in the sack he carried slung over his shoulder, then neatly returned what he didn't take.

"He's coming closer," said Victor anxiously. "What should we say?"

"I don't know. We should say something."

"Yes! Think quick."

"Let's wave. He's our friend now—he saved us, didn't he?"

Victor's bruised face lit up. "That's what we'll say—'Thank you for saving us.'"

We waited for Rancho Grande to get closer. As he neared, something prompted us to hold hands. There was no trash

outside Victor's house, and it seemed as if Rancho Grande would pass us by altogether; it seemed as if we didn't exist, as if he hadn't found us a few days ago hurt and bleeding by the highway, and carried us to the club.

I wanted him to recognize us and be friends with us so badly that I yelled out to him from across the street, "Thank you for saving us, Rancho Grande."

"Thank you for saving us!" we cried in chorus.

We waved to him and repeated our cry until it became a chant, a chant piped only a few times, because without warning, Tía Milita descended upon us.

"What are you doing?" she asked sharply. "Get the hell inside!"

She never swore.

"That's Rancho Grande," I said. "He saved us from the river kids."

"He carried me," explained Victor.

"Talking to bums," she said savagely, and pushed us into the house.

Mother tried to calm her friend and at the same time be polite to Rancho Grande. She had always liked him. "*Buenas tardes*," she called to him in her American accent. "*Grácias*."

Then to my aunt she tried explaining, "That man brought our children home. He carried your son in his arms. Hector has been trying to find him to give him a reward."

My aunt would have none of this. She asked Mother, "Is this what went on while I was gone? Is this your idea of caring for children?" My aunt slammed the front door shut. Her face was red as she confronted Mother. "Now I know how everything happened."

"No you don't," snapped Mother. "That man had nothing to do with anything. He helped our children. Why won't you listen?"

"To what?" my aunt challenged fiercely.

That brought everything to a standstill.

"To an explanation," Mother said humbly. "Just an explanation," she repeated in a lower voice. "Milita, it hasn't been easier for us. Hector has been like a madman. Why do you think I've been here daily knowing you hate the sight of me? We're so ashamed . . ." Mother covered her face with her hands.

Embarrassed, I went to look out the window; Victor came with me. Again, I wanted to tell them the truth. But it was the same feeling as being with Father. I knew what I could do for them and refused to do anything about their anguish. Victor's face was next to mine and together we saw Rancho Grande standing in front of the house. We waved to him and, before leaving, he nodded slightly in our direction. I felt victorious.

Mother cried alone for a while and then Tía Milita's arms went out to her. Their arms wrapped around each other, the women wept, apologized, sputtered regrets, and held us so tightly that Victor had to scream to remind his mother that his ear was still healing.


SUNDAY came. I woke up before Petra came to dress me for Mass. I went into my closet, and took out bills and divided them into two wads, one for Victor and another for myself. I tried stuffing the money into my shoes, but had to pull out some as it made walking painful. I stuffed the rest into my underwear. I checked in the mirror and saw that nothing showed.

All dressed up, I joined Mother, who approved of the way I looked, and we drove to pick up Tía Milita and Victor to take them to Mass with us. Our fathers never went unless it was a holiday or something important like a baptism.

Sitting in the backseat, I passed Victor his share of the

money. Quietly he crammed it into his front pocket. I could tell he had forgotten about our plan to give some to the beggars. Despite the bruises and cuts, his face was the happiest it had been in days.

I had no idea so many people in town had heard about what had happened to Victor and me at the river. Before Mass, women friends of our mothers walked up to us and patted our heads. I had to laugh at the women patting Victor's head. It looked like half a volleyball. Some women hugged us, thanking God we were all right. We stood by as our mothers were consoled by other mothers and we thrilled to the admiring gazes of our peers.

After Mass more people stared and pitied us. My emotions were divided: part of me reveled in the pity and concern, a more urgent part of me wanted them to leave us alone—at least long enough for us to pull our money out and dole it out to the poor. I was eager to experience the gratitude of unfortunates.

It wasn't easy. After the crowd left, we followed our mothers behind the altar to the sacristy so they could meet with Padre Lozano to discuss their plans for our upcoming Holy Communion. Our mothers talked of the Communion breakfast and flowers for the church; the priest interrupted and addressed himself to Victor and me.

"Jesus will enter your bodies, your souls, for the first time," he said slowly, then he fell silent.

We knew all that; he knew we knew all that; but he still held his pause and rocked back and forth on his heels. Armida's money was in my pants.

"This is the most important moment in your lives. Your souls must be pure and ready to receive your Savior."

He folded his small hands across his chest. Our town priest for over forty years, Padre Lozano was old, lined, sad. Perhaps it was the bruises and stitches on our faces which prompted

him to add, "And you must obey your parents during this time of preparation, as they are the guardians of your souls."

He paused again and rocked awhile longer. Our mothers and Victor and I shifted uneasily at this last admonition.

"I want to light a candle," said Victor to his mother.

His request freed us and we hurried out the side exit and ran to the front steps where the beggars were. It was nothing for Victor to pull his money out; I had to double back to pull out mine.

Finally, there we were, in front of the beggars. There were five of them: one blind, two deformed, and two with their legs missing. We walked by them a few times; they ignored us. This made it even better. Dramatically Victor reached into his pants and slowly pulled out his money and gave it to two of them, the blind one and the deformed one with shrunken arms.

"*Gracias, Dios lo bendiga*," they said.

The blind man rubbed his bills with both hands and grinned inaccurately where he thought Victor stood.

I had three beggars to give to. It was wonderful. I prolonged it as long as I could; then, ever so slowly, I peeled out my bills, one by one, relishing the moments as their faces lost their well-practiced sorrowful, miserable look.

It was magic.

"Thank you, child. Bless you," they bleated, kissing the bills and crossing themselves with them. Then the beggar who wore cut-off pants to highlight his amputated legs reached over and grabbed my shoe and tried to kiss my leg. His smell was foul. I tore myself away from him. Victor took my hand and led me back to the sacristy.

They were discussing seating arrangements with Padre Lozano and debating what flowers would best decorate the church. The moment we entered, my aunt opened her arms to Victor, and he nestled right into them. His sudden abandonment hurt me; I needed to talk to him about our doing charity.

I was excited about sharing our money with beggars. I felt like a truly good person.

I also needed to talk to him about the revulsion I had felt when the legless man tried to kiss my leg. I had wanted to kick him, not only because his hand had touched my skin, but also because he was ugly and was surrounded by a smelly wall of filth—worse than anything we had smelled at the river. Had my feelings erased my good act?

Beggars had always been outside the church. They were part of Sunday and Mass, and ever since my parents trusted me to venture alone within six feet of them, I had always dropped change into their palms. That had never meant any-thing to me until I had my own money to give away. This was a new ecstasy. I was really giving, but part of it made me sick. Victor's words "I hate the poor" echoed through my head, and now I understood his feelings.

I could only ask Victor whether I needed to love those I helped. Was it permissible to hate the cripples, the poor, the weak?

They spoke of the breakfast. Hot chocolate for everyone. Of course it would be held at the club. The Hotel Río Bravo couldn't serve that many people. I looked around the sacristy. Pictures of Jesus at different ages were everywhere. One pic-ture showed Jesus in agony hanging from the cross. His mouth was open, blood poured from His side, and the fingers on His hands were curled like claws on a dead bird. What troubled me was that the nails did not pierce His palms, as was usually shown; the nails were driven through the wrists.

That inconsistency disturbed me, distracted me from my other worries. Was that how it had actually happened, or had the artist made a mistake? Then I noticed that the feet weren't crossed over each other as I was accustomed to seeing. In this painting, Jesus had a nail through *each* foot.

This was an important difference. I walked to a smaller

picture on the wall and saw that crucifixion was the way it was supposed to be: the nails driven through the palms and a single nail holding down both feet.

I calmed down. The extra nail on the big crucifix had troubled me because the nun who had taught us catechism told us the story of the Three Kings, Melchior, Gaspar, and Balthazar. Later, Mother had told me the story of the Fourth King who arrived too late for Jesus's birth.

This king spent the rest of his life searching for Our Savior, and he finally found Him, on Good Friday, when Jesus was crucified.

That story always made me cry. It made me angry too. Poor king. I wondered if there was a fourth nail to be found somewhere; so many miracles had been attributed to the three nails, what could come from the fourth? If I found it, would I too be a saint?

As we walked toward the car, the beggars besieged us.

"*Los niños! Los niños!*" They cried. The children! The children!

Their voices were joyous rasps. The blind one groped after the ones who were crippled and all three landed in a heap. Only the deformed ones reached us.

I grabbed onto Mother and yelled, "Run!" We ran to the car. Victor and his mother hesitated long enough for one of the beggars to wrap himself around Victor's feet. He screamed, horrified at the hands that touched him, but he seemed unable to reach down and pry himself loose.

Mother had opened the car door, and I dashed in. Tía Milita was still standing around shouting at the beggar, "*Lárguese! Quítese de aquí! Viejo cochino!*" Get away from here. Filthy old man.

From the safety of the car I called out to Victor, "Kick him. Kick him."

Mother ran back and ordered Tía Milita, "Get in the car."

Then Mother reached over and plucked Victor out of the beggar's grasp, and carried him back to the car. She threw him in as if he were a small melon and then dashed around and started the car.

"Roll up the windows," urged Tía Milita as we were half-way down the street.

"They can't possibly catch us," Mother said. "I don't understand what happened to those people."

Victor was crying out of control and shaking his legs as if some imaginary hands had gotten hold of him. Mother pulled the car over to let Tía Milita sit in the back with him and cuddle him. His cries died down eventually. I looked back and saw that he was half asleep. He's putting on an act, I thought. Good, that way we won't have to answer questions.

The drive home was easy. Once again our mothers were talking to each other in a natural way. Perhaps it was the incident with Rancho Grande or the planning of our Holy Communion breakfast that brought them together, but they were talking, happy to be with each other; their smiles were soft, gentle, their voices had high and low melodies, something that had been missing since Tía Milita had come home.

Mother kept me home the next day. We shopped, visited Father at work, and played with my sister. Tuesday was no different. I pressed for permission to visit Victor. Mother called Tía Milita to check if it was okay. It wasn't. He wanted to be home with his mother.

Thursday after Mother left to go somewhere, I walked the four blocks to Victor's house and knocked. Rosario, their new maid, answered the door.

"Is Victor home?"

"He can't see anyone," she answered and shut the door. From behind the door she added, "He's sick."

I went home and told Mother about this. She called Tía Milita and later Mother told me to leave Victor alone.

"Why?" I asked.

"Because that's the way things are for now," she stated flatly.

I knew that was no explanation; I also knew that was all I was going to get.

That same day I was taken to the doctor to have my stitches removed. I was looking almost normal except for a few shadows around my eyes and mouth. Mother brought me home and left; apparently her friend Betty from college was still around and I was free for a while.

I went into the closet, took a few bills, went to the toy store, and bought two cars like the ones we had taken to the river. Then I walked the four blocks to Victor's house, knocked on the door and ran. I hid around the house and saw Rosario come out. She picked up the cars and took them inside.

There was no sign of Victor. I started to go crazy with doubt and jealousy. He has told, I thought. His mother held him; he got weak and told. I could see it happening so clearly, I wanted to kill him. How could he do this to me for her? I let Father cry, I was loyal to our secret. Victor had told—I was sure.

That night was long and painful. The whistle of the watch-man was my only solace. Somehow the sound of his wail in the night connected me to Victor. I imagined him sleeping with his mother, telling her over and over again how I had made him do everything. I was sorry I hadn't peeled off his ear, hadn't kicked his wrapped head. I tortured him all night.

The next day I lied and said I was going to the playground. I knocked loudly on Victor's front door. Rosario opened it and I walked in, knowing full well that she was too new to the household to physically prevent me.

I walked into Victor's room. His toys were strewn all over the place. The cars were not among them.

I swallowed my anger. "Hi."

He nodded. He was involved in cutting out pictures from a comic book and pasting them onto a large sheet of paper. I saw no apparent purpose to what he was doing. He cut out a few more pictures of Captain Marvel.

"MMMmmmmmmmmmmmmm! ZOOOOOOOM!" he exclaimed.

"What?" I asked.

"I can fly in the air . . . I'm straahnnngg." He was baby-talking. "Zzzzzzzzzzzzzzzz. Mnnnnnnnnnnn. Shazammm!"

He pointed Captain Marvel at me and pitched him across my chest.

I waited a few more minutes hoping for something important to happen. Nothing came.

"Why are you baby-talking?" I asked impatiently.

He didn't answer; he just kept making the same dumb sounds.

"Victor, I came to play with you. Did you forget our plans?"

He shook his head, then returned to his comic books.

"Why are you acting like this?"

"I want to." He was still baby-talking—mouth pursed tightly.

"If you won't talk to me in a regular way, I'm leaving."

He picked up his scissors and leafed through a comic book.


FATHER didn't come home for dinner that night; Mother and I ate alone. It was nice. I had become more interested in her, ever since I had seen her carry Victor into the house. I told her she was strong and that seemed to please her.

"When I lived in Los Angeles, I played a lot of tennis. When I take you there, I'll teach you how to play too."

That excited me; I had never done anything with Mother.

On the spot I decided to tell her about Victor's baby-talking, my lying about going to the playground, my barging in on Rosario.

She wasn't surprised. "Your aunt and I had lunch. Victor's had a terrible shock. He needs to be a baby again—just for a while. You have to leave him alone, understand?"

"I can't play with him?"

"Not for a while."

"How long?"

"Until he feels safe again. These things happen sometimes when there's a big change in our lives. You did it when you were smaller, right after Cristina was born."

"I did?" I loved hearing baby stories about myself.

"Yes, right after we brought her home from the hospital. You baby-talked, only you don't remember."

"I remember when you brought her home. Daddy had a big party. She kept crying. Did I baby-talk?"

"You wanted to be the only baby in the house. Don't you remember you were jealous of Cristina's eyelashes?"

"I remember. I wasn't a baby, though."

I hated her for reminding me of that. Cristina had inherited Mother's long eyelashes and her American complexion. I looked like Father; my lashes, my coloring were exactly like his. When I was seven years old, I had tired of Mother's friends admiring Cristina's lashes. I was sickened by the words "She's so different from Andrea." This really meant, I was sure, *She's a lot prettier than Andrea.*

One day when I was alone upstairs with the baby, I took a pair of scissors and while my sister slept, I tried to cut off her lashes. I also cut off part of her eyelid. From the blood that spewed I thought I had cut out her whole eye. I was seven when I did that. I knew what I was doing.

I decided to forgive Mother for bringing up the incident. These new moments of intimacy with her well worth reliving

past misery. I said nothing. I did, however, once again become acutely conscious of our physical differences. Her hair was blonde, mine almost black; her body was long, almost fragile, mine compact, tight; her body movements were flowing, deliberate, mine fast, unpremeditated.

After the problem with Cristina's lashes, Mother tried to pay more attention to me. But I was either too embarrassed or too guilt-ridden to allow closeness to develop between us. I made Father and Petra my centers of affection. After that came Victor. Matters had stayed pretty much that way until now. Victor was sick, Petra was busy with Candelaria and Cristina, and Father had stopped coming home for dinner. Mother and I had no one to turn to but each other. It was good, and I got to find out about her life in Los Angeles.

She showed me photographs of her in college and told me about living in a big city.

"You wouldn't be able to walk around as you do here," she warned. "You'd get lost. It's big—but beautiful."

"Do you wish you still lived there?"

"I want to live with my family, you, Cristina and your father." She kissed me. "And," she added, "pretty soon you are going to have a baby brother, or maybe another sister."

I didn't like that. "Baby?"

"Your father wants a son."

"I don't want a brother. I love Victor. He's my brother."

"You can have two. Or maybe one more sister."

"We don't need it," I argued.

"Too late," she said gently. She put my hand on her belly. "It's already in here."

"In there?" I jerked back my hand.

"Andrea," she said softly, "don't be afraid. Give me your hand."

Reluctantly I gave it to her, not because I wanted to, or

because I was curious, but because I liked being physically close to her. But now that we were close, she was telling me that another person was coming into the house. Inside, I felt myself turning away from her. I couldn't help myself, and wished I wasn't the way I was.

# 10

AFTER talking with my mother, I was filled with
hate and suspicion. I hated the thought of an
unknown being invading my family.

Why did Father want a boy? What about
me? What were those fights between Mother
and Father all about? Why was going to bull-
fights with Father so important? I had come to
love Manolete almost as much as Father loved
him. I learned to shoot for Father.

"But she's a girl, Hector!" I had heard
Mother protest countless times.

"But she's my daughter!" he would answer.

I had always believed that being his daughter
was an important difference. Weren't the Durcals special? Grandfather had brought the railroad to town. Even old Candelaria knew that.
What did Father need a son for? He had me.
How many times had he told me that he loved
me more than anything in the world? I was
glad I hadn't given in and told him why Victor
and I had been attacked.

I suspected everyone. Where was Victor?
What was wrong with him? Had he told? That

was driving me crazy. Yet a part of me was certain that he would never tell about spying on Armida—I knew Victor could never explain that to his mother.

I suspected my parents of trying to replace me. Petra seemed to have abandoned me as well. She was always busy with Cristina, was worried about Mother and her problems with Father, was making sure Candelaria did things right. I feared I wasn't special to her anymore.

FOR two days I sulked in my room. With a vengeful obsession, I went through every coloring book I had. Mother had always tried to get me interested in coloring, hoping perhaps that I would become more involved in painting.

Mother was transparent to me. Now whenever she came in I delighted in painting wrongly in front of her, and purposefully outlined in black the figures of Raggedy Ann and Andy. Once she tried to join me by coloring on the opposite page I was working on. I moved on to another book altogether. The more she tried to come close to me, the more I rejected her. I enjoyed it.

For those two days my house was inhabited by people who seemingly had no connection with each other. Father never came home for dinner, and in the morning he was quiet and cold. I wanted to be cruel to him, to reject him for wishing for a son, but I was denied the opportunity; he barely noticed me.

On the third day Mother came into my room and laid out some of my nicer clothes.

"You're coming with me to visit Mimi," she said.

Mimi was the daughter of one of her friends. I liked her, though she could never replace Victor.

"I don't want to go," I said. "Maybe Victor will call or something."

"You're coming whether you want to or not. I know what's bothering you—it's the baby. That's natural, but you're car-rying it too far. Besides, Mimi's been asking to see you."

That pleased me; no one else seemed interested in me.

Mimi lived on the American side. As we crossed the bridge, I looked down at the shacks that lined the Mexican side. I had seen them countless times before but now they were personal; now they were important to me, a part of me, paid for in blood. I loved them.

"Have they always been there?" I asked, pointing to the shacks.

"Ever since I came. I imagine they were there long before that."

"Will they always be there?"

"Probably. This is a poor country."

"Are there poor people in Los Angeles?"

"Poor people are everywhere."

"When I have my house I'm going to help the poor."

"I don't understand you, Andrea," my mother said sadly.

We stayed at Mimi's until after lunch. The visit went well. Our mothers left us alone most of the time.

Mimi was a pretty, friendly girl. Her hair was always combed away from her face and she wore barrettes. I liked that. Hers always seemed to stay in place as I wished mine would do. They didn't; no matter how much hair Petra put in them to make them tight, they still traveled down my hair until even-tually they came to rest on my ears.

Mimi knew about my getting beat up and asked me to tell her about it. I did and it was wonderful to see her squirm as I described Victor's ear. I didn't tell her the full story.

"We went walking past the club and suddenly there were some river kids and they wanted money. We didn't have any and they beat us up."

As I said, the visit went well.

When we left I was glad I had come. But something was wrong about the whole thing.

It was me. I was different now, and I kept wondering if Mimi would be so generous with me if she knew I was a thief, that I had watched Armida sell touches and that I had a stash of stolen money hidden away with my Holy Communion dress.

I felt older than Mimi because of what I knew, and somehow she must have sensed my change, because all the while I was there we only did what I wanted to do. She followed my ideas enthusiastically and thought every one of them wonderful. It was flattering, I suppose, but terribly unfulfilling for me. I found myself wishing I could forget all I had learned that summer even for just a day. I wished I could erase the events of the past weeks altogether, or else be free to talk of them, to understand them, to make them wholly mine.

I knew I had stumbled onto something big about life, something I wasn't supposed to know about yet. I had seen the secret adult world, the part that is always there but never talked about, the part that I sensed and feared. Maybe I should have been happy that I knew. I wasn't. I had seen terrible dark things at the river and at Armida's and I had changed. My visit to Mimi's confirmed it.

After Mother brought me home, I walked over to Armida's. It was the first time I had been there since we had taken her money. I don't remember having a purpose for going; I just had to go.

The smell of Popeye's brought back the fears I had experienced the first time we crept up to the loft. I could hear the clicking of billiard balls in the bar. I heard Armida's voice as she answered the men's demands for more beer.

The sound of her husky voice made me eager to see her again, much more than I had looked forward to seeing Mimi that morning. Armida was an indelible constant part of my thoughts and naively I expected her to be pleased to see me.

Two customers entered the store with me and rang for ser-
vice. Armida came to the front, waited on them and rang up
the sale. Suddenly I found myself alone with her. I looked up
and smiled.

"What do you want?"

I had come unprepared; I was without money.

"I, I just came to look . . ."

"At what?" Her voice got lower.

"At things . . . to see if there is anything to buy."

"If you're not buying anything, leave."

I did. But I sneaked back in. When I was sure she had gone
back to the bar I crept upstairs to the loft and once again I
found myself doing what I had promised I would never do
again—spying on Armida.

I had barely positioned myself when two boys arrived. The
procedure hadn't changed. No words were exchanged; apparently she could tell by their faces what they were there for.
The curtain snapped back, then closed. Up went the dress and
the boy touched her. His friend did the same.

Things were the same and yet they weren't. This time I
noticed that when they were touching her, she didn't smile. I
couldn't see the gold in her teeth. Maybe it wasn't fun anymore.
Was it because we had stolen her money and she had to start
all over again? Another change was that she didn't put the
money in the coiled rope.

I found this change exciting. Was I to discover her new
hiding place? I wanted to scream with anticipation. I wished
ever so hard that Victor were with me.

Armida scanned every aisle, making sure no one was there.
I could barely breathe. Then for some reason she returned to
the dressing room where she sold touches and looked at herself
in the mirror. I flinched with embarrassment as she smiled at
herself and checked her teeth.

I expected her to hide the money somewhere in the dressing

room. Instead, she started climbing upstairs toward the loft where I lay. I realized I was going to get caught.

I scurried on my belly across the floor, but every time I dragged across the floor the boards creaked. Armida climbed slowly up the wooden stairs; they too creaked with increasing loudness as she came closer. In a matter of seconds I would be caught, be accused of being a thief. Police would come to Popeye's to drag me to jail. Had I been in the most searing part of hell, I couldn't have repented harder or more bitterly than I did in those moments.

I felt her tight grip on my ankle. "What are you doing? What do you think you're doing?"

She jerked my ankle up to her chest and shook me violently up and down. I saw the floor pull away from my face and then race back toward it.

I screamed, "Jesus! Help me!"

She screamed louder, shook me harder. "Answer! What are you doing here?"

My head bobbed back and forth; I thought my jaw would fall apart. My arms splayed out, searching for something to hold on to.

I pleaded, "Let go of me!" I had to stop her shaking me. I was suffocating. In desperation I reached out to one of her legs and held on with every ounce of strength I had. My head was about to explode with my own blood.

Mercilessly she continued swinging me up and down by my ankle until I thought my foot would snap off. "What have you been looking at?"

"Leave me alone," I shouted. I let go of her leg and slugged at her thighs and knees with all the strength I had left. Then I reached down and found the fleshy part of her thigh and I dug my nails into her softness.

She reached down, took my wrist and wrenched it back. "Tell me what you want, little bitch."

I looked deeply into her mouth and saw her gold.

She pulled back my wrist even tighter. Pain shot up to my shoulder. "How long have you been here?"

I sputtered, "A few minutes."

"I sent you out of here before. Why did you come back?" Another sharp pull on my wrist.

Bursting into tears, I shouted some incomprehensible gibberish.

"Liar!"

She let go of me and the moment I hit the floor, I scrambled to my feet and dashed toward the stairs. She caught one of my braids and jerked me down to the loft floor; she placed a heavy knee on my chest. I could smell her then.

She ordered, "Give back my money."

Her knee pressed down harder on my chest; her arms pinned my shoulders to the floor. "Give it back!"

I turned and twisted under her weight. "I hate you. I'll tell my father."

She released me. I stood and faced her. Billiard balls clicked in the background; knuckles rapped loudly on the bar. Armida's face registered all this.

She looked into my face. "I know who you are," she said. You're Hector Durcal's daughter."

I shrugged.

"Does your father know his daughter's a thief?"

"Does Don Pancho know you're bad when he's asleep?"

Armida moved toward me again, her lower lip puffed out, her arms outstretched. "I don't care whose daughter you are—you—you demon."

She grabbed for my braids and yanked me full circle around the room and flung me against the wall. Her red fingernails reached for the side of my face. Holding me by the hair, she banged my head several times. The room blurred. With both fists I hit her across the chest. She let go. My teeth found the

inner part of her forearm and I bit until I felt her flesh open in my mouth.

She let out a muffled cry and stared unbelievingly at her bleeding arm. I inched away and sidled toward the stairs. She didn't stop me. I put one foot down and then another. Our eyes locked. I continued walking sideways down the stairs, careful not to turn my back on her.

"You are a thief." Her voice had a tiny quaver. "Thief. Thief!"

"I don't like you anymore." I dashed out of the store.

I'm not sure if Armida hollered "Thief" to me again or whether my own guilt kept the word drumming inside my head. I do know that I heard it all the way to Victor's house.

My aunt's car wasn't there. I banged loudly on the front door. Rosario answered; she seemed annoyed to see me.

Out of breath I said, "Tía Milita."

She let me pass. "Wait in the living room."

My aunt came immediately. "Andrea, what's the matter?"

"I'm scared," I said, holding back tears.

She sat next to me and put her arms around me. "Tell me."

I felt like a fraud, letting her comfort me. I didn't want to see her; I needed to see Victor.

"The river boys."

"Are they after you again?" She whirled to the window and peered out.

"No, but I'm scared they'll find me again."

"Are you sure you didn't see them?" she asked, looking both ways out the window.

"I'm afraid they'll come to my house . . ."

"Andrea, nothing will happen to you if you stay away from the river. It takes time to get over things."

"Is Victor almost well?"

"He's napping. His ear is better."

"When can I see him?"

"I don't know," she said cautiously, then added, "Maybe you two should try playing with other children for a while."

"I don't want to!"

"It will be better for both of you. Diane and I have talked about it."

"But you didn't talk to us. No one talked to us. I have to see Victor. I can't play with anyone else."

She wasn't hearing me. "You'll see him again—you just have to wait awhile—till his father gets home."

"That's not until September. It's when school starts! Can't I see him now for a little minute?" I struggled to keep the panic out of my voice.

"He's napping."

"Can he call me on the phone later and can I come over? I'll be quiet, I promise."

She walked me to the door. "We'll see. Have Diane call me."

She brushed my forehead lightly with her lips before opening the screen door for me.

That was that. I walked home full of pain and loneliness. My aunt had meant well, but she had only made my world smaller. I had gone to Armida's to find something, something that my visit to Mimi's that morning had told me was gone.


ONLY Candelaria was home. Barefoot, she was ironing in the kitchen, her pipe lit and resting on one of Mother's silver ashtrays. This was unusual; she only ironed in her room.

"Your mother and Petra have been looking for you."

"I went to the park."

She looked at me. "They went to the park."

"Then I went to see how Victor was. What did they want?"

"Your mother wanted you to go with her. She's not feeling well."

"Who?"

"What's the matter with you?" she scolded. "You look funny. Come here."

I walked over to her expecting her to place her hand on my forehead. She turned up my chin and stared into my eyes. "You have sorrows," she said.

Something more than gentleness, more than understanding, touched me. Tears rolled down.

"Crying helps—not too often, though. Best you learn that soon." Candelaria held on to my chin until I nodded okay. "Now I need help. I don't like ironing in the kitchen."

I helped carry our clothing back to her room. She carried the board and iron. Then she came back into the house, washed off the ashtray, dried it, returned it to the living room. I followed her to her quarters.

"Mother is sick?"

"She went to the doctor's. She didn't want to drive alone."

"She wasn't sick this morning."

Candelaria chuckled. "She wasn't, huh? You got no eyes but for yourself, Andrea. No eyes but for yourself." There was no anger in her voice. "That's not bad," she sighed.

"What's Mother sick with?"

"Woman's sickness."

"Is Father coming home?"

"Don't know."

I didn't want Father around. Armida knew who I was. Would she come to my house? Knock on my door? Come into my house? I had to get to Victor.

"Can I call Tía Milita and tell her Mother's sick?"

"Don't make your mother's business anyone else's but hers. Stay with me till they get home. Why are you so sad-eyed?"

"Things."

"What problems can you have?" She drew on her pipe and looked at me.

"I have lots of problems," I answered rudely. "*Lots* of them."

"Adult problems, kid problems—all the same."

"*You* don't know." Stupid old fool, I thought.

She shrugged and continued ironing. I looked around her room, relieved that she had never moved the dresser. How worried we were the day we stashed our money behind that pine chest. Those early problems were small now. I had Victor with me then, I wasn't alone; I hadn't been found out yet. Once again I felt Armida's grasp around my ankle and was unable to control myself.

"Don't!" I blurted.

Candelaria looked around at me. "Here," she said, handing me some matches. "My candle's about to go out. There's more wrapped in the newspapers, over there by the wall."

A red votive candle flickered before a series of tattered holy pictures. The Baby Jesus, Our Lady of Guadalupe—Patroness of Mexico—hovering above red roses, the Holy Family. A host of other saints rested on the dresser top.

I rummaged through newspapers and brought out a new candle. As I bent over, I spotted a bottle of liquor under her bed.

"Don't put that one out until the new one is lit. Bad luck."

"I won't," I said, distracted from my misery by the opportunity to use matches. "I know how to do it. Father showed me." Mother and Petra had never allowed me to touch them.

I opened up the box of matches. The wax stems were soft; the heat of the day had gotten to them. "Look, Candelaria, I know how to light matches even if they're soft."

Inside I said a prayer: *God, if I light Your new candle with just one match, will You please keep Armida from coming to my house?"*

I put my index finger on the back of the match head to provide support, then I struck it across the rough surface. It exploded into the miracle of a small flame. My heartbeat quick-

ened; I thought it would go out. I pointed the lit head down and the flame became stronger.

"See?" I said proudly.

"Light the candle. The old one's gone to the Lord." I put the match to the wick; the flame expanded. My index finger was burning; I held on to the match.

*Watch, God. It's burning me. Watch. I'm not letting go.*

I pulled away the match and saw that the wick had taken hold. I replaced the old candle with the new and handed it to Candelaria.

"First try," I said.

She gave me a wide toothless smile. The blackness in the center of her mouth caused me to stare, perhaps impolitely.

The last mouth I had seen was Armida's and hers had glittered.

# 11

AFTER lighting Candelaria's candle, I went into Father's study. The picture that Alma and Rosa had ripped apart had been replaced by baby pictures of me in Mother's arms. I didn't like them.

Armida. Would she come? Would Father believe her or me? I felt far way from him. Was I still the most special part of his life? If he knew the whole story, would he hold and carry me close to him?

I was grateful for the bargain I had made with God. The successful lighting of Candelaria's candle gave me some security. It hadn't been easy. A small white blister was appearing on my finger. I hoped God was noticing it.

The fights between Mother and Father had become the center of our family life. Their kissing, their pressing, had disappeared. I felt especially sorry for Mother, whose whole life now consisted of waiting for Father to call or show up for dinner. Well, that's what they get for wanting another baby in the house, I thought.

I longed for someone to like, someone to be nice to. My bitterness, my anger, was souring, rotting my blood. I could taste it in my mouth, smell it in my breath. I thought no one deserved any kindness from me.

I remembered Candelaria.

I went upstairs, took bills from the trunk and returned to Candelaria's room. She was sitting on the bed watching her candles and smoking her pipe.

"No one's home yet," I said.

"Won't be long."

"Can I stay with you?" I asked. I sat on the chair in the corner, the bills rolled tightly in my fist.

She shrugged, "If you want."

"I mean, can I stay here—will you talk with me?" She looked at me for a long time. Unable to withstand her gaze, I shifted my eyes to different parts of the room.

"Why?"

"I want you to tell me things," I said.

"What?"

"I haven't thought of them yet," I said. I doubted that this was such a good idea. Moments ago she had been nice to me. Now she didn't seem to care.

"Thank you for letting me light the candle," I said. "Candelaria, I want to be friends. I can't find anybody to talk to. They won't let me see Victor. He's my best friend."

"There are other children to play with."

"I just want Victor."

"Then I guess you'll have to wait." She drew on her pipe.

"Mother said I was getting a baby brother or sister before Christmas. I don't want it. I hate it."

She laughed. "That's your big problem?"

"It's not the biggest one," I said edgily. "I got lots more, bigger ones. Only Victor knows. We have secrets."

"You do, eh? Well, don't tell me about them."

"I'm not." I suspected she was laughing inside.

"Secrets always come out, you know, somehow, they do."

"Ours won't." Now I was worried. "I want to talk to Victor," I sighed.

"Maybe he's told," she teased. "Maybe he told his mother your secrets and she's going to tell your mother."

"He didn't!" I shouted. "Victor would never tell. You're mean."

She shuffled over to me and cupped my face in her dark coarse hands.

"I'm playing with you. Stop worrying your head. Your face has no light in it," she said. She took my lips and moved them all around. "Your mouth should move more. Laugh," she urged.

I pulled away, but not too far. "When Victor was here I laughed all the time."

She went back to her bed. "Look," she said, stretching her hand out toward me. "What do you see?"

"Half a finger's gone." I had never noticed that before, not even when she had had her hands on my face and mouth.

"Look," she repeated and opened her mouth wide. "What do you see?"

"I know, you have no teeth. That's not funny."

"When I lost half my finger I thought the worst had happened to me—never figured any man would want a woman with half a finger. When my teeth fell out, I thought I could never eat right again."

"I know, you can eat meat." I grew impatient. "You showed us. That's still not funny."

Candelaria laughed, laughed at my angry statements.

"If you keep laughing, I'm going to hate you too," I threatened.

"I laugh because when these things happened to me, I thought they were a punishment from God. They weren't."

"How do you know?"

"Because lots worse things happened. And when God got around to punishing me for my sins, He didn't go around taking part of a finger and all my teeth. What's funny is, I thought those problems were big." She reached for her pipe and relit it. "Problems come, but they go away. I couldn't hold on to my teeth. Your father can't hold on to his hair. You can't hold on to your problems. They're going to leave you. So stop think-ing they're forever. Nothing is—and it's a long time till we die."

She leaned over and rubbed the bottoms of her feet. I focused on the missing finger and desperately wished she hadn't touched my mouth.

"Are you a mother?"

"Fourteen times."

I was speechless. I figured fourteen was two more than a dozen, four more than all the fingers on my hands.

"Yes, fourteen," she said, looking at me. "Mostly boys."

I chose not to believe her. "Where are they?"

"Only five left. Two went across the river, to the other side to work in the fields. My girl lives in Veracruz. One of my boys is a policeman in Monterrey, the other one comes and goes."

"You mean the rest are dead?" I asked.

I wanted to apologize for the question, at least tell her I was sorry that her babies had died, but something about Candelaria stopped me. I could not express grief or pity for what had happened to her.

"Yes, they're dead," she said tonelessly. "Some were babies when they died—the revolutions of '14 and '15 took some . . ." She paused, then added, "Took their fathers too."

She reached under the bed and took out the bottle. The contents looked milky and I recognized the pulque, a drink Father said Indians like to drink. She took a long swallow from the bottle.

"Did you cry?"

She rolled her eyes back—maybe she was trying to re-member.

"I cried for the ones I had with me. They died hungry. The rest died angry."

Her voice was plaintive—as if she was releasing some lost secret. I didn't feel she was speaking to me. Besides, the dates, numbers and deaths of her children and their fathers were incomprehensible.

I had never heard Candelaria say so much before. I didn't understand what she was saying, I had a gray sense, a strange yet clear-cut feeling that I was hearing a frightening story, something worse, something darker than the tale of the prince whose father had been murdered, something blacker than the death of Alicia. I didn't want to hear or understand.

Candelaria's stories were not in books; Mother would never read them to me. Hearing her talk gave me the same feeling I had felt when I first saw Armida. It wasn't exciting like seeing Armida had been; it was powerful. All I could do to protect myself was to breathe in deeply.

Then suddenly I saw that Candelaria was a *girl*—like me. She had always been . . . just *her*. I had never been aware that we were similar—connected somehow. I had felt bound to Armida, perhaps because her actions had awakened something raw inside of me, and whatever came as a result, I had thrilled to what she did; but intuitively I recoiled from Candelaria's story.

"Where's your head, Andrea?" Her voice was familiar once again to me.

"Did you know Alma and Rosa?"

"Saw them at Mass sometimes."

"Did you like them?"

"Never talked to them."

"They killed Alicia," I said.

Candelaria reached down for her bottle and took another long drink.

"They stabbed her," I continued. "The police never found them."

She took one more drink before corking the bottle. I expected the room to smell like when Father was drinking; instead a sweet, thick odor of pineapple wrapped itself around me.

I asked, "Who do you think stabbed her, Alma or Rosa?"

"Why do you care? she asked.

"I think it was Alma," I said with certainty. "And I *do* care."

She stood up. "Are you hungry? I'll fix you something."

"No!"

She sat down and stared at me. "Little girl, why are you here?"

"I want to tell you something," I said coyly.

"I know."

"In a way it's a secret. Do you tell secrets?"

"Depends."

I worried. "Would you tell mine?"

She rubbed the soles of her bare feet together. "I don't know."

"Please don't," I begged. I looked into her eyes and lied. "Victor and I found some money in the park—we kept it."

She blew out a long stream of smoke. "In the park?"

I nodded. "We gave some to the poor outside the church."

"And?"

"Don't you think that was good?"

"And the rest?"

I held out the tight roll of bills to her. "This is for you."

She ignored my outstretched hand and looked at me with unfriendly eyes. "I'm not poor."

"But this is a present," I argued. "Take it!" I ordered. "Please?"

"Why?"

"To buy things. Don't you like to buy things?" I asked.

She rose slowly from her bed. "People don't lose money in the park." She stood looking down at me and added in a low voice, "Children who *find* money don't keep it secret. Children who *steal* money have secrets."

I dropped my gaze and looked at her feet; my hands, tucked deeply into my lap, were kneading nervously.

"It's not stolen money," I whispered. "I wanted to give you a present."

"Let me see the money."

I handed her the sweaty wad of bills. She fished through them and took one out. "For my drink," she said, and returned the rest. "You gave me a present, Andrea."

I followed her into the kitchen.

"I'm cooking dinner. Want to eat now or wait for them?"

"I'll wait," I said.

"Could be a while."

"That's okay."

I noticed that she didn't thank me for the money.

In my room I put away the rest of our treasure. There was still so much left. What were we going to do with it? What was wrong with people? Only the beggars had been grateful. Maybe we should return it to Armida. The thought of her made me nauseous. She knew about me.

I lay down. The day had been a long one and the sun had yet to set. An invisible weight pressed down on my chest and even though I turned over on my stomach, it stayed, forcing me to take deep breaths. Breathing through my mouth helped.


THAT Mother was sick, truly sick, dawned on me as I watched Petra half-carry her upstairs and then put her into bed. Mother bent over to take off her shoes and nearly toppled

over. She held on to her stomach with one hand and with the other broke the fall. Petra raced over to her and helped Mother regain her balance.

"*Señora, por favor, tenga cuidado*," pleaded Petra.

Mother smiled weakly at her. She said to me, "Put on your pajamas, Andrea. Get in bed with me. We'll eat upstairs to-night—just you and me—here in bed."

The dark circles under her eyes gave her a haunted look. I looked at Petra.

"Do as your mother says, Andrea. I'll bring up dinner for you both."

"I'll help," I said.

"You'll help by getting in bed with your mother," said Petra. "At least I'll know where you are."

I understood the barb in Petra's voice and quickly undressed. It was sundown; the house was starting to cool off. Mother held up the sheet to let me slide in. I snuggled next to her, content that even though she looked ugly, she still smelled good.

"What's wrong with you?" I asked.

"Problems with the baby."

"Inside?" I pointed to her stomach.

"Doctor says I have to stay in bed a few days. Will you keep me company?" She stroked my head as she spoke. It was soothing.

"Will I have to stay in bed too?"

"Not if you don't want to. It might be fun, though. We could play and color—listen to the radio—whatever you want."

"Could Victor come over? You could read us stories."

She pressed me to her. "You miss him so much, don't you?" I nodded.

"All I promise is that I'll ask Milita. If Victor's better, she may let him come over for a little while."

"What made him sick?" I asked, still not understanding.

"Maybe too many things happened while his mother was away. He needs rest too."

"Everyone in this town needs rest," I snapped. "Now there's nothing to do."

"There are many things to do. Find enjoyment in quiet things too."

"Why?"

"Because running around isn't the only way to have fun. I worry, Andrea. You're so restless."

"Like Daddy, huh?"

She took a long pause. "I'm afraid so."

"Why are you afraid? Isn't he good?"

"Your daddy is wonderful. He's a wonderful affectionate man."

"Then why isn't he ever home?"

"His feelings are hurt. He'll settle down in a while."

"Why do you fight so much? I hate it."

"It's not fun for us either," she said sadly.

"But you do it so much," I complained. "Don't you love each other anymore?"

"I love him very much." She took my hand and squeezed it.

"Does he love you?"

"I believe he loves me. And he adores you."

"Then why isn't he here? Doesn't he know you're sick?"

She looked ready to cry. "I don't think he does."

"Then tell him. Why don't you tell him? I'll tell him."

"Andrea, calm down. I'll tell him. I'll tell him when I see him, or when he calls, or when I can find him." Her voice was weak.

"Where is he? At work?"

"No."

"Then he's at the club. Call Tony. Want me to?"

"He's not there either. He's probably with friends playing dominoes. Dr. Salas said he would find him and send him home. He's a man. He'll know where your father is."

"He's drinking, isn't he? And he'll come home falling on the stairs and you and Petra will have to carry him and undress him like a big baby. And in the morning he'll be real mean to everyone and then we won't see him again. I know."

"And I'm sorry you know, Andrea," she said.

Her face looked so sorry that I felt ashamed for what I had said. "I still love him a lot," I assured her. "When he drinks he gets strange, and . . ."

"And what?" she pressed.

"And then he smells bad. How can you kiss him when he smells so bad?"

She held up her hands in a gesture of helplessness. "I love him. Someday, you'll meet someone, and you'll fall head over heels in love with him." She chuckled to herself. "I'm going to love watching your father when that happens."

I laughed with her. "Why? Will he think it's funny?"

"No," she said, still laughing. "He won't think it's a bit funny."

We stopped talking when Petra and Candelaria showed up, each carrying a tray of food. They straightened out the sheets for us and placed the trays on our laps. Candelaria had made soup with meat and vegetables; Petra had made me a peanut butter and jelly sandwich.

Candelaria looked out of place upstairs in Mother's room. I had never seen her there before. She looked small and old, and incomplete without her pipe. I smiled at her and she playfully wrinkled her nose at me. I felt I had a new friend.

When they were out of hearing I confided to Mother, "Candelaria keeps a bottle of pulque under her bed."

Mother seemed truly interested. "How do you know?"

I was encouraged by her curiosity. "I was in her room today waiting for you and I saw it. She took a drink from it."

I was careful not to say that Candelaria let me light her candle, or that I had given her money, and I was afraid to mention her nine dead kids.

"Well, she's harmless. I don't know what we'd have done without her. She's been such a help to Petra. I've been absolutely useless since . . ." Her voice cracked. Hurriedly she sipped several spoonfuls of soup.

"Since when?" I asked. "Please don't cry."

She sighed. "It's been a hell of a summer."

"I know—since Alicia was killed, huh?" She nodded. "That's when everything bad started happening to us. I like it when you cuss, Mommy."

"Did I?"

"You said, 'It's been a hell of a summer.' "

"Well, it has." She smiled at me. "It's been the worst *damn* summer of my life."

I laughed. "You're being silly."

"That's probably what I need—laughter and silliness. I wish my friend Betty had stayed longer. We laughed so much. But now I'm laughing with you and that's wonderful too."

We finished dinner and stayed in bed talking, and after a while Mother asked me to go for her sketch pad and pencil and then she had me sit down in front of her while she sketched my face. She drew me frowning and laughing; she drew Cristina from a picture in the room; she drew Victor from memory. I felt pride watching her do this. I loved watching her face as she worked, with her tongue barely peeking out between her teeth. She looked like a little girl. At times I felt I could see myself in her face. And then I remembered the feeling I had had when I realized that Candelaria was a girl, like me, and I remembered Armida, and now here was Mother, and Petra was downstairs.

We were all girls.

These women had once been my size. There was Armida with her dress up behind the curtain, Candelaria with her pipe

and her dead kids, Mother waiting for Father, and Petra who seemed to have no other function in life but to care for us.

I didn't want to be like them; I wanted to disconnect myself from them. They had no laughter inside. And what would happen to me when I grew up?

I said to Mother, "I don't want to grow up." She continued sketching. "Everything bad happens to grown-ups," I persisted.

"Not everything. Things happen to people of all ages."

"But mostly to grown-ups."

"That's because we don't have parents to watch over us," she explained softly. "Come here." She put down her sketch pad and motioned me to her side. "What's frightening you?"

"I'm afraid to grow up. It's ugly."

"Is that how you see us—your father and me—as ugly people?"

"It's the fighting and the quiet. I don't want those things."

"But there's joy too. There's love and having a home and children that you love. There's caring for them, talking to them like now. Andrea, there are many wonderful things."

"Is sitting here with me wonderful?"

"Yes. It is. *This* is wonderful, Andrea." She kissed me.

"You're sure using that word a lot. You said it about Daddy, me—everything. And you're sick—you almost fell."

"It's because of the baby. I just need a few days' rest."

"See? That baby's causing trouble already."

She laughed at me. "Come here, you grump. Let me draw you as you look this moment."

Up went the sketch pad; that's the last I remember. Mother told me to lie still and not to move my face; in those moments of quiet, I fell asleep.


THE sound of metal hitting metal followed by a loud screech of brakes woke me. I was in my bed, unable to recall how I

got there. Then I must have fallen back to sleep, because I was awakened again by loud voices outside.

The voices grew louder; then I realized that they were getting closer; then the voices were *in* the house. Through the bottom of my bedroom door I saw that lights were on.

Fragments of Mother's and Petra's voices—loud horrible wailings—filtered through. Their cries were incomprehensible, unrecognizable to me, and so I stayed in my room—afraid to leave for fear of what I would find.

I called loudly for Mother and Petra; I yelled, screamed— still no one came. I got out of bed and turned on the light.

I opened the door and yelled downstairs, "Mother! Petra!" Male voices drowned out my cries. I went back to bed and waited for a long time before the door opened.

It was Candelaria. She had on a worn faded blue robe; her hair, which was usually braided around her head, hung loose. She looked like a *bruja*. She carried Cristina and was rocking her back and forth in a futile attempt to quiet her.

"Tell me what's down there," I begged.

"Stay in bed. Lots of noise and yelling right now."

She tried to calm Cristina; the baby squirmed away from her, pulling at the long stringy hair. Patiently, Candelaria pried open my sister's fists to free the hair.

"But where's Mother? Who's down there?" I wanted to know, yet I feared hearing the truth. The noise, the shouting, had told me that something terrible had happened to my life. I could feel it, could almost touch it.

Candelaria busied herself with Cristina, avoiding me.

I demanded, "Candelaria, go get my mother!"

"I have to stay here. That's all I'm supposed to do. Things can't go your way right now, Andrea. Understand that."

Candelaria continued to struggle with Cristina, who was demanding an explanation of her own.

I took my sister from her and drew her to me. She wrapped

her little arms tightly around my neck. For the first time in my life, I felt loved and needed by her. I responded spontaneously with tears and kisses.

"Don't cry," I whispered. "Mommy's coming soon."

Cristina quieted down.

The sound of another siren invaded the room, causing the baby new fears.

"Candelaria, *two* ambulances?"

She gathered her hair and pushed it back. "*Your* parents are all right."

"When can I see them?"

"Don't know." She sighed. I smelled the pineapple.

"You drink pulque, don't you?" I sneered.

She shrugged.

"It smells."

Candelaria got off my bed and went to sit on the extra bed—the one Victor used.


LATER that night, Petra finally showed up. From her I learned that Father had crashed his car, that Mother had become sick and had been taken to the hospital. Father had gone with her. When I asked about the two ambulances, Petra grudgingly told me that the second was for the night watchman.

# 12

THE heat in my room warned me I had slept late; downstairs, voices painfully reminded me of the previous night. I lay there trying to guess who was down there.

Petra. Tía Milita. A man. Dr. Salas?

And then I heard him ask, "Can I go see if she's awake?"

Victor.

I hurried to meet him. He stood near the base of the stairs; I stopped short as I came close to him. Something kept me from hugging or pulling at him as I usually did whenever we had been separated for a while. His color was different, his tan, the result of our playing freely in the summer sun, had faded to an uneven pallor. His curls no longer fell loosely around his head. Now his hair was combed straight back—the curls shorn. I saw his mother in him.

Perhaps he sensed something different in me, because he too held back. We approached each other, fully aware that three adults were watching.

I had been right as to who was downstairs,

and more out of duty than desire, I kissed Tía Milita, shook hands with Dr. Salas, and sat on Petra's lap. In her hands was one of Father's handkerchiefs with his initials embroidered in maroon, which she twisted around and around.

I looked around my living room and instantly realized that everyone knew more about my life than I did. I hated the way they looked at me—faces with uncertainty and pity. Angry and resentful, in my head I ordered them all out of my house. I wanted my parents—my weak Mother, my wild Father.

"How are you, Andrea?" asked Dr. Salas.

"Where's my mother?"

He came closer to me. "Resting."

He placed his hand lightly on my head. Instinctively I sank deeper into Petra's lap.

"Is my mother dead?"

"No!" they answered.

"Hector's with her," explained Tía Milita. "Petra and I will help take care of you and Cristina until they come home."

"Where's Cristina?"

"In the back with Candelaria." Petra's voice was a tired whisper.

I wanted my sister with me; but I needed to know more.

"When is Father coming home?"

Dr. Salas knelt before Petra and me and spoke so that only we could hear him. "As soon as your mother is well enough. She needs him to be with her. Do you understand?"

I looked at Victor; his eyes avoided mine. I'd get the truth from him later, I figured.

I turned to Petra and asked, "If I dress myself, can I go out?"

"After you eat."


WHEN I came downstairs, the doctor and Tía Milita were gone. Victor was in the kitchen with Petra and Candelaria

and Cristina. He smiled at me, a weak perfunctory smile. He looked almost like his former self. I ate enough to buy myself permission to get outside to question Victor.

Petra took me by the shoulders. "Play in the front or the back. Milita doesn't want him at the park, the plaza, or the *river*," she added dramatically. "She'll be calling to check on you, Andrea."

The moment we stepped outside, Victor slipped a note to me. It was a tiny square and I had to unfold it several times before I could read the message that was scrawled out in his tiny writing.

"Don't look at it now," he ordered.

"I can't read this. Why are you being so funny? What's the matter?"

He snatched back his note and whispered to me, "It says, 'Andrea, never talk to me about when I was sick.' "

"You mean when you were baby-talking and your mother wouldn't let me see you?"

"Yes. Now, don't do it. Promise me."

I saw that it was important. "All right, Victor, I promise."

Together we walked toward the street. The trail of Father's accident was a block long. Tire marks lined the street. They swerved erratically left and right, ending at the house of a quiet family without children. Resting in a wrinkled heap, almost inside their living room, was Father's bright banana Oldsmobile. Only the right side of the car was damaged.

We backtracked, following the trail of the tires, and I saw where the stucco of the Muñoz, the Elias, the Gómez homes had been crushed by Father's car. In some parts I could put my finger through the holes down to the chicken wire in the wall.

I said to Victor, "I was asleep, but I heard it."

He surveyed the site and shook his head. "This is very bad, Andrea."

We approached Father's car, and I felt growing horror and fascination. Father's car, a car that raced furiously or proudly to and from the house, a strong, fast, powerful vehicle, the newest and prettiest in town, was now remnants, the right headlight strewn on the street.

Victor shook his head. "This is really bad, really bad."

"Don't talk," I pleaded.

He disregarded me. "This is the worst crash we've ever had in this town."

"Shut up, Victor. You don't know."

He pointed to the houses and their broken fronts. "Look at that." He continued talking, mainly to himself. "This is the worst crash I ever saw." He put his hand to his forehead and once again shook his head.

I walked over to check the tires; the ones on the right side were flat. Three spokes stuck out of the front tire. We squatted and looked at them. Victor snapped them back and forth. They made a low humming sound.

I got on my stomach and checked beneath the car and then I saw it—the watchman's bicycle—now a barely recognizable jumble—irretrievably welded to the car. We walked around to the undamaged side. What must have at one time been handlebars was now a braided piece of wire. Untouched, a few feet away, was the watchman's whistle.

I picked it up. "Look, Victor." I blew through it. "It still works."

"Get that out of your mouth!" he screamed.

"Why?"

"Because, because, it's dirty . . . it's *his*. It's a dead man's thing."

"He's not dead," I answered. "He went away in the ambulance. Petra told me."

"He's dead. I know."

"Who said?"

"I heard them talking. They didn't really say it, but I knew what they were talking about."

"When?"

"Before you woke up. I wanted to talk to you. They said you had to sleep."

I believed him. Since I had first seen him that morning, I had known he had something to tell me, something no one else would say to me. Perhaps they thought it best if he told me—it probably was.

I slipped the whistle into my pocket and headed for home. Victor followed. I had heard the news. The watchman was dead—killed in front of my house by my father. That was that. I looked up to the balcony of my house and saw Petra standing there. Had she been watching us all the time? I waved at her and she waved back.

I turned to Victor and asked, "Is Father really at the hospital?"

"I don't know."

"Is he hurt too? Like the watchman?" I asked with great fear.

"No, not like that," he answered quickly.

"How do you know?"

"Dr. Salas said he'd talked to him."

I squeezed both his hands. "Remember *exactly* what he said. Think."

He closed his eyes while he spoke. "He was talking to my mother in your living room and he told her, 'Hector wants you to watch the girls until he handles the police.'"

I let go of him. "The police?"

"That's what I heard. So he can't be dead."

I was confused. "He's with the police, not at the hospital?"

"That's what I heard," he repeated. "But maybe he . . ." He was reluctant to continue.

"Maybe what?" I threatened.

"Maybe the police have him," he suggested cautiously.

"In jail? Why because of *this*?" I pointed to the broken stucco. "He'll fix it."

He lowered his eyes and stepped away from me. "The watchman's dead. Your father killed him. That's very bad." He believed his words.

It was true. That didn't matter to me. Maybe it should have, but it didn't. I felt nothing. No remorse that Father had killed someone—only anger that he might go to jail. It was an accident. Father had liked the watchman. Had hired him to take care of us, to take care of the whole neighborhood. No, Father couldn't go to jail, and Victor shouldn't think that he should.

"He didn't stab anybody," I argued. "He's not bad like Alma and Rosa. This was an accident. Think he would ruin his car on purpose?"

Victor had loved riding in Father's car.

"No," he conceded. "But when people kill someone, they go to jail. That's the truth, Andrea. You know it is. Besides," he added slowly, "killing is one of the biggest sins."

"Why are you talking like this?" I shouted.

"Like what?"

"Like you're someone real good, or like a teacher. You're talking like one of the sisters." I wanted to hurt him. "You're talking like an old good lady—not like my friend."

He flushed. "I'm going home, Andrea. It's not good for me to play with you anymore."

"See?" I yelled. "You're sounding like your mother. She told you that, didn't she? Didn't she?"

"I only do bad things when I'm with you," he said softly. He quickened his pace.

"Victor, you're lying. You're sinning. Right now, you're sinning," I called to him.

He stopped walking away from me. I felt relieved. "I'm not," he said.

"Lying is a sin. You've told me that a million times, and now you're lying. You're blaming me for everything—everything! I didn't want to steal Armida's money. That was your idea, remember? I wanted to look for Rancho Grande's treasure. True?"

"That was before," he murmured.

"Before what?"

He lowered his voice even more. "Before I got sick."

I was confused. "Before Beto beat us up? When did you get sick? Getting hurt isn't getting sick."

"I got sick afterward, after Mother came home."

"That's a lie. I saw you. You weren't sick. You were hiding. Your mother didn't want you to play with me. You let her hide you, and I had important things to tell you." I wanted to tell him about Armida's knowing I had stolen the money but I held it back.

He started to say something; I quickly cut in, "Anyway, you're lying again because you weren't really sick, and because it was your idea to steal the money."

He shook his head sadly. "I was sick, Andrea. I was sick in a different way."

"How?"

"I can't explain it. I was scared all over, all the time. I kept shaking, even in the night."

"Victor, being scared isn't being sick. You were just afraid that Beto and the river kids would get you, weren't you?"

"It was more than scared," he said. His voice shook; tears were beginning to show.

"I believe you." I spoke as gently as possible. "Don't go, Victor. Don't leave me. You're my best friend."

He hedged. "What are we going to do?" He chewed the inside of his mouth.

"I want to find Father. I want to know about jail."

"Andrea, nobody is going to tell us anything."

"We haven't asked everyone." I was thinking of Candelaria. "Come back to the house with me," I urged. "Don't you care where he is?"

"I care. It's just that I don't want to get in trouble again." He was wavering.

"I promise. We won't do anything bad. No lying, no stealing. We'll talk to Candelaria and ask her where Father is. She's my friend now. You liked her."

"I didn't like her. I liked watching her eat meat, that's all."

"Okay, we'll ask her to eat meat for us if you want."

Light returned to his eyes. An impish smile spread across his face. "Know what I really want?" he teased.

I warmed to him. It seemed that in him tears and smiles were never very far away from each other.

"I want to get those spokes out of the tire."

"Why?"

"I just do. I'll stay with you if you help me get them out."

We returned to the wreck; we yanked, pulled, and jerked, but they held fast. Finally, one of them snapped off and that satisfied him.

Under the car was a large pool of oil. A small white object lay in the center of its blackness. I plucked it out.

"What are you doing?" asked Victor.

"Look," I said. "Know what it looks like?"

He took it from me, studied it, and then threw it to the ground in disgust. "It's a tooth!"

"I know. Why did you throw it away? I want it." I retrieved it and relished the horror on Victor's face as I dropped it into my pocket.

"Why do you want it?" he asked.

"Why the spoke?"

"It's part of a bicycle. I'll throw it away if you'll throw *that* away."

"Nope, it's mine," I said. "Come on, let's talk to Candelaria."

By the time we entered the house his look of revulsion was almost gone.

CANDELARIA wasn't in a talking mood. Her hair was loose, as it had been the previous night. The room was dark, the familiar smell of her pipe was absent; her votive candles were lit, but the holy pictures that usually rested on the dresser were propped on her pillow. Rosary in hand, she sat on the bed and prayed to the holy cards. Her eyes were closed and her toothless mouth moved rapidly as she ululated Hail Marys over and over. She crossed herself three times, kissed every one of the pictures, then kissed the wooden beads and wooden cross on her rosary.

Thinking she was finished, I asked, "Can we talk to you?"

I stepped in slowly. When she frowned at my feet I stopped walking.

"Candelaria, look, Victor's back," I said.

She didn't bother to look at him. She pulled out a sack of straw from under her bed and threw the straw all around the floor of her room, covering every inch with various shades of yellows and browns.

"Don't come in," she ordered. Victor pulled at my shirt. I ignored him.

Next she pulled out a bottle of what I figured to be holy water and sprinkled it over the straw, all the while praying, "*Madre Santa, Madre Purísima . . .*"

The ritual continued until the bottle was empty. Then with a small broom which was really no more than a bunch of dry twigs tied together at one end, she swept the straw out of the

room. She pushed us back roughly, and ordered, "Don't let *this* touch you."

Once the straw was outside, she scooped it up, put it in the original sack, and walked to the middle of the backyard, where she set fire to it, all the time continuing to chant, "*Madre Santa, Madre Purísima . . .*"

When the fire extinguished itself, she took the ashes and threw them in four directions. There wasn't much wind, but eventually they did waft away.

It was only when we followed Candelaria back into her room that I discovered Petra had been observing us. I expected her to order us inside, but she didn't say a word.

Petra is acting strange, I thought.

Inside her room Candelaria took a wooden comb and ran it through her hair several times. We watched her plait one side, then the other. When she finished, she wrapped her braids around her head. She seemed like her usual self again; this gave me the confidence to speak.

I spoke as politely as I knew how. "Candelaria, please talk to me."

"What do you want?"

"Will Father go to jail for killing that man?"

"Rich men don't go to jail."

"But Dr. Salas said he was with the police. Victor heard him."

"Rich men don't go to jail."

"Will he come home today?"

"Don't know."

"And Mother?"

She looked at me. "Love your mother when she comes home, Andrea. Love her very much."

She frightened me. I felt close to tears. "I will . . . I promise."

"Go away now."

We had no choice. I wanted to ask about the straw. The

holy water made sense to me, but I had never seen straw used in a *cleansing* before. Later on that day Victor and I sat in the dining room and listened to Petra explain Candelaria's doings.

"Jesus was born in a manger, on a bed of straw," said Petra. "Some people believe that since God chose straw for His Son's first bed, straw is holy and has special powers."

"More than holy water?" asked Victor.

"I don't know," Petra answered humbly.

"What was Candelaria cleansing?" I asked.

"Candelaria believes in certain things—*mal de ojo*, for example."

The evil eye.

"Mother told me those things aren't true. Are they, Petra?"

She waited a long time before saying, "I know the Lord Jesus will protect the good and punish the evil," she said firmly. "Finish your fruit. Leave Candelaria alone." She hurried out.

Petra had surprised me. I had expected her to speak with the usual derision she and Mother used whenever I had asked them about Indian rituals. This time Petra had said nothing against *mal de ojo*. Did this mean she believed in it?

Were the bad things that were happening to my family because of the evil eye? Were we being punished for being evil? I thought of Armida's money. *God forgive me.* I hoped God remembered that we had done *good* with that money.

I thought of Father. Was he evil? Why had I felt guilty when Candelaria had said, "Rich men don't go to jail"?

Father had killed the watchman. Victor was right—it was a terrible sin. But it was an accident. God surely knew that.

So why the cleansing? And if needed, shouldn't the whole house be cleansed? I knew my parents wouldn't allow it, but then they weren't home. I ran after Petra.

"Petra, let's do the whole house with straw and holy water,"
I begged.

Vehemently she shook her head no.

"Why?" asked Victor. "It would be good."

"The señor would never allow it."

"No one's here," I argued. "Me and Victor will do it. We'll
do it real fast, won't we, Victor?"

His eyes lit up. "Yes."

"Please let us, Petra, please," I pleaded. "We won't tell.
It'll be a secret. It can't be bad. That way Father might come
home sooner—Mother too."

I tried to put my arms around her neck. She stiffened.
"There's been enough trouble in this house," she said and
walked away.

Victor and I looked at each other.

"I want to go look for straw," I said.

"I don't want to get in trouble."

"What's bad about looking for straw?"

"Petra said no. She'll tell my mother and then I'll get in
trouble."

"Well, Candelaria knows more than Petra about this. She
knows more than anybody—she's the daughter of a priest,
remember?"

"That's right," Victor conceded.

I saw my opening and spoke as forcefully as possible. "Listen,
if there's a curse on this house maybe it's because of the money
we stole, and if the curse is on my house, it's going to move
onto yours soon."

His eyes widened.

"The money is still upstairs," I added. Again I deliberated
telling him about Armida's catching me the day before; again
I held on to my secret.

He wasn't convinced. His mother had changed him. My
mother didn't have the same power over me. Earlier that sum-

mer he would have jumped at the chance to do magic. Now he was being cautious.

"It could be something else other than the money," he said.

"What?"

"Alma and Rosa. They killed too—on purpose, remember? Besides, we blessed our money."

"You mean Alicia might have put a curse on the house?"

"That's possible," he said. "And if she did, it's going to stay in *this* house only. We never did anything to her."

He was right—for the most part. "Okay," I said, "if Alicia put the curse on the house, didn't Candelaria just get rid of it when she cleansed her room?"

"Maybe."

"So then it can't be Alicia either, right?"

"I guess not."

"So what is it, Victor? Talk to me!" He was being so lazy about this, I was ready to hit him.

"I don't know what it is. If it's not Alicia and it's not the money, there's only *one* thing it can be. It's the only thing left."

I felt sick. "It's Father and the watchman, isn't it?"

"I think so," he said sadly.

It had to be. By every law of life I had learned up to that point, the watchman's death was the cause of my family's misfortunes. If Father went to jail, if Mother died in the hospital, it would be because of the curse.

"Victor, we have to do something important."

Again we went to Candelaria; she still wasn't talking much.

"What can we do to bring Father home?" I asked.

She shrugged. Her indifference was painful. She had been my friend the day before, had stayed up with Cristina and me during the night when we were alone; now she acted like she hated me.

Victor asked, "Does the whole house need a cleansing?"

Candelaria ignored the question.

I tugged at her skirt. "Please help me, Candelaria," I begged. "We asked Petra, but she won't let us do it. Talk to her. Please. I want Father home."

She made a series of guttural sounds, then hissed, "The watchman had seven children."

# 13

HE came home two days later.

Too late. Victor had smuggled newspapers from his house to mine; I had seen the front pages.

I saw the face of the dead watchman; the bottom half of his mouth was gone. The eyeballs were distended; the eyelids would not cover them. I saw his wife and her seven children, one of them Smelly Hands. The worst picture was the one of Father hiding his face with his hat. I felt angry and ashamed.

I read the headline, "*Irresponsáble Acción de Hector Durcal*," and Victor and I sounded out enough words to realize the papers were against him. I remembered how people used to turn and wave at us as we sped by in Father's yellow car. They were so friendly to us. But now the papers hated Father. I was embarrassed in front of Victor.

Father called Petra in the morning and told her that he would be arriving. After she told me, she hurried around the house making everything cleaner. She bought flowers and put them

on the dining-room table; she ordered Candelaria to start making lunch for Father; she dressed Cristina and me as if we were going to Sunday Mass.

I went upstairs and out onto the balcony to wait for him. The day was promising to be hot; a cloudless blue sky would let the sun come directly through to us. Two cars parked down the street. Six men got out. Two carried big cameras. They walked to the front of my house and stood around talking and laughing. I heard the name "Durcal" several times. They smoked and crushed their cigarettes on the front sidewalk, which Petra had hosed down earlier that morning. Neighbors peered out their windows. Mr. Gutiérrez came out and stood in front of his house, arms crossed, and waited. Father's Oldsmobile was still embedded in the Gutiérrez home. A reporter asked him to pose next to the car and he obliged. I sent a death wish.

Father arrived in a police car. There were no other policemen with him other than the driver. The reporters swarmed noisily around, making it difficult for him to get out; the driver stayed behind the wheel and stared straight ahead. Father pushed the door open, forcing the reporters to step away.

He got out; he was hatless, unshaven; his eyes were red, his gaze burned with anger. For a moment he stood straight up and glared at the newsmen; they stepped back and stopped their baiting. Then the police car pulled away and left him alone. That was some kind of signal, because suddenly the reporters were all over him.

"What's it going to cost you?"

"Did your wife leave you?"

"Are you going to fix it with the judge?"

Father walked toward our front door and the closer he got the louder their questions. The reporters seemed to take turns standing in front of him. A fair-skinned young man was the most eager to stand before Father.

"Why is your wife *really* in the hospital, Durcal?" he taunted.

Father stopped walking; I thought he would explode as he stared at the young man.

Father turned to the rest of the reporters and warned, "Keep *that* little son of a whore away from me."

Two of the reporters pushed back the upstart; the young man was delighted with himself. Father moved closer to the front door. I found myself yelling, "Hurry, hurry!"

Just as he reached the front door the young man was in front of him once again. "Were you really behind bars?" He grinned.

"You're dead, you son of a whore dog," said Father. He took a hard wild swing.

The young man easily stepped aside. Father missed and fell. The reporter roared, "*Ese toro, olé!*"

Later, as a result of Victor's faithfulness, I was to see that picture of Father, facedown, on the ground, on the front steps of his home.

I raced down to meet Father. Petra had the screen door open, and she stood between Father and the reporters until he came inside. Cristina was in the center of the living room crying. Candelaria stood in the kitchen watching us. Father pulled Petra into the house and slammed the front door. We all stood and stared at each other. The doorbell rang several times and the noise outside subsided and we heard the cars go away.

The anger in Father's face was diffused by tears which flooded down his cheeks. "*Mis niñas*," he called, and held his arms out to us.

I rushed to him and Petra carried Cristina over to him; her cries had died down to little whimpers. He was smelly and sweaty; Cristina pushed him away and called for Petra. Father let her go.

I allowed myself to be hugged and stroked, and I answered his "Andrea, Andrea," with "Daddy, Daddy," but I didn't mean it. Too suffocated by anger to feel anything other than my own rage pulsing through my body, I dug my nails deep into my palms and focused on the pain; that pain kept me from pummeling Father's face. Biting my lips prevented me from ordering him back out to the street or demanding that he chase down those reporters and make them scream like the river puppy.

Father held me long enough to steady his breathing, then he went into his study and made several phone calls. His voice was strong, its timbre ringing throughout the house that had been so silent for three days. Although his voice sounded the same, and though his sentences, as always, were nothing but a sequence of commands, I no longer believed. The power of Father was gone. I doubted him. Worse—I pitied him.

I soon saw that it was not all his doing. Petra had contrib-uted to my change of heart. The day after Victor and I ques-tioned her about the straw, we found a thin strand caught in the couch's slipcover. We searched further, moving slowly and carefully so Petra wouldn't notice us, and found more straws in all parts of the house. I didn't know if it was Petra or Candelaria who did the cleansing; I did know it could not have happened without Petra's approval.

Petra's decision to cleanse the house planted in me the seed of doubt and distrust toward Father. Would Father be able to fix our lives? Return them to the way they were before we saw Armida? Before going to the river? If Petra doubted him, why shouldn't I?

After he came home that day, I followed him around the house. He seemed to feel some strange need to check doors, windows, mail. He questioned Petra about food several times. He went into the bathroom, bathed for a long time and came downstairs dressed in one of his best suits. He called the ware-

house and one of his men came for him in a small truck. It
didn't matter to me that he was shaven, or that he wore a hat,
or that he smelled as he usually did. I had already seen the
lesser part of him and that became a permanent addition to
the way I would always see him.

Before leaving, Father sat with me in his study, stroking and
kissing me all the while he spoke. I sensed a nervous person.

"I'm going to see your mother," he said. "Do you want me
to tell her anything?"

"When is she coming home?"

"I'll tell you when I return tonight."

"When's that?"

"Before dinner."

I looked at him. "Really?"

"I swear it." He made a large cross over his heart. He was
trying to be funny.

"Will you get a new car?"

I could tell the question made him uneasy. "In good time,"
he said softly. He dropped his hands to his sides and his eyes
drifted across the objects on his desk. "Your daddy has a lot
of business to do and first is to get your mother home from the
hospital."

"What made her sick? The accident?"

"Andrea, you're a little girl. Some things are not for little
girls to know. Your father has a lot of business to do for the
next week or more."

"You'll have to fix people's houses," I said, expecting to see
some sign of embarrassment on his face. None came. I pushed.
"What about the watchman? Victor said when people kill
people, they go to jail."

His lips whitened. "Victor is a child. Children know nothing. You are a child. I will take care of everything."

His voice was strong; perhaps at another time, maybe before
he missed hitting that reporter, I would have believed him.

"You're not going to jail?"

He stood, looked down at me, anger still in his eyes, and lifted me to his height; his hands bruised my upper arms. "I will never go to jail for an accident. Do you believe I did that on purpose, Andrea?" He shook me. "Do you?"

"No." I pulled loose.

"When you have questions, ask me. Nobody, not Victor, just me, understand?"

"Yes," I lied.

He leaned over and gave me a long suffocating hug.

After he left I tiptoed into his closet and buried my head in his clothes trying to recapture his smell, trying to repossess the fervor I had directed only toward him. Nothing returned.

Later that same night Father came home and told me Mother would be home in three days. During that time he worked like a madman to erase all traces of the accident.

From the balcony I saw him directing workmen as they replastered the neighbors' walls. They patched holes—but the houses could not be repainted by the time Mother came home.

The worst day was when they came for the car—Father's car. Four men came with Father, who was driving a flatbed truck; a smaller truck with a crane followed. It was hard work. They had to lift the car off the sidewalk to put it in the street. I could tell Father's warehouse workers weren't too sure what to do. He had to keep showing them where to go and how to drive the truck. They used chains which were too thin and consequently snapped; the car crashed down.

"Son of a bitch!" he screamed.

The men stood idly by.

"Son of a whore!" he said louder.

The men looked at the ground and shuffled their feet nervously.

Father got in the smaller truck and sped away, leaving the men behind. They smoked in silence. Half an hour later Father

returned with huge chains. The men seemed pleased; they moved eagerly toward the chains, seeming to approve of Father's selection.

Together Father and his workmen positioned the chains underneath the car, and then Father directed the crane operator to begin hoisting the wreck onto the flatbed truck. The metal screeched against the concrete as the car rose slowly off the ground. A few bolts and pieces fell from under the engine.

When the car was about two feet off the ground, Father ordered two of the men to guide the wreck onto the truck.

"Push it lightly. I don't want her swinging loose." Father moved in to show them how. Then he ordered the man working the crane, "Speed up. Get this carcass out of here."

A high-pitched whir filled the street. I put my fingers into my ears. I saw Father gesticulating to his men to guide the car carefully onto the truck. The car must have been nearly six feet off the ground when suddenly it broke into three pieces. One fell—almost as if on purpose—on a workman's leg.

The man collapsed under the piece of metal. His cries filled the street. Father ran around like a crazy man trying to lift the piece off the workman.

"Help me!" he ordered.

It was useless. They couldn't lift it. The injured man screamed and growled; his fists pummeled the street. Then he passed out.

I raced into the house and got Petra. "I'll call an ambulance," she said.

"Get pillows, blanket, a rope," Father snapped.

Neighbors came out. Father put them to work. In unison they freed the man from under the metal.

Petra emerged from the house with everything needed— including several pieces of rope I didn't know we had. Father tied the man's leg and then lifted the man onto the back of

the small pick-up and drove away. The remaining workmen stood around nervous, lost.

Petra took over. "There's enough of us here to get rid of this thing," she said, pointing to the car pieces.

The neighbors and workmen followed her directions. They pushed, lifted, sweated. In the end all three pieces were finally hoisted onto the flatbed truck. Everyone clapped. The truck pulled away; we waved the workmen goodbye and then the street was empty, nearly clean—except for the bolts that had fallen out—and a familiar silence returned to the neighborhood.

FATHER came home for dinner. He looked tired. He assured us that the man would be all right. He was kind with us; but he spoke in phrases that went unfinished. He tried to play with Cristina, but he was pretending and he couldn't fool her. She refused his caresses and eventually Petra came and took her upstairs. He finished his dinner in silence.

I sat with him. Under the table, I played with the dead man's tooth, something I had taken to carrying around since I had plucked it out of the oil. I don't remember a specific reason for my action; it just seemed logical, as logical as cleaning the house with straw. The tooth, I figured, could well have special powers. Like the straw.

Father stared at his plate as if expecting something to come out of the center. I sensed that he was thinking something sad.

"Do you believe in curses?" I asked.

I startled him. "Curses?" He looked annoyed.

"Yeah, bad wishes that come true."

"I know what they are. Why are you asking? Who have you been talking to?" He stood and threw his napkin over his plate.

"I'm trying to talk to you. If you're going to get mean with me, I won't say anything. Who do you think I've been talking to? No one's around. No one comes here anymore."

"I'm sorry. No, I don't believe in curses. That's all super-stition." He took in a deep breath. "Why are you asking?"

"I'm wondering if the accident that the workman had today might not have been a curse of the watchman."

"That's ridiculous, absolutely ridiculous."

"I'm just asking."

"And I'm just telling you. Get that garbage out of your head."

I felt myself getting mad. "How can you be sure? How do you know that your accident wasn't part of Alicia's curse? You don't know. You believe it, but you don't *know*."

"I know goddamm it because I say I do and that's that!"

"You'd better not hit me," I warned.

"Hit you? When have I ever hit you?" He seemed thor-oughly confused. I was too. Everything was getting away from me.

I took the edge off my voice. "You've never talked to me that way before."

"I've never felt this way either," he said hoarsely.

I looked up at him and nodded.

He walked past me and put his head on my head. "Sorry, Andrea."

"It's all right, Daddy."

He walked over to the china closet and took out a bottle, then went into his study and shut the door.

I stayed in my chair, clinging to the tooth. It gave me some comfort. Perhaps I needed something definite to cling to, some-thing that was part of a safer, happier time in my life, a time when the club and Tony the waiter were a source of laughter, a time when discovering secrets with Victor promised limitless wonders.

Cristina had taken to me since the night of the accident, and I found solace in her need for me, found joy in hearing her call my name, "Anda." Life was changing too rapidly, and I knew it; I had stopped feeling safe in Father's presence. Cris-

tina's dependence on me somehow restored balance to my life. If Father wasn't strong and powerful to me, then I would be strong and powerful to someone else.

I did as I was told that night and went to bed at the first command. Alone, I grieved at the vacuum left in the space Father had occupied so fully.

I lay in bed and ran the town and its people through my head; every place and everyone seemed soiled to me. My bed was the only place where I felt safe. The club reminded me of the river with the tortured dog and Beto. Besides, Smelly Hands worked at the club, which reminded me of the accident, and of Armida, whose money was in the chest with my Holy Communion dress; and thinking of Armida reminded me of Alma and Rosa and Alicia with her throat slit.

Victor didn't come around once Father was home. I didn't care; his presence would only have burdened me. No, I was content with the tooth, content with staying in the house playing with Cristina, taking naps with her, staying as close to her as possible.

Deep inside I knew that if Victor and I hadn't gone back into the maids' room to talk to them about confession, they would not have been sent away and none of this would have happened. But we had gone back and inadvertently set off a chain of events that was strangling my family and me. And all I had to ward off more disaster was a tooth.

## 14

A RAIL-THIN old crone was helped up the stairs by Father and Petra while Cristina and I watched from a safe distance away. Mother was in nightclothes, and Father stood aside, pain etched in his face as he watched Petra carefully undress his wife and put her to bed. Cristina kept pulling away from me, demanding to go to Mother.

"Take her to your room, Andrea," Father ordered.

Mother spoke sharply to him in English. "I want them with me, Hector."

I let go; Cristina climbed eagerly onto the bed and threw herself around Mother's neck. Mother tottered under the baby's weight, but only when she was about to collapse did Father lift off Cristina.

When Mother was resting comfortably on her pillows, I walked over and kissed her many times—more than I wanted to; her breath was bad. The last time I had seen her we had been in bed talking and she had been sketching, and I had been pouting about the new baby. I no-

ticed her stomach was flat, and, God forgive me, I thought at least some good had come out of this.

Candelaria stood in the doorway studying Mother for what seemed hours before telling Father, "Give me money to buy oxtails. Soup will make her strong."

Silently, he gave her a handful of pesos. Father said little the rest of the day; even when the smell of boiling meat per-vaded the house, he said nothing. He followed Candelaria upstairs and stood by while the Indian woman spoon-fed Mother, whose trembling hands had spilled soup over the bedding.

I stood behind Father, overwhelmed at the change that had taken place in Mother in less than a week's time. The hands that had dexterously moved a pencil over her sketch pad were now unable to hold a spoon. Yes, everything bad happens to grown-ups. No matter what Mother or anyone else said, it was the truth.

I had what I had thought I wanted: the family was united again—only because we were in the same house. But we had changed; we were strangers who had nothing to share. The only reality we had in common came to us through our noses when Candelaria faithfully boiled oxtails, and, almost reli-giously, padded barefoot up the stairs to feed Mother six times a day.

Father never left the house; he remained in his study barking orders over the phone, or sitting on the couch reading about himself in the papers—something that was sure to send him back cursing to the phone.

The first two days Mother only slept and ate. When al-lowed, Cristina and I went in to see her and, true to my promise to Candelaria, I was good to her. I loved her with as much love as I had.

After the third or fourth day I noticed specific changes in Mother. The important differences were subtle, but the

changes pronounced. She spoke only in English to me. She did the same with Father and Cristina. Her eyes were different, too; they were scrutinous, clear, penetrating, and liquid in that they followed every move we made. She saw us through the eyes of a stranger who was trying to learn about us through observation.

Another change was how she reacted to Candelaria. Barely a week ago when I had told her that Candelaria drank pulque, she had smiled and called her "harmless." Now it seemed that she wholly depended on Candelaria. My mother drank obe-diently from the older woman's hands, demanding more soup, completely trusting that the potion would make her strong again. When she finished eating, she would lie back and allow Candelaria to pray over her. Candelaria stretched her arms over Mother's supine form and feverishly entreated to the Virgin Mary, "Look and take pity on your daughter." I had walked in on them by accident the first time, expecting the ritual to halt because of my presence, but they continued. After that, I spied on them again and learned that it was a rite that always accompanied the feeding.

What was all this? Mother had consistently discounted our servants' beliefs as superstitious nonsense. Had not Alma and Rosa been sent back to the river for frightening Victor and me? Wasn't I forbidden to speak to maids about God and religion?

I wanted to tell Father what was going on, but I feared his reaction. Never had I seen him stay in the house so many days; the strain of being caged was showing. The sweet caresses he showered over us when he first returned after the accident gave way to perfunctory pecks on Cristina's and my foreheads. Only with Mother did he remain solicitous and caring; but Mother was not responding. She barely spoke to Father. No, I couldn't tell Father about Candelaria's prayers.

I did tell Petra.

"You stay away from there, Andrea," she warned.

"Why?"

"It's none of your business."

"You know Mother doesn't believe in *that*," I pressed. "Do *you*?" I was thinking of the straws Victor and I had found and waited for a wince or a sigh that would belie whatever answer she gave me.

Her pockmarked face revealed nothing. "There are many ways to reach God," she answered.

I continued to spy on Candelaria and Mother. It was easy—they were both so involved with what they were doing. Besides, there was little else to do. I wasn't allowed outside; under Father's orders the curtains in the front room remained closed. Curious onlookers paraded in front of our house almost daily surveying the site of the accident. The replastering was finished; the paint never went on.

Mother got to where she could sit up after Candelaria prayed over her and then the old maid talked to her.

"Señora, it is bad for you here," whispered Candelaria.

"Why?" asked Mother.

"I can feel it."

Mother laughed weakly. "Can you?"

Candelaria picked up the tray and left without saying more. But she continued to talk to Mother every time she came upstairs to feed her. She never said much. Candelaria's Veracruz accent was thick and Mother's ear lacked the sharpness to understand the rapid speech common to people from the tropics.

"You have a mother on the other side?" Candelaria asked her one afternoon. I stood in the doorway; they knew I was there.

"In California."

"Go to her when you are strong again," Candelaria urged. "Take your children with you."

"I can't leave my house, my husband. Tell me why I should leave."

"It's time for you to move. Bad airs are around. They bring suffering to this house. You know this is true, señora."

Mother was silent and handed back the tray of food. I stepped aside to allow Candelaria to leave, then went in to talk to Mother.

I asked angrily, "Do you believe her?"

She spoke softly—barely above a whisper. "She means no harm."

"I've heard what she says. Why do you listen? You always told me not to listen to what the maids say."

"I don't want to be rude. She's worked so hard cooking for me. I am getting stronger. I should be up in a day or so. Where's your father?"

"Probably in his study. Isn't he ever going back to work?"

"Get Daddy for me."

"Will you tell him what Candelaria said?"

"Maybe later if you want. Meanwhile, let's keep it a secret."

I'd never had a secret with Mother in my entire life. This was a good one.

Father went upstairs immediately. Of all of us he saw Mother least. Since she had returned from the hospital he slept either on the living-room couch or in the big chair in his study. He went to see her only when she called for him. It seemed peculiar watching Father do what Mother told him.

He locked their bedroom door. I tried listening, but they spoke quietly and in English. Then Father yelled out in Spanish, "You'll never see them again if you go."

I don't know what she answered, but he calmed down.

SUNDAY morning Father allowed me to stay home from church.

He, Cristina and I were having breakfast when suddenly Mother appeared. Her hair was combed, and she had on lipstick and rouge on her cheeks. She wore her yellow bathrobe with matching slippers, things she wore on trips when she wanted to look extra nice in hotels.

Father couldn't move fast enough to make room for her.

"Petra!" he called. "We have a guest!"

Petra clapped at the sight of Mother at the table. "*Señora, por fin!*" she exclaimed. Hurriedly she brought in the same thing we were eating, chorizo and eggs.

Mother looked at the eggs and laughed. "At last, no soup!"

Candelaria peered out from the kitchen and saw Mother eating.

"*Está bien?*" asked Mother pointing to the food.

"*Sí, señora,*" answered Candelaria and gave us her widest toothless smile.

Mother ate and Father beamed with pleasure. He seemed foolish to me. All she was eating was eggs and sausage yet Father was the happiest I had seen him since the accident. His eyes followed Mother's fork as it went into her mouth and then he moved his own mouth in unison with hers.

She swallowed and he piped, "*Olé!*"

He did it a few more times until he got Cristina and me to follow suit. It felt stupid to cheer while Mother ate eggs. I did it for him.

"Andrea," Father said, "your mother has been eating so much oxtail soup she's growing horns. Come, feel the bumps on her head," he challenged.

I shook my head in refusal.

"Come," he said in English. "There's two bumps—baby horns. Your mother is the bull of the corral. She gets everything she wants from now on."

Cornered, I got up and felt Mother's head. "Nothing there," I said and sat down.

"Sure there is," he said, touching her gently and kissing her forehead.

He was trying to be funny; it wasn't working. He was speaking in English, and I wasn't used to hearing Father clown in English. He had an accent and his silliness lacked the bite I associated with his morning romps.

I also found myself speaking English, which added to the strangeness of the morning scene. An occasion that should have been full of spontaneous laughter was a farce as we assumed these unfamiliar sounds. Apparently I was the only one who noticed or cared. But to me it was as if our insides had been replaced by something foreign, some counterfeit sound borrowed to make do. Everyone, including me, was shocked when I burst into tears.

The tears sprang forth. I lunged and covered Father's mouth and pleaded, "Stop that!"

The whole room stopped.

The whole house stopped.

Mother, after a second or two, asked, "Stop what?"

Father caught the moment. "Come here," he said gently and pointed to his knee.

I went and sat on it—barely.

He spoke in Spanish. "What's the matter with you, Andrea?"

I screamed at the top of my lungs, "I want us to stop the way we're acting! We're acting stupid!"

"Why do you say this?" asked Mother in English.

"I don't know! Something's scaring me!"

"Speaking in English scares you?" asked Mother in English.

"Yes. No. It's that we're pretending."

"Pretending what?" continued Mother.

"I don't know," I said. I turned to Father and asked, "*You* know, don't you?"

"I'm trying to understand."

I believed him.

I looked at both of them. "Do you still love each other?"

"Yes," they answered.

I nodded. "I don't feel it anymore. Something's gone." I got off Father's knee and walked to the staircase. Petra followed me from the kitchen; her cheeks were wet. In the doorway stood Candelaria; her eyes swept across the room, stopping at every face.

"Go away," I said.

She sat next to me and held my hand. "Tell your Petra what's wrong."

"I hate everything. I want things to be like they were."

She sighed. "They can't. And you don't need to act the way you did. Your parents need you."

"For what?"

"They need your love."

"I hate that word. People just use it. The new baby's not coming, is it?"

Petra shook her head.

"Good."

"Andrea, sometimes the devil comes out of your mouth."

"I don't care. You know this house has a curse on it. That's true, isn't it?"

"No, it's not. There was an accident and your father is trying to fix everything. He doesn't need his daughter crying and yelling all over the place." She spoke to me like an adult.

"Tell me why we're speaking English now."

"Your mother wants it."

"But why now? What does it mean? Why right after the accident and after the hospital?"

"I don't know."

"You do know, Petra. Something's happening. I can feel it

and Candelaria is a witch. She prays over Mother and tells her to leave."

"How do you know?"

"I heard her say it when she brought up the soup. She told Mother this was a bad place and for her to go home to Grandmother's."

"Well, she hasn't gone, has she?"

"She started walking today. What's going to happen when she gets all strong again?"

"Andrea, you're acting like a spoiled baby. You shouldn't be spying on your mother. Be sweet. You can be so sweet when you want to. Don't ruin things like you did this morning." She let go of my hand. "You need a good spanking."

That made me smile. "Are you going to spank me?"

"If you don't stop sulking and adding to the troubles of this house I sure will."

"You won't spank me." I took her hand. "I'll be good. Tell them I'll be good."

"No, you come down and say you're sorry."

My parents were speaking softly to each other; I could tell Mother had been crying. I felt ashamed. I apologized; my parents opened their arms and embraced me.


THE next day Father left the house for the first time in days. While he was gone, Mother called long-distance to Los Angeles.

"No, there's nothing to worry about. I'm all right. I want the children to see Los Angeles. They've never had an American Christmas. . . ."

She was speaking from Father's study. I kept out of sight.

"Hector's doing the best he can. It's been rough—and very costly. Anyway, I want Andrea to see more than this town. She's a little savage. . . . You'll see for yourself. Cristina's fine.

. . . Yes, really. . . . Of course I can have more children. . . . I don't know. I don't want to think of that right now. I need time. . . . Love you too. . . ."

After she hung up, I stepped into the doorway. "I'm not going to Los Angeles," I said.

She looked surprised.

"I'm not going. I'm never going. You can't make me."

She held her hand out to me. "What are you talking about?"

"I heard you. You said I was a savage. I know what a savage is," I said.

She laughed. "Good, tell me what a savage is, Andrea."

"I hate Los Angeles."

"You've never been there."

I banged the doorframe with my fists. "I don't care," I screamed. "I still hate it."

"Look at you!" she said mockingly. "You are a savage."

"You want to take us away because of what Candelaria said to you. You believe her. You're stupid."

Now she was angry. "That's not true and watch your tongue."

"Does Daddy know?"

"I'll tell him when he comes home."

"Good. You tell him in front of me. I want to hear you tell him."

"You're impossible."

She walked away.

I sat in the living room waiting for Father to arrive. It was a long boring wait. I fought off sleep. Mother remained upstairs. I hated her for talking to Grandmother about me.

Grandmother loved me. I had only seen her twice in my life, but whenever she came to visit, she came loaded with presents for me. Father liked her too.

Three loud beeps sounded. I ran to the door; it was Father, finally. He stood by a car, a brown muddy-colored car, not nearly as nice as our yellow one. One of the doors had a dent.

He smiled and pointed to the car. "Well?"

"It's brown," I said, "not new."

"To us it's a new car."

"I don't like brown cars."

I walked up slowly. I felt Father's eyes following; I tried to hide my disappointment. I knew I was supposed to feel excited about this.

All I could think of to ask was, "Does it go fast?"

"Of course it does!"

"I wonder if Victor will like it."

Father shrugged. "It's better than what his father drives."

He reached into the car and beeped the horn several times. Mother came out. She looked sleepy and lazy and strolled casually toward Father and his car.

"It's fine," she said without enthusiasm.

Father's face fell.

"Diane," he said in a guarded voice, "how would it look for me to buy a new car after what happened? People would talk even more."

"Since when have you concerned yourself with what people say?"

"You've never learned, have you?" he asked bitterly.

I sensed a big fight coming. I didn't want to hear the ugly angry words they were going to say to each other.

"I like the car," I blurted. "The seats are nice. Look, Mother," I begged and pointed to the inside. "The seats are white like in our real car."

She ignored me and looked at Father. "Cars don't matter to me. You know that, Hector."

"I'm tired of your so-called sensitivity. Tired of your suffering face. I'm sick of you trying to change me." His voice grew louder with each phrase. "You've been trying to change things since I married you, trying to make us better. Don't say it isn't true. You can't do it, Diane—you just can't."

I stood behind the car and watched as my parents tore at

each other. I didn't understand everything—but my sympathies were with him. I knew what it was to do wrong—I was a thief. I was a liar. I knew that those who do wrong suffer.

Mother could list all that was foul about Father. Was there not the body of a dead man to point to? Father had killed the watchman, a man who had children to feed. Yes, Father was the bad one—and he was all the more pitiful for it.

Spit gathered at the sides of Father's mouth after he exploded at Mother. His fury failed to change the unfocused, cold gaze she cast on him. She could have been looking at a stranger from a mile away.

She turned to me. "Tell him about Christmas," she said, throwing the words over her shoulder. She turned and headed toward the house.

Father and I watched her walk back with slow, measured steps, the pace of a woman gathering her strength.

"It is a good car," he said. His voice was unconvincing.

"She called Grandmother today. We're supposed to go there for Christmas. Did you know?"

He shook his head.

"I don't want to go," I said. "Don't make me."

Father took my face in his hands—as Candelaria had done. "Your parents are just people, Andrea," he said. "Believe me, we're trying to do the best we can. We make mistakes. Like you and Victor, we sometimes flunk, understand?"

His hands were cold; his fingers had white lines running through them, the kind I had when I was scared, the kind I had when Armida caught me in the loft. I pitied Father.

I pulled away from him for fear of finding myself unable to breathe. He was trapped; he was too much like me. He had expected Mother and me to like his brown car; we had failed him miserably.

"I want to go inside," I said apologetically. I followed the same trail back into the house that Mother had trod moments before.

I sensed Father looking at me; I heard his shallow breathing as he watched me move away. There was nothing I could do for him. How could I tell him that he was not an evil man? That the killing of our watchman was *only* an accident?

I lacked the courage to tell him about my willful sins. I had pity for him, but no loyalty.

When I opened the screen door I felt him behind me. He shoved me aside and bolted up the stairs, two, three at a time.

"Diane! Diane!" he called.

Doors slammed shut and the yelling began. They took turns. I cowered in the kitchen with Petra and Candelaria. All three of us waited in fear as the upstairs shook with crashing objects and the shock of bodies slamming against the walls.

In the end, blood streaming down his face, Father ran downstairs, hurried through the front door and ran down the street, leaving his brown car behind.

# 15

I HEARD his drunken steps in early dawn.

"Diane!" he bellowed. "Petra!"

I went back to sleep. They must not have heard him. They must have decided not to hear him, because when I finally got up later in the morning the house was unusually still.

Mother's door was closed. I went downstairs and found him, fully dressed, passed out on the living-room couch. The cut over his eye had sealed and the front of his shirt was soiled. His alcohol breath filled the room.

I poked him a few times; he turned over. Petra tiptoed in and led me to the kitchen, where she quietly fed Cristina and me.

"Where's Mother?"

"Still asleep."

"Why is Father on the couch?"

"Your mother thought it best if he stayed downstairs."

I looked at her and asked, "You don't like him anymore, do you, Petra?"

"Your father is a wonderful man. I work for him."

"But you didn't help him last night. He called for you. I heard him."

She shook her head helplessly. "I do as I'm told."

"Mother's not eating?"

"She'll eat later. I'll take her some coffee. Don't cause trouble."

"I think I'm going to hate this day."

I watched Father sleep most of the morning. Finally near noon I poked my finger into the cut over his eye. He sat up. His cheek was creased and his eyes were red. He tried to smile at me. His lips barely moved.

Father's eyes scanned the room. I was the only one around. There was none of the usual family support that ordinarily accompanied his hangovers. Mother was in her room; Petra was upstairs with Cristina; Candelaria was in her quarters.

"To hell with all of them," he muttered.

He rubbed his face with his hands several times, then went to the bathroom. He didn't shut the door and the sound of his urine splashing into the toilet bowl was the only sound in the whole house. It seemed to last forever.

Father went to the refrigerator and pulled out a cold beer. He always said that a cold beer was the only friend a man had when *el demonio* had taken his soul. He leaned against the refrigerator in his wrinkled clothes and rolled the cold beer bottle across his forehead.

"Don't stare at me, Andrea."

"What's wrong with our house?"

"Not you too," he groaned. He downed the rest of the beer, then let out a long burp, the kind that made Mother flush with anger. "Ahhh. That felt good. I don't know what's the matter with this house, baby. I don't know what's the matter with me." He pulled playfully at my braids. "You still my friend?"

"Yes."

"Well, that's one. After I shower, do you want to go for a ride with me? Spend the day together, like the old days?"

"Mother said I had to go to catechism with Victor. You could make me go with you."

He smiled. "Sorry, Andrea, you'd better go."

"*Make* me go with you, please. I want to be with you."

"I know, baby, but it's near the end of summer. Pretty soon you'll be getting ready for your Holy Communion. Your grand-mother from California will be here. Your dress came from Madrid."

"Who cares?"

He walked over to the sink and let the cold water run over his head. "I'm dying."

"Does your eye hurt?"

"Not just my eye."

He kissed me and went into his study and closed the door. I followed and knocked. "Can I come in?"

"Not right now."

"Aren't you going to take a bath?"

His voice sounded tired. "Later."

"Want me to get someone to cook you breakfast?"

"Your father doesn't need anybody."

"Should I get Mother?"

"What for?"

"Want another beer?"

He waited a long time before answering. "No."

I went for a beer, opened it, and put it in front of the study door. "Daddy, a beer is here."

No answer. I spoke louder. "I'm putting a beer here." I banged on the door as I spoke.

"Huh?"

"Daddy, it's me, Andrea. I put a beer here for you, okay?"

"Okay."

Then he didn't say anything more. He wasn't mad. He was just asleep.

I was relieved to get away from the house even if it was for

religious instruction. Victor and his mother picked me up and I listened to all they had done that day. They had been shopping in the morning and he was wearing new clothes and behaving very dressed-up.

I wanted to tell him about Mother and Father's big fight, but I suspected he would say something bad about them. I could tell when Victor was in one of his good moods. Those were the times when we had our biggest fights. So I suffered through his goodness and answered his "How've you been, Andrea" with a "Just fine, Victor, and you?"

Tía Milita smiled to herself. I could tell this would later be told to Mother and they would laugh and talk about how cute we were. And if Victor was around spying, he would believe them, and then he would prance around and overact. Then I would feel like hitting him and I would keep myself away from him to prevent myself from hurting him. Being without him was harder than being with him and wanting to kill him.

It was midweek, so the beggars that usually lined the church steps were not there. Tía Milita parked her car around the side of the church and escorted us inside. Doña Sara, Padre Lozano's housekeeper, opened the door for us.

Doña Sara had served the padre of our town since anyone could remember. Our fathers had tried to figure out her age— it was impossible. She went back to before the time Grandfather brought the railroad to town.

Doña Sara had no Indian blood in her—she made sure everyone knew that right away. She considered herself an equal to anyone but the padre. When she opened the door she briskly directed us to our proper places. Victor and I were taken to a side room where an old nun, Madre Angelica, sat in a small pew. Doña Sara took Tía Milita to another pew.

"This is today's meditation," Doña Sara told my aunt.

My aunt nodded gratefully.

Always dressed in widow's black, Doña Sara spoke mainly

with her body. The eyebrows went up and that said "Ah, it's you." She half bowed and extended her arm and she was saying "Come this way." If she pointed her index finger at Victor and me, that for sure meant "Go in there and be quiet." If the brows went up again, we both heard "Hurry."

I was delighted to have Madre Angelica instruct us. We had had her before; she was the nicest of all the sisters who taught catechism. Once we had Madre Encarnación. She would often pull our hair if we answered incorrectly. I told Father and he made sure we never got her again. Later we found out that she mainly taught converts.

Anyway, Madre Angelica made me laugh. She had a small wrinkled face and her eyes were brown and set deep in her head. She also had short whiskers around the sides of her mouth and along the side of her chin—not much, just a few bristles, but enough for Victor and me to take one look and choke with laughter.

She began:
*Who made us?*
*God made us.*
*Who is God?*

We had learned all this months ago, though we didn't dare tell her. She continued until we got to the part about confession.

*What is confession?*
*One of the Seven Sacraments instituted by Christ to give grace.*

That's the part that always got me. What was being in a "state of grace" all about? I understood how sins stayed on your soul until you went to confession, but what if you weren't really sorry and you confessed anyway just because someone told you a certain act was a sin? And what if you didn't confess a sin but were truly sorry?

This was too much for me. I started to think about First Communion instead and who I would give my First Com-

munion kiss to. Such an important gift. Wouldn't Petra be surprised if I chose her! I wondered how a kiss, a kiss from *my* lips, could ever save someone's soul.

But first I had to make a good confession. I knew one was supposed to tell priests everything, but I had seen Padre Lozano at my house drinking with Father. They would drink until Father had to drive the padre home.

Tía Milita once said about my father, "Hector could get the Blessed Virgin drunk if he wanted." I believed her. So confessing to Padre Lozano would have been like telling Father, and that was simply not possible.

We gave Madre Angelica the right answers and then Doña Sara reappeared and gave her brows an extra high lift which meant "You're finished. Good." Our religious instruction was over.

"Mother," said Victor, "she's got hair on her face."

"Don't be fresh, Victor."

Suppressed laughter is painful and Victor and I suffered until I saw that we were nearing my home.

"Tía Milita, don't take me home yet."

My voice surprised me. It had a frightened, desperate sound.

"Andrea, what's wrong?"

"Nothing."

"Then why don't you want to go home?"

"I like being with you and Victor." I sounded false.

"It's five o'clock—near dinnertime," she said.

"Please take us by the plaza." I looked at Victor and pleaded with my eyes.

"Just for a while. We never get to go there," he lied.

Moments later we were watching vendors laughing and peddling their wares. It was like early summer. Feelings rushed back. I recalled parading across the plaza flashing Armida's money in the faces of expectant vendors. I remembered the power I felt when I refused to buy their goods.

Tía Milita waved away the vendors as if they were nothing.

The men's smiles faded as they moved back from our car and I felt like one of the American tourists. I was sorry for the vendors and wished that I had brought money to buy some-thing—anything. I recalled how carefully they dusted their goods in the early morning by the river. I asked my aunt to take me home.

Victor looked at me and asked with his face, "Are you sure?"

I nodded yes. On the way home we stopped off and got some ice cream cones, not the kind they sold in the USA but ices, the soft runny kind we had in Mexico.

The sun was setting as we pulled up to my house. Only one light was on. Something told me that Victor and my aunt should not come inside. I got out of the car, hastily kissed my aunt goodbye, and gave Victor's hand a weak squeeze.

I heard Father's angry voice before I opened the front door. The whole room seemed to take a deep breath until they saw that it was only me.

Sitting on the couch in the dimly lit living room were Smelly Hands and his mother. She was dressed in black. Her legs were covered with thick black stockings and she wore a black ban-danna knotted lightly under her chin. Smelly Hands had on a white cotton shirt with a black band around the top of his arm.

"Andrea," Father said curtly. "This is Mrs. Sánchez and her son Rodrigo."

I shook hands and noticed the woman's four front teeth were missing. I thought of her husband's tooth upstairs.

"Please go to your room," Mother said softly in English.

I could barely see Mother; she huddled in the shadows of a large chair. I went upstairs to my room and shut the door—only I never went in. I stayed at the top of the stairs and spied.

Mrs. Sánchez said, "I have only my son to help me. It is not enough."

"I already paid," Father cut in. "I know who sent you here."

"There are six little ones—too young to—"

"And what have you done with what I gave you?" he asked.

"We're not asking for much. Until we learn to live without my husband's income . . ." The widow's voice broke.

Father let her cry. Smelly Hands put his arm around her. I didn't want to hear or see any more.

Mother spoke to Father in English. "You have to help them, Hector. What else can you do?"

He answered in English. "Don't talk. You're my wife, not their lawyer. I already paid more than necessary."

"Don't speak to me that way."

"Then shut up," Father ordered in English.

He turned to the widow and Smelly Hands and spoke to them in Spanish. "You will not get another cent. You will not come here again. If your son wants to keep his job at the club, I will not see him near this house, nor will I see you or any of your children here."

Father opened the front door for them, and they left without saying a word. He slammed the door after them, then turned around and said to Mother, "Don't you ever speak against me."

She laughed, a dry, bitter laugh—low, almost manlike. She showed no fear of him.

I came downstairs, hoping to stop whatever was about to happen. "Hi."

They ignored me. I moved closer to them. Restlessly, Father paced across the living-room floor. Mother sat in the shadows of the darkening room.

"I will not be blackmailed because of an accident, Diane."

"Do you really think you can ever pay enough, for a human life?" When Mother stood up and walked over to him, I saw her for the first time since their fight. An ugly blue mark marred her face under her right eye.

There was no denying it: Father had hit Mother. It didn't make sense, but the anger I felt was toward her.

All my life I had witnessed Mother's failure to understand

our town. Petra and Father had tried explaining to her about life in a town like ours, but it never seemed to sink in. So when I saw her bruises I couldn't help but feel that she had finally received her just punishment.

Yet it wasn't that simple. She was still my mother and I didn't like to see her hurt—not on the face. Not by him. Did she deserve that? She must surely have been bad for Father to have struck her to leave such a bruise. She had upset the order of our family life. She had changed what she and Father meant and I could never forget or forgive her for that.

# 16

**M**Y parents had hit each other. I was sick.

GROWING up was never anything I had
longed for, waited for, never anything I wanted
to happen to me. Seeing cut and bruised parents
confirmed my belief that everything bad happens to grown-ups.

I was one of those unfortunate females
whose breasts grow at an early age. They had
started growing a few months before Victor
and Alicia came to stay with us. One day I
woke up to find these things sticking out of my
chest. I tried walking bent over for a while,
but eventually it was impossible to hide them.

One day, before this summer, I had gone over
to Victor's. I was wearing a T-shirt. Halfway
there I suddenly noticed I had really grown fast.
I should have gone home and changed, but I
didn't.

Victor and Alicia were in the kitchen making fruit drinks. Victor was dropping cut-up

bananas into the blender. Two glasses were set on doilies. Alicia frowned when she saw me.

"We're making banana malts," said Victor.

"I hate bananas," I said, hoping that would in some way pay back Alicia for not being happy to see me.

"Good," Victor said lightly. "There's only enough for us."

"I'm not asking you for anything," I countered.

I wanted to leave, but I would have felt dismissed. Besides, now I was mad at both of them. I sat right in front of them and watched them mix, pour and drink their malts. I suspected they enjoyed not sharing their treats with me.

I saw Alicia's eyes on my breasts. I tried to bend over. With her eyes she directed Victor's attention to my chest, and he nearly choked on his malt.

Together they stared at my fronts and tried not to laugh. Suddenly Victor got up and tweaked my breasts. He just got up and pinched my things. He and Alicia burst out laughing.

I ran home and spent the day plotting my revenge.

It would be at school during physical education. Victor was terrible in sports; I usually covered for him. He was always the last to be chosen. I was always the first; whether people liked me or not, they chose me because I was a good player.

For the next week I ignored Victor and felt absolutely guilt-less to see him the last one chosen. If someone teased him, I laughed at him. I controlled any impulse to give in to his pain. I made sure he didn't exist for me.

The following weekend he came to my house and sputtered, "I'm sorry about what I did last week."

"Prove it."

"What do you want me to do?" he asked. His face paled; he had that pretty look he got whenever he was scared—all color drained away, leaving only his black eyes and dark hair visible.

"Let me hit you."

He took a deep breath and said, "Okay."

He braced himself, waiting for the blow.

"Turn around," I said. "I want to hit you in the back."

He turned.

Then I took the biggest swing of my life and hit him in the back—dead center. I felt wonderful.

He doubled over—breathless. Tears framed his eyes. I was joyous beyond words to see him suffer. After that, it was understood that if he did anything to me I could and would physically pay him back.

Maybe that's why Alicia's death hadn't been such a big deal for me when it happened. She had laughed at me.

I enjoyed Victor's newly gained respect. Other kids had always respected me. They didn't like me, but they respected me. I was never afraid of fighting, nor was I afraid of getting beat up. Father had always told me, "Andrea, you never lose so long as you connect once."

The incident about my breasts was all tied into growing up, and what happened then had prepared me for what I had to do next.

My parents had taken to hitting each other, and Smelly Hands and his mother were asking for money, and Father was not about to give them any.

I felt it was up to me. I had to do what grown-ups were supposed to do. I had money. I knew that some of it belonged to Smelly Hands.

The day after Father threw Smelly Hands and his mother out of our house, I went into my closet and took out some bills—two of each. Then I was good throughout the morning: I dressed myself and ate as if I was hungry; pretended I didn't see Mother's and Father's messed-up faces during a silent family breakfast; pretended I didn't feel anything when he left the house without kissing Mother goodbye. I ignored the fact that Mother hid out in her room all morning. I played with Cristina

as if she was the cutest thing that had come into my life. Then when everyone was busy with their lives, I took off—alone.

The sun was overhead and sweat poured down my face long before I arrived. The walk had been hard—not because of the time or length, rather because I had never done this alone. Victor had always been with me.

Something was bound to go right for me. Smelly Hands was in the parking lot washing down the cement with the hose. Normally I would never have noticed such an act, but given my condition at the time, this was the most beautiful scene I could ever want. No one I knew was around.

He saw me and kept watering.

"You were at my house with your mother last night."

He checked around as if to see if anyone was watching us, then continued washing down the cement.

I got closer to him. "I want to tell you something."

He was silent.

I stood almost beneath him. "Don't you remember seeing me yesterday?"

The veins in his throat pulsed. "I remember. What do you want?"

"You asked for money. Still want some?"

He turned his back to me and hosed down another part of the parking lot. "Why?"

I didn't know how to talk to him. He was just a busboy, I told myself, not really important, yet in the last few hours he had become the most important person in my life.

I feigned a cough and repeated my offer. "I got money for you, if you still want some."

He closed the hose nozzle. "Why are you here?"

"I told you. I have money."

"How much?"

I showed him my bills.

"Why are you doing this?"

I shrugged. I couldn't very well tell him I felt bad my father had run over his father.

"Your mother said she needed it," I said.

"Your father said he wasn't giving us anything."

"He's not. I am."

I held out a sweaty roll of bills. He snatched them and quickly slipped them into his pocket.

"Is it enough?"

"For what?"

"Your family."

He avoided my eyes. "Maybe."

"Why don't you count it."

Again he looked around, then rushed over to a shed where garden tools were stored and quickly counted the money.

"Well?" I shouted.

"Well what?" he called back.

"Is it enough?" I shouted louder.

He didn't bother answering. He came out of the shed frowning in disapproval. As he walked toward me he stuffed his shirt roughly into his pants and tightened his belt. With both hands, he carefully pushed back his hair. He stared at me all the while. I felt small.

"*I* have six brothers and sisters to feed. This is good for only a few days."

I didn't know what my next move should be. Should I offer him more money? I wished I had brought Victor with me.

"How much do you need?" I asked.

"Where did you get this money?"

"It's mine." My mouth was dry. "Mine."

"*You* have money?"

"Yes."

He's being careful, I thought. Quickly I killed the suspicion that Armida had confessed to him her money had been stolen and that she had caught me up in the loft.

"Who gives you money? Your father?"

"Sometimes. Sometimes Mother does, sometimes my aunts or my grandmother gives it to me. Is that enough?" I longed to leave, to be rid of this whole mission.

"Where's your friend?" he asked.

"What?"

"The doctor's son. Where is he?"

I shrugged.

"Come on, tell me. Where is he?" His voice took on a bite. I felt afraid; I sensed I had reason to.

He looked around again, then whispered. "You know, Beto has been looking for you and your friend."

"Beto?"

"Yeah. They've been asking me and Tony where you two live. He's the doctor's son, isn't he?"

I turned as if to go. "I just came to help you." I was trembling. I hated my body for announcing my terror so clearly to the busboy.

"I'll be needing more than this," he said slowly. "Newspapers have been talking about how your father was drunk . . ."

"So what? I'm paying you."

"This won't feed us for long." He hitched up his belt. "I work here all day. My mother's doing ironing."

"I'm giving you what I have."

He looked at me for a long moment. "You can get more, can't you?" he challenged.

My trembling increased.

"Maybe."

He uttered each word slowly, evenly. "I work here every day, and every day Beto and his friends come around wanting to know where you and your friend live. I've never told them."

"You want more?"

"I need more."

"How much?"

"How much do you have?"

I didn't know. The thought that he might set Beto on us paralyzed me.

"I have more money," I said quietly.

"I don't want to tell them where you two live. I've seen what they did to your friend."

I hurried away from him. When I was almost out of the parking lot I called, "I'll bring more later."

"When?"

"I don't know."

"Remember your friend. You don't want him to get hurt."

"My father killed yours. Leave him alone. I mean it."

He laughed at my threat.

"Did you read what the papers said about your father?" His voice was low, secretive. "They say your father *murdered* mine."

"Leave Victor alone. I'll bring more money."

"Where will you get it?" he jeered.

"Goodbye."

I shook all the way to Victor's. I knew that if I told him about Beto, he would get sick again. He was terrified of getting hurt. I was more afraid for him than for myself.

I practiced several approaches. Blunt truth was out of the question. I tried to sound excited. "Guess what we have to do?" I sounded phony. I didn't trust my voice.

I knocked on his front door and I remembered how attached he had become to his mother since she had come home. It was then that I decided to play up the sin angle. He always responded to that. Victor was determined to receive Christ for the first time without a sin on his soul. I let that be my guide.

"Victor," I said, once I knew we were alone. "You were right. Father did a terrible thing when he killed the watchman."

He swelled with pride at hearing my admission. "Yes, he did."

"The man had a family, a big one."

"Seven children."

"Can I tell you a secret?"

His eyes lit up. "What?"

He was so eager to hear something exciting that for a moment I almost told him the truth. "My parents had a fight. A *big* fight."

He was disappointed. "Oh. Why?"

I had every intention of telling him about the cuts and bruises on their faces. But when I formed the words in my head they sounded so hateful, so horrible, that I could not mouth them.

*My parents hit each other. They threw things and hurt themselves.*

I could never say that to him or to anyone.

"It was over the watchman's widow. Mother thinks Father should pay the family more money."

"Smelly Hands too?"

"He's part of the family," I said.

Victor wrinkled his nose. "But he's a dirty boy."

"He came with his mother to the house. They asked for money and Father threw them out. She has no teeth in front."

He laughed. "Is she ugly?"

I laughed too. "She dresses in black."

"Widows have to."

"She cried in the living room when she asked for money."

"Uncle let her cry?"

"He told them he had already given them enough money," I said.

"How much did he give them?"

"I don't know. But the mother was very sad."

"Uncle should have paid her," he said.

Now was the time, I figured. "I agree, Victor. I went to the club today."

He looked interested.

"I took money from our chest."

He grew serious.

"I gave it to Smelly Hands to pay him for what Father did."

"You gave him our money?" he asked loudly.

I stammered, "Not a lot."

"Why?" Color rushed to his cheeks. "We didn't owe him anything. Andrea, I hate you. You're a traitor!"

"Stop yelling!" I ordered. "Your mother's going to hear us."

His breathing was loud. "That boy's bad, Andrea, and you gave him our money," he whispered roughly.

"Not a lot. I had to. I could have caused a curse if I hadn't. You know that's true. Think about it."

He had no answer to that.

"There's more," I said, taking advantage of his temporary silence. "Smelly Hands wants more money." Victor jerked his head up. I spoke faster. "He wants it soon. He said Beto and his friends are looking for *you* and they want money. He said he won't tell them where you live if I give him the money."

He blanched. A faraway look came over him. The anger of a few moments ago vanished instantly. He looked sick. I felt compelled to touch him. I put my hand on his arm; he pulled away and protectively covered his ear.

"Go home, Andrea," he said, shrinking from me. Tears came quickly. "Go home." His voice shook.

Afraid that he might start screaming, I hit him in the chest with all my might. I flattened him. He lay on the floor struggling for breath, trying to cry. He released only a few girlish whimpers.

"Victor, don't make any more noise. Listen to me. We're in a lot of trouble."

"I haven't done anything."

He put both arms around my neck. His hold was strong. I felt awful. Why had I gone to the club without him? In the midst of all that confusion I found myself experiencing joy that Victor would reach out to touch me in a plea of help. Hands were forbidden between us ever since the time he pinched my breasts. I liked his holding on to me.

"Will they get me again?"

"No. We'll pay him, that's all."

He was still for a while. Slowly he unwrapped himself from me. He was recovering.

"You did the wrong thing, Andrea."

"No I didn't. You agreed that the lady should have money. If Father won't pay her I have to."

"But you gave it to Smelly Hands too. You should never have paid him. He's bad. We saw him be bad."

"The lady said it was for her children. It's not my fault he's one of them."

He pulled back, farther than arm's length. "Uncle killed that man. We didn't. You told him we had money. In the end he'll get all our money and want more. We're going to get hurt again," he said. His body trembled.

"Victor, when we run out, we'll tell him there's no more."

"He won't believe it. We may have to tell someone, a grown-up or something."

"I'm not telling anyone—neither are you," I challenged.

"Padre Lozano won't tell."

"So what? He can't stop Beto and them. He's an old man. I'd rather tell Father instead. Father would kill those boys. A priest can't do anything."

He nodded his head slowly. "You're stupid, Andrea. You keep forgetting you have to confess everything to Father Lozano sooner or later."

I wasn't going to argue with him. My mouth said yes; my heart knew different.

"Think, Andrea. This is our worst problem."

We sat in silence and thought. I tried to figure out how much money we had but lacked the skills to compute the total. Besides, where were we going to find the space to sort out the money? Just when I was deciding that Candelaria was the only one to turn to, I learned that Victor was looking elsewhere for salvation.

Solemnly he announced, "The Virgin Mary will help us."

I couldn't believe him. "What? She's up *there* and we're down here. Now who's stupid?"

"We'll pray real hard. On our knees. We'll put thorns under us to make Her hear us. We'll ask Her to make Smelly Hands stay away."

"How is She going to do that?"

"That's up to Her!" he answered angrily.

"Victor, I know what you're thinking. It's those Fatima kids, isn't it? They were good kids. That's why the Virgin appeared to them. We're bad and we've done so many bad things this summer we lost count. She probably doesn't remember us. Victor, I have to pay Smelly Hands more money."

His face was losing color again. "Andrea, what if he takes the money and in the end he tells Beto where I live?"

"It won't happen that way."

His face was full of pain and fear. "How can we be sure?"

"No one will hurt you, Victor. I promise you. We'll pay and pray at the same time. I swear to you I'll pray the hardest in my life. Okay?"

It took a while but finally he sucked in a deep breath and nodded.

# 17

THEY were nestled in Father's study in each other's arms, not unlike the way Victor and I had been earlier that day. She was holding him—as I had held Victor. They had both been crying. Nothing seemed to matter: not my walking in on them, not my staring at them, not my listening to them. Her lips brushed his bruises—not really kissing his hurts, more like caressing them with her open mouth.

She hadn't bothered to dress that day and her mouth was the regular natural color. Mother looked sickly without lipstick. Father didn't seem to mind.

He whispered softly, ". . . try to understand . . ."

"I don't know how. Everything I do seems wrong," she said plaintively.

He chuckled, a private, self-indulgent laugh. "Everything I do seems wrong," he repeated, imitating her helplessness. Then his voice changed and it was husky again. "It's truer for me than for you, my dearest woman."

He turned to me. "Where've you been?"

"Victor's. Are you two made up?"

He kissed her. "I love your mother."

"Your father and I love each other," Mother echoed.

"Does this mean you're going to pay them?"

Father disengaged himself from Mother's grasp. "What are you talking about?"

"Smelly Hands. Are you going to pay him and his mother?"

Father asked angrily, "Who's Smelly Hands?"

Damn, I'd said his name. "The busboy, you know, the boy who came here," I stammered. "We call him Smelly Hands because his hands are dirty when he works at the club."

They looked at each other.

"That's very rude," said Mother.

"That's not the point," said Father stiffly. "Why ask *me* questions like that? Who've you been talking to?"

"Hector," pleaded Mother, resting her hand on his leg. "Don't be cross with her." ,

"Answer me," he demanded.

"I haven't talked to anybody," I said. "I swear. I saw that boy here last night, remember?"

"Go to your room, Andrea."

"I haven't done anything," I protested. "I'll go and *pray* for you. On my knees!" I yelled dramatically. "For all the good it'll do you!"

"Where does she learn these things?"

"Calm down, Hector. Children only say what they hear. The maids, the neighbors, they all talk."


VICTOR arrived early the next day; we were barely finished with breakfast.

"Come to play?" asked Mother, a forced friendliness in her voice.

"He came to pray with me," I announced. "To get ready for our First Holy Communion."

"Petra!" shouted Father. "Bring hot chocolate for my daugh-

ter's praying partner." Hurriedly he wiped his mouth with a napkin, took Mother by the hand, and pulled her into the study. Victor and I ignored the noises and waited in silence until they came out again.

Mother walked Father to the door; she moved as she had in the past: her eyes had a sleepy look, reminiscent of times earlier that summer.

"You came to pray with Andrea?" she asked, playing with Victor's hair as she spoke.

"Yes," he answered, apparently enjoying her caresses.

"What will you pray for?"

I looked nervously at him.

"The Chinese," he answered casually.

"Good," said Mother and she drifted upstairs.

Petra brought him the hot chocolate. He sipped it cautiously. "It's American. No cinnamon."

"Let's pray," I urged.

"Andrea, did you lie about Auntie and Uncle's fighting?"

"No, they fight and stop. I don't care what they do anymore. Yesterday they were arguing, today they're kissing. Mother still wants him to give the watchman's widow more money."

"He should." Victor blew across the cup.

"He's not going to. He got mad at me for asking. Hurry with the chocolate."

"Do you have a rosary?"

"We're not going to pray a whole rosary, Victor."

"Yes we are. You agreed to."

"I agreed to praying."

"The rosary is the best prayer."

"It's long and boring," I argued.

"It's the best prayer for the Virgin Mary. I brought thorns. And don't say prayers are boring."

He downed the rest of his chocolate, dug his hands deeply into his short pocket, and pulled out a handful of rose thorns.

Too late for me to get out of it. If Victor was going to allow me to pay Smelly Hands from our money, I would have to pray on thorns. I was ready to, but not with the rosary. Saying the same prayer more than fifty times seemed an impossible task, I thought.

"Where are we praying?" he asked.

"You know the altar Candelaria has in her room?"

"With the candles?"

"Yes. I want to pray there instead of in my room. I don't want Mother looking in on us."

Candelaria gave us permission. She too asked what we were praying for and again Victor answered, "The Chinese."

"They're far away," she said. "Make your prayers 'specially loud."

It took the better part of an hour. Victor was obsessed with making sure my thorns did not turn over on their sides. He was as zealous with himself.

"If they really hurt, we might get a vision," he said.

"I don't want a vision. Don't hope for one. What if She comes?"

"She'll tell us what to do. Maybe She'll say, 'Give your money to the poor,' maybe She'll tell us to build her a church. I bet She won't say anything about giving anything to Smelly Hands."

Kneeling on thorns, we prayed the rosary to the Virgin Mary. It was long, boring, and painful. The only thing that kept me going was my own personal secret prayer to the Mother of Jesus, "Don't come down, don't come down, don't come down."

It was a miracle that She didn't. Victor prayed the entire time arms stretched out, eyes shut, his back straight as a board. Head tilted back, he prayed so loudly that I thought for sure the ceiling would open and a cloud would descend and there She would be.

He was exhausted when we finished. Beads of perspiration dotted his nose and upper lip. "Maybe She'll come tomorrow," he muttered.

We helped each other up and checked out our knees. The thorns had penetrated the skin but there was little blood, a few pinpricks' worth.

"Now let's think about my part," I said. "I have an idea. We'll take half our money, no more than that, and pay him a little at a time. We'll do it slow so—"

"Not half!" he said hotly. "How much did you give him last time?"

"Two of each."

"Twenties too?"

"Yeah. Two of each. Victor, the widow has seven children."

"He's grown. Doesn't count. Besides, he probably eats at the club."

"Six," I conceded. "All right, six. We saw their picture in the paper."

"How much to feed six?"

"We'll ask Petra or Candelaria."

First we figured what two of each came to. Seventy-two pesos. Victor was appalled.

"That's very near a hundred, Andrea, very near."

"So what? There's lots of money up there. Come see."

"There's too much in there," he said after taking a cursory peek into the trunk. "We can't possibly give him half. I'd tell my mother first."

"Okay, not half, but most of half. Victor, this has to be enough to get the curse out of my house."

"There's no curse anymore. Stop talking about it, you'll make it true," he said.

How could I make it truer than it already was? Everything was wrong with my life. My parents were either kissing or hitting each other. Mother was sick, and her baby had died.

Mother was talking about taking us to Los Angeles. There *was* a curse. It only made sense.

If I had been the watchman and a man had killed me with his car, and I couldn't take care of my family, I would have put a curse on his house and his family, even the maids. Candelaria's straw might have helped; it certainly didn't fix everything.

When I had come home the day before and found my parents kissing, I hadn't been convinced that they were really made up. And the way Father had acted when I asked if he was going to give money to Smelly Hands proved to me that he was never going to. It was up to me.

I knew Father hadn't meant to kill the man. I believed he was sorry, but he wasn't *ashamed* of himself. That is what everyone else wanted him to feel. *They* wanted Father to act ashamed. Even though he had given the widow a plot of land, *they* wanted him to suffer. *They* were the newspaper people, the neighbors, yes, even Mother, Tía Milita, and Victor.

I regretted telling Victor about going to the club. He didn't seem to care what happened to Father or to me. All he cared about was the money. He was being so damn cheap about it I found myself wishing Beto would show up and give him a good scare. Not hurt him—just scare some of the cheapness out of him. I became resigned to the fact that the only way to get Victor to release some of the money was by praying on rose thorns.

But I prayed to the Holy Virgin to please let me figure things out by myself. I was tired of my life; laughter and playing had vanished.

Petra did help us. "One hundred pesos would buy lots of beans and rice."

"Enough to feed six children?" I asked.

"For a while."

"A long while? A month?" prodded Victor.

"Maybe. Yes," she said absently, "if you're careful. Just beans and rice?"

"Yes," Victor answered.

"We don't know," I countered.

We returned to the chest and three times took out two of each.

"That's more than two hundred pesos. Now you take it to him in little parts. Make it look like you can't get any more," he said in a motherly tone like his mother's.

"I know what to do, Victor. There's so much more money in there. We'll never spend it."

"We can still do good works with it. Maybe later we'll need some of it. Andrea, you can't give it to that boy, please."

"What about Beto? What if Smelly Hands tells him where you live?"

That stopped him only for a moment. "We're praying against that."

"On thorns?"

"Yes."

"That's going to keep Beto away?" I asked in disbelief.

"Yes." His face became uncertain. "If not, I'm telling Mother and Uncle and Padre Lozano and the whole world—"

"All right! We'll tell the whole world if you want. But not until we pay Smelly Hands enough money to make my house good again. I'd do it for your house if you needed it. I swear I would."

"You swear for everything."


IT was two days before I returned to the club. Two days equaled four rosaries prayed on thorns in Candelaria's room.

"It must be raining gold in China by now," Candelaria said to Petra when we paraded back to her room. They laughed.

Victor prayed as fervently as before. At one point I tried

praying with my arms held out, but was forced to put them down after a few Hail Marys.

I was stronger than he, at least I saw myself as stronger, able to beat him up and all that. Yet I was incapable of keeping my arms outstretched for an entire rosary.

I came to respect Victor's intensity once I had attempted and failed to match his endurance, and realized that his ability to pray as he did came not from physical strength, but rather from faith—something I had never considered.

"You're shouting!" I yelled at him after Petra peeked in to see if anything was the matter. He never heard me. Instead his pitch grew louder. His eyes were closed tightly and he seemed oblivious to the drops of sweat that streamed over his eyes and slid down his nose.

After we finished praying we helped each other up, checked our knees—more pinpricks.

"You bled more." He sounded a little disappointed. His attempts to leave the room proved difficult: he took two steps and fell.

"Are you all right?" I asked.

"I'm dizzy." His face was pale, his eyes looked to the ceiling for some stability. "I'd better sit," he stammered.

"I hope it isn't a vision," I said. "I don't know the symptoms, do you?"

His eyes lit up. "Do you think?"

"Here, lie down on Candelaria's bed—just in case."

He let me lead him.

"Water?" I offered and left without waiting for an answer. The urgency with which I filled the glass alarmed Petra, and she followed me back. She saw Victor down the water without stopping for breath.

"Does your mother know you're praying like this?" Petra asked.

"She knows about China."

She grunted and left the room. I knew it was only a matter of minutes before she would go upstairs and tell Mother. Tell her what? I asked myself. What could Petra say we were doing wrong? Praying for heathens? It was beyond my imagination, but I knew Victor's excesses would draw adult attention to our actions. If I was going to take more money to Smelly Hands, I'd better do it fast.

"Victor, we've been praying really good. Tomorrow we'll go to the club, okay?"

"I'm not."

"Why?"

"I don't want Smelly Hands to see me."

"He knows about you. I told you what he said."

"I don't care. I don't want to go."

"You're scared," I said angrily.

"Yes, I am, Andrea," he admitted. He waited awhile, then added, "I'll pray while you go."

"Think that will help?"

"Of course."

"You'll be praying *all* the time I'm there?"

"Yes, even if it takes two rosaries—I'll pray them."

I didn't like that. He was getting strange about this whole business. When you do things with people it's supposed to bring you together, yet praying with Victor only separated us. He went somewhere else when he prayed. I didn't like him pulling away from me.

At Petra's suggestion, Candelaria went with me when I walked Victor home. It was fun being with her outside the house. She strolled down the street barefoot, pipe in her mouth, jaw forward. She reminded me of Popeye, and I thought of Armida. Why was her store called Popeye's?

Half a block away Victor turned to us and said, "Don't come farther. Watch, I'll get home all right."

He ran the rest of the way. I watched him as he darted from

us. His legs were so skinny. He was so thin that I could only marvel once again at his ability to hold his arms out as long as he did.

"Goodbye, China boy," Candelaria called.

He turned and smiled at us. The sun was setting and his face was lost to the glow of the sun resting behind him.

Candelaria and I waited until we were sure he was home safely, then she held her calloused hand out to me in a gesture of friendship. "*Amigas?*" Her toothless face spread out in a wide smile.

"*Sí.*" I felt secure with her as we walked home in silence. She hummed a Mexican tune which ended precisely as we reached the doorstep. I was impressed.

"How did you do that?"

"Do what?"

"Know when to end the song?"

She laughed. "It's a trick. All Mexican songs can end whenever you want to."

"No they can't."

"Sure they can. Everything can. You just go 'tan-tan' and end the song."

"But what if there are more words to the song?"

"Andrea, when you're singing, no one can tell you when to end your song."

"All songs?"

"I just know Mexican songs."

"No Indian songs?"

She laughed again. "A few."

"Let me hear."

Right there in front of my house she chanted, "*Antu, nanchi, tuta ma jai, mata tu tanchi ana man guey.*"

"What are you saying?"

"Something you don't believe."

"What?"

She whispered in my ear, "When you go to the marketplace, make sure you have the horse before the cart."

"Who cares about carts and horses? What did you really say?"

"That's the truth, Andrea. It's just a song." She pushed her flat nose against mine. "Laugh more," she chided.

"It's not funny. Do you know any magic songs?"

"Magic songs?"

"For curses."

"There are no songs for curses."

"Candelaria, you're lying. I saw you pray or sing over Mother when she was sick."

She opened the door as if to get away from me. "I asked God to help your mother get well. That's all you saw."

She went inside, leaving only the screen door between us.

"Candelaria?" The light was on in the living room and I could see her very clearly. "Is that the truth?" I could see her but I knew she couldn't see me.

She opened the screen door. "Come inside."

"I didn't say anything bad," I protested.

"Next time you go praying for people you don't know, include a prayer for those around you. Seems to me you and your little boyfriend need to do some praying for yourselves once in a while." She lowered her voice. "And don't go thinking I don't know you're trying to pray yourselves out of some devil's net. You can't bargain with God. His rules are for your salvation—break them and *snap* . . ."

She underscored her words by forming two fists and twisting them as if she were breaking a twig in half.

Nothing more was said. She took her pipe and emptied its ashes onto one of her hands and left me standing in the entry.


I WAS right. Petra told Mother that Victor and I were praying "too hard." The matter was brought up at dinner. Father

was there and they were still in their making-up mood which meant they were cooperative and polite with each other.

The summer heat had come indoors and we were eating what Father described as "one of Diane's *gringa* dinners," which included cold cream of spinach soup, shrimp salad, cheese, cold cuts, and iced tea.

Petra had cooked a separate order of beans and rice for Father. No matter what the rest of the family ate, Father always had to have beans, rice, tortillas, and cold beer. Although he was always given a glass, he drank beer directly from the bottle. "Beer gets hot moving it around," he would explain to any new guests.

Mother asked, "Still praying for the Chinese, Andrea?"

"Yes."

"How long will this go on?"

"Until China is converted," I said and feigned a serious interest in the food.

"Converted into what?" said Father and laughed at some kind of joke I didn't understand.

"Catholics," I answered. "They're persecuting missionaries. Sister said we'll only have world peace when China's been converted."

Father smiled softly at me. "That might take a long time, baby."

"There is such a thing as going overboard," Mother said. "Petra tells me you two have been saying whole rosaries on your knees and on thorns. Don't you think that's too much, Hector?"

"Is that true, Andrea?"

"It's true. We have been praying for the Chinese." I heard myself sounding like Victor. "It's only for a while." I heard my voice getting weak. "Please don't make us stop." My voice was feeble.

I needed them to let us keep praying. I needed them to let Victor pray in whatever manner he chose to if I was to pay

Smelly Hands the money he needed, and if I was to save our
house from any further curses. It was something I could never
tell them. Never. They sat there eating, not knowing that I
held their salvation in my hands.

*FATHER* came into my room when I was nearly asleep.
"Gone for the night, baby?"
"Hi, Daddy."
"What are you?"
"Your girl."
"My what girl?"
"Your best girl."
"Who loves you?"
"You do, Daddy."
"Why?"
"Because I'm the best."
We laughed. We hadn't performed our ritual since the be-
ginning of summer.
He pulled the sheet up to my chin. I knew he was getting
ready to have a talk with me. I worried. The next day was to
be my second payment to Smelly Hands.
He took a deep breath. "Your mother tells me you've been
praying in Candelaria's room."
"She has an altar with saints and all that. We don't have
anything like that in the house." I tried to sound reproachful.
"And this is for the Chinese?"
I yawned, although I suddenly felt very awake.
"I already told you. World peace."
"*All* that is up to the Chinese?"
"Yes. The sisters said so. Don't you believe them?"
"Of course. But I like the Chinese. I don't think they're bad
people, do you?"
I'd never even seen one.

"I don't know."

"Well, they're not, and praying on your knees the way you two have been doing will not change anything."

"Doesn't God listen to children's prayers more than he does adults'?"

"The sisters told you that?"

"Yes." That part was true and I believed them.

"Well, they know more than I do, I guess. But what about the thorns?" His face was grave. "Do you think Jesus wants you to pray on thorns?" He spoke slowly, evenly. "Think He expects you to hurt yourself before He listens to you?"

He was making me sad. I felt my throat get tight.

Tenderly he stroked my hair. "Answer me, baby."

My face burned with embarrassment.

I shrugged. He waited for me to say something. I couldn't talk. I swallowed hard. From somewhere, from his touch upon my head, perhaps, came a desire to cry.

It was more than that. It was a desire to empty myself out, to spew out the whole summer, to tell and tell until I cleaned myself of all that I had seen and done. Alma, Rosa, Alicia, the money, Armida, Smelly Hands, everything.

I came close—the closest ever to breaking down. I knew Father would understand my lying, my stealing, my curiosity for knowing what adults did, my desire to peek under the layers of skin that hid people.

Father wasn't afraid of being bad; neither was I. But he loved me too much and so I didn't have the strength to tell him. I couldn't take the chance that he might find me too similar to his weaker self and therefore love me less.

So I lay there that night stalling, parrying, any way I could to keep him away from my core.

"Are the Chinese Catholic?" I blurted.

"I'm sure some are."

"Isn't Catholic the real religion?"

He paused.

"Did the sisters say that too?" He seemed weary.

"It's what Jesus started. The rest are Protestants," I explained. "Don't you know all this?" I felt confused.

He scratched his forehead and smiled sadly. "I remember thinking like that. Now I trust God to love all people."

"But God's Catholic, isn't He?"

"No, God's just God," he said quietly. "Someone once told me that God is . . . well, God is like an egg. Some people like their egg scrambled, some fried, others like their egg poached. But no matter how they like it, it's still an egg."

I put my hands under the covers. "You're going to get in a lot of trouble talking like that."

"From who?"

"Everybody—the sisters, Padre Lozano." I almost included Victor. "Besides, if God is an egg, why did Mother have to become Catholic to marry you?"

"You know about that?"

"Victor told me."

"That's not the whole story. I didn't *make* your mother become Catholic. She wanted to. She wanted to be married in the Church. That's all."

"She wanted to be married in the Church?" I found that unlikely. Mother never impressed me as being particularly thrilled about Mass and all that.

His patience grew thin. "My mother wanted it," he said loudly. "You're old enough to know that sometimes we do things just for our parents. Don't you do things for me?"

"Yes."

He fixed my covers. I knew he was getting ready to leave. "I don't want you praying on thorns anymore. Pray for the Chinese, for anyone you want, but don't hurt yourself. God is good. He doesn't want children hurting themselves when they pray to Him."

He kissed me good night. It was a special kiss. As he pressed his lips to my forehead, he seemed to be breathing me.

When he was at the door I asked, "Daddy, do you believe that God is an egg?"

"God is an egg, Andrea."

He left my room forgetting to turn off the light. I lay there feeling comforted. Weight had been taken off me. True, I hadn't confessed anything, everything was still locked inside, but I liked the egg idea. It gave me greater bargaining power with God—and maybe with Victor. Years later I learned that his metaphor was not original; that didn't matter. But at that time in my life it worked.

I got up, went into the trunk in my closet and stuffed the allotted money into one of my socks, a dirty one. In the trunk I saw the watchman's tooth wrapped in a wad of toilet paper. I laid it on the dresser to take with me the following morning when I went to pay Smelly Hands his money.

# 18

HE met me at the door the next morning.

"I have the money," I said.

Victor was still in his pajamas even though it was midmorning.

"Two of each?" he whispered.

"Yes."

"Just two?" he emphasized.

"Yes, I swear it. Will you be praying for me?"

"Of course. I'll start as soon as I figure you're there."

"Why are you whispering?"

He looked around behind him. "Why do you think I'm whispering?"

"Goodbye, Victor. I'll come back and tell you what happened."

He slammed the door.

It was a lonely walk. My pocket bulged with bills. Damn Victor, I thought as the August sun baked my head. He had stayed in his pajamas just so he wouldn't have to come with me.

I held the watchman's tooth still wrapped in toilet paper. I carried it for luck, an amulet

against Smelly Hands. As I neared the club I unwrapped the tooth and rubbed it nervously.

God is an egg.

God is an egg.

God, if you make this go right, I promise to give lots of money to beggars. I swear.

Before reaching the club property I renewed my vow several times, I looked at the sky and proclaimed it loudly when I walked onto the parking lot.

I walked around the outside of the place looking for him. I ran into Tony the waiter first.

"Where's Victor?" he asked.

"I don't know. I gotta find the busboy, you know, the guy with the dark hair."

"Why?" Tony was polite but suspicious. He knew who had killed the watchman.

"I have to talk to him." I fingered the tooth.

"Your parents know you're here?"

"I have to tell him something. He knows me. Really."

He nodded sympathetically. "I'll get him."

He came back after a few moments. "He said he'll meet you outside. I'll go with you if you like."

"No!"

I went around the back to where weeks before, Smelly Hands had washed the vomit off Victor's shoes. I waited for what seemed a long time before he finally came out—impatient and looking at me in irritation.

"What do you want?"

"I brought you more money." The sock felt thick in my pants pocket.

In a barely audible voice he asked, "How much?"

I threw the sock at him. It fell a foot short of where he stood. He took his time picking it up. All the while his eyes never left my face. I rubbed the tooth harder.

He picked up the sock, inspected the money. "I expected

you sooner," he said, putting the bills into his back pocket.

"I had trouble getting it."

"Where did you get it?"

His eyes bored into mine. I feared my mouth would give me away. My upperlip trembled uncontrollably.

Smelly Hands turned his head and spat into the air. "Where's your friend?"

"Why?"

He looked away from me. Then at me. Then away from me again.

"I needed the money sooner," he said quietly.

"I told you. I had trouble getting it." I was trying to sound nice, but anger was rising in me.

"Too bad. I already told Beto where your friend lives." I could barely hear him.

"Why?" I yelled. "Look, I got some of this from my grand-mother, the rest from other people for my birthday!" My mouth was completely dry. I held the tooth across my chest.

He sighed; the corners of his mouth drooped, giving him a sorrowful look. He was acting and there was nothing I could do about it. He nodded his head slowly. "Wish I'd known about this money sooner. Sure would have made the whole thing easier."

"Made what easier?"

He shrugged. "Everything. I only told because I needed to feed my family."

"Now you have money!" I screamed. "Lots of it!"

"To buy what?"

"Beans and rice."

"What?"

"Beans and rice. My maid said this would buy lots of it. She knows."

"Your maid knows what I need to feed my family?"

"She buys what we eat."

"You eat beans and rice?"

I didn't answer.

"Well?" He demanded loudly.

His voice frightened me. "What?"

"Do you eat beans and rice?" he repeated savagely.

I held the amulet out against him. "My father does."

Again he spit into the air. "Your father's a drunk." His discharge almost landed on top of me.

"Your father is dead and I'm glad," I yelled and left him standing in the parking lot staring at me. I could feel him even after I had run for two blocks.

I never looked back. I made a quick turn around a corner, a turn I would not normally have made but necessary if I was to get out of his sight.

I stopped when the pain in my side forced me. Fear about Beto kept my breathing shallow, tense. I needed water on my head, in my mouth. My whole body craved water. I decided to go home before reporting to Victor. Using the faucet in my front yard, I drenched myself. The spigot was barely two feet off the ground, so I lay down to let the water pour over my head. At first the water was hot; after a while a sweet coolness came and I drank until the dry patches disappeared from my throat.

Refreshed, I decided to run to Victor's. The water in my stomach bounced heavily, and after the first block I stopped and vomited bitter water on the sidewalk. Steam rose from the hot cement.

Victor's face was pale when he opened the door.

"Something's wrong."

"Did you pray?" I asked.

He lifted his pant legs. Deep thorn scratches and punctures crowned both of his bony knees. "I said two rosaries."

"Victor, you really hurt yourself."

"I know." He smiled. "Now tell me what happened."

Brusquely, I pushed him into his house. "Let me tell you."
I frightened him.

"They're going to get me, aren't they?" he asked.

"Shut up. Let me talk."

"Andrea, you're going to tell me something bad. I can tell."

"Pull your pant legs down. You look like an old lady. That
blood looks awful." I sounded angry, but in truth I was doing
all I could to prevent myself from throwing myself on the
ground and declaring to Beto, Smelly Hands and anyone else
that we were open game. My trip to the club, Victor's bloody
offerings were pointless.

"Tell me quick, Andrea, please." His face broke my heart.

"He took the money and then told me it was too late."

"So?" His eyes contained every possible fear.

"He told Beto where you live," I said weakly.

He rocked back and forth, both hands on his forehead. "I
prayed, Andrea. I prayed so hard."

"We both did. The money came too late, that's all."

"They're going to get me, I know."

"No, Victor. We won't let them. Maybe we'd better get
help from someone bigger than us—I don't mean family. We
have money still. We'll pay someone."

"To kill Beto? Andrea, that's the worst sin!"

"Don't be stupid. We don't know any killers. Let's get Tony.
He likes us and he saw what the river kids did to us. Why
don't we pay him to keep those guys away? He's friends with
both our fathers. He'll know what to do."

"Andrea!" He grabbed me by the shoulders. "Father!"

"What? Let go, you're sounding crazy."

He was shaking me and jumping up and down and laughing. "I forgot to tell you!" He couldn't stop wiggling. "I got
the answer! This morning—the phone—Father, he's coming
home."

"Your father?"

"Yes." He nodded vigorously. "Don't you see? He can help us."

"Victor, you can't tell him."

"You don't understand. They can't get me if he's here, if he's home, can they?"

I let him pace around his living room and said nothing about the fact that we had been thoroughly thrashed while my father was home. If he believed his father could protect him, I was not about to take that away from him.

"Are you going to tell your father?" I asked again.

"I won't need to. When he comes home his picture will be in the paper. It's always in the paper. They'll see it."

He was right; his father's picture was always in the paper. I didn't believe my uncle's arrival would change anything. All we could do was hide inside our houses. Victor was dreaming again.

"You think the river kids will see the paper?" I asked sarcastically.

"Smelly Hands will. He'll tell them. Don't you see, Andrea, my father's the biggest doctor in town. They can't hurt me."

I reached into my pocket and fingered the watchman's tooth. I saw Victor's face: deluded, complacent, but at peace. Too weary to argue, I went home.

News of Uncle's arrival had reached my house, too. Mother and Petra were racing around—happy, excited. A reception was scheduled for my uncle the next day.

I was amazed how easily people could go on with their lives even though mine was going crazy. Couldn't they hear my insides churning? I sat on the couch and watched the excitement.

There hadn't been a party at the house all summer. Tía Milita had sent her maid to help with the preparations. Petra had rounded up some extra help and they were in the kitchen making handmade tamales, my uncle's favorite.

Candelaria was supervising the tamale making and it was obvious she considered her assistants inferior. "This *mixtamal* is lumpy," she scolded, "unfit for beggars." She threw back the dough to the two Indian girls, who looked about fifteen years old. They cowered beneath the older woman's orders.

Mother and Petra had moved the dining-room table against the wall; the dining-room chairs were moved into the living room so the guests could visit. Mother was the happiest I had seen her all summer.

Father came in, sweaty, his shirt open. Two of his warehouse men helped him unload cases of beer and liquor from trucks. They made several trips bringing in piñatas, cases of glasses, dishes from the club, boxes of silverware.

Father opened one of the cases he had brought in from his warehouse; he pulled out a bottle and said to Mother, "Diane, look. Scotch. American." He beamed. I saw love in her face.

Father explained, "The blocks of ice won't come until to-morrow afternoon. One of the warehouse boys will be here with an ice pick to chip it real fine."

"Who's going to tend the bar?" asked Mother.

"Tony. I'm stealing him from the club for the night. Besides, everyone will be here, so what's the difference."

She kissed him. "You're wonderful, darling."

"Tony said he'd bring some extra help," added Father.

My heart sank at the words "extra help."

Smelly Hands? Not Smelly Hands. Dear God! I wondered if Tony knew about Father's threat should he ever see the busboy near our house again. The busboy wouldn't dare show up, I reasoned. He couldn't.

Mother was on the phone. "I want at least two photographers," she demanded. "Good ones, *comprende*?" she emphasized in her best Spanish.

Father wrested the phone from her. "Javier, if you send any of the shits who were here after the accident, send another

group to photograph me shooting them." He slammed down the receiver.

"Hector, why did you do that?" asked Mother. "He was being so cooperative with me."

He didn't bother answering her.

Throughout the rest of the afternoon everyone worked. There was joy, excitement in the house. The adults were happy and it had been a long time since I had seen grown-ups laugh and work at the same time. Their energy flowed over onto me and I found myself being drawn into their pool of celebration. I smiled and looked forward to the next afternoon. The threat of Beto and Smelly Hands paled as I sat in what seemed the middle of a carnival. Maybe Victor was right. Maybe his father's arrival would make matters right. Maybe we would feel safe again.

Mother continued on the phone inviting people, their special friends. She went through several telephone lists and checked people off by titles rather than names: the "other" doctor and his wife and kids, the owner of the two movie houses, Father's business associates and their wives and kids, two bankers and their families, the club singer and his band and other special people who belonged at such an occasion. This was most certainly a special day. The doctor, our town's polio specialist, was coming home.

The day came to an end; the extra help was paid and sent home. My parents, Cristina and I, Petra and Candelaria stood in the dining room amid stacks of dishes, rows of glasses, linen, liquor, food, and tableware—none of which could be touched until the next day.

Father looked at Mother and the maids. "Girls, you look exhausted. I'm treating you all to dinner—at the club."

The maids stood paralyzed.

Candelaria said, "I don't want to go anywhere, señor. I'm fine right here."

"I'll stay with her," Petra offered. "Take the señora and the girls."

Father was adamant. "Come on, Candelaria, find some shoes to fit you. Andrea, get a dress on. Petra, get yourself and the baby ready. I'll go shave."

"Hector, maybe we should do as Petra suggested," Mother said.

"Absolutely not. We all worked our asses off today. We should go celebrate. Let someone else wait on Petra and Candelaria for a change." He was growing impatient. "Let's move, ladies, now!" he bellowed.

He got his way. Moments later all six of us were crammed into his brown car. It wasn't easy. Father literally pushed Candelaria into the front seat with Mother and him. The old woman looked miserable. Petra sat in the back with us and talked with Cristina all the way.

"Car," Petra would say, pointing to a car.

"Car," Cristina repeated.

And so it went.

"Store."

"Store."

"Tree."

"Tree."

Every time the baby repeated something, we'd clap for her. She was having a wonderful time. She was the only one. The adults weren't talking.

Candelaria said nothing throughout the entire ride. I felt sorry for her. I avoided looking at her feet. It was the least I could do. She had wrapped her braids neatly around her head and she wore a long black skirt with a pink satin blouse I had never seen before.

Getting Candelaria out of the car was almost as hard as getting her into it. I opened the door for Petra and Cristina; I tried opening the front door, but Candelaria was stronger and

held it fast. She looked at me as if to say, Leave me alone, little girl. I did and said nothing.

We were already going into the dining room before Father noticed that Candelaria was still sitting in the front seat staring straight ahead, her face rigid, resentful.

Father went back, stuck his head through the car window, and warned, "If you don't get out, I'm going to carry you in." He opened the door, took her hand and led her out. His arm draped around the old woman's shoulders, Father entered the club dining room.

"Tony!" yelled Father. "*Tengo toda mi familia!*" he announced loudly, his arm still around Candelaria.

Tony saw him and shook his head incredulously. He ushered us to a large table—dead center in the main dining room. Father placed Candelaria next to him. Right away he ordered two shots of scotch for him and Candelaria. The rest of us drank 7-Up.

"My *compadre* is coming home tomorrow, Tony."

"We've all missed him," said Tony, pouring Dad a third scotch.

Father downed his; Candelaria sipped hers slowly.

Nervously, I looked around for Smelly Hands. I didn't see him. Thank you, dear Jesus.

"Yes," Father continued, "I've needed my friend. Bullfights aren't the same without him."

"*Sí, señor,*" said Tony. He glanced over at me and gave me a slow, lingering wink. From that I concluded that I should relax. Smelly Hands would not appear in the dining room while my father was present. I allowed myself to be hungry.

Father ordered everyone's entree and motioned to Tony to pour him a fourth shot. Mother gently placed her hand across Father's glass; he flicked it off as if it were a fly. Embarrassed, the waiter set the bottle on the table and left.

Father poured Candelaria another shot. Mother and Petra

exchanged glances. I sat in the middle watching, waiting for some new experience to come my way. It had to come. Dad was pouring.

"You remember my father, don't you?" Father asked.

"The men of the Revolution were men," Candelaria answered.

"I bet you knew a few," laughed Father.

Candelaria chuckled. She held her glass out to Father. He refilled it.

"We'll get the sherbet in the afternoon," said Mother. "There's so little room in the refrigerator. It might melt."

"We can get some dry ice," Petra said.

"I hadn't thought of that," said Mother.


*DINNER* was chicken and rice.

"I saw Carranza the year he was murdered," said Candelaria. "A great weight came upon me. I knew then something terrible was going to happen to him."

"He was a good president," Father said sadly. He refilled their glasses. "That was 1920. Long time ago."

"One of my sons was killed in the same ambush."

"Cowards. Sons of bitches," slurred Father.

"In the morning we'll stuff the piñatas with coins instead of candy," Mother said. "Candy leaves such a mess. Besides, there's so much food . . ."

"We'll mix in some peanuts too. That way they won't be so heavy."

Father started humming; Candelaria followed suit.

Father sang the first line, *"Ya no quiero ser borracho . . ."*

Candelaria came up with the second. *"Ya me, voy a detener . . ."*

They smiled at each other and continued in chorus. *"De ventanas y paredes pa'no dejarme caer."*

People were looking at us.
Oblivious to all, they sang the second stanza:

> *"Ya no quiero ser borracho*
> *ya me voy a confesar,*
> *a ver que me dice el cura*
> *y me vuelvo a emborrachar."*

They laughed and beat the table with their hands. The song seemed most appropriate.

> I don't want to be drunk
> I'm going to hold on
> To windows and walls
> So I won't fall down.
> I don't want to be drunk
> I'm going to confession
> To see what the priest tells me
> And I'll get drunk again.

Mother asked for the car keys; Father gave them to her. We got up to leave. I tried to get Father's attention to tell him that everyone in the dining room had stopped eating and was looking at us, but he and Candelaria were swaying out of the club singing "El Corrido de Cananea."

Mother drove home. Father and Candelaria were passed out in the backseat. I sat next to them, my nose out the window to escape their smell.

# 19

"No, Milita," Mother assured my aunt, "we have everything."

Throughout the day Mother and Petra dashed in and out bringing more food, more decorations for the party which was to welcome home our town doctor.

The August heat had fixed the hour. When Mother wasn't shopping, she was on the phone making sure everyone would arrive at exactly six that evening. According to plan, when Uncle arrived at six-thirty, all his friends would be there to surprise him.

In our town it was customary for entire families to come to events such as this. They came with their maids, who spent time in the kitchen visiting, trading stories, and making sure we children left the adults alone. Often, if parties ran late, the children would go upstairs to sleep. At the end of the evening they would be carried out to the car. I remember many times dropping off to sleep at someone's house and waking up in my own bed the next morning with no memory of how I got home.

That day my job was to stay out of the way and make sure my toys were safely out of reach of the visiting children. Petra warned me several times, "I don't want to hear any complaints if something is broken."

My toys were of little concern to me. I worried about Victor, my skinny lifelong friend. Would Beto show up at his house? I figured Victor was busy opening presents Uncle was sure to have brought him. I hoped Victor wouldn't forget our problems just because of some new toys. Beto was after him, not me. I knew Victor couldn't withstand physical pain. That's why his praying on thorns had impressed me so much.

THE dining-room table had been extended as far as it could go. Every inch was covered with platters of multicolored cheeses on crackers, olives, pimento, celery and cold meats brought over from the other side.

Tony came early dressed in a black uniform; he wore a red sash around his waist. He looked different outside the club— handsome, taller, less like a waiter, more like a movie star. Immediately he moved in and sorted the various liquors. Father's study had been converted into a bar. I ordered a Shirley Temple.

It was good—just like at the club, cherries and all. It made me feel special about my house, about my mother, who could arrange our house to look so pretty.

I wanted to ask Tony who was coming to help, but decided to trust him to keep Smelly Hands out of Father's sight. I was right to trust him; two other busboys showed up. Tony told them that they were to carry drinks and food to guests in the backyard. Father had set up chairs and tables so that people could enjoy the cool evening breeze—should it decide to appear.

Smelly Hands didn't show.

Two photographers and a reporter arrived first.

"Here come the brown shoes," Tony said sarcastically. He offered them scotch and soda. "American," he said and held up the bottle for them to admire.

They saw the label and laughed. "Black market," one said. Drinks in hand, they walked around the house checking things out. Tony watched them; I watched Tony.

"They'll start on the food soon," he predicted.

Sure enough. They walked by the table stuffing one of everything in their mouths; food flowed out but they crammed the next bite in anyway.

"The party hasn't started yet," I said to them. "My mom's upstairs. You should wait until she comes down—it's only polite."

A short squat man with a fat face turned to Tony and asked, "Where's the *king* of the house?"

"I'll tell the king you asked for him as soon as he gets here," Tony answered. "I'll tell him exactly what you said."

The man's eyes opened wide. "Hey, fella, we're here to take pictures, that's all." He smiled anxiously at Tony. He had celery and cheese stuck between his teeth.

Tony glared at the newsmen. He was as close to being rude as I had ever seen him. He refilled their glasses and said, "The chairs outside are comfortable."

After they were out of sight I said, "You don't like them."

"Brown shoes and greasy hair," Tony muttered under his breath.

"What does that mean? Are brown shoes bad?"

"Just a joke, honey. Some people don't know how to act in other people's homes. You know, no manners."

"Why did he call Daddy king?"

"He's a silly man. Forget him. You look really pretty today, Andrea. Is that a new dress?"

"No. It's something I hate to wear. It looks new because I hardly ever wear it. I only put it on when Mother makes me. Sometimes she likes me to look like a girl."

"Well, you're a very pretty girl," he said and winked.

It was a different kind of wink from the one he had given me at the club the night before. This wink had fun in it; the other had contained a secret. This made me want to talk to Tony more. I liked him—always had—even though I usually had to share him with Victor. Now I was alone with him and my mind raced to some new place—to some new area yet to be experienced.

"Tony, what's a *puta*?"

"Where did you hear that?" He frowned at me.

"Don't get mad. I heard it last Easter when Victor's cousins came to visit. Two dogs got stuck together and they threw rocks at them and yelled, '*Puta, puta.*' "

"Victor's cousins said that around you?"

"The ones who came from Monterrey. You remember them. They had glasses. Tell me. Every time I ask someone he does what you just did."

"It's not a nice word, Andrea. No one should tell a nice girl about things like that."

"You might as well tell me," I argued. "I'm going to keep asking until I find out."

"Andrea, I'm here to work. Your father has done more for me than anyone in this town. What would he think if I taught his daughter bad words?"

"I already know the bad word, Tony. I'm just not sure what it means. If you don't want me to go on saying it, tell me what it means. Is it like fucking?"

I don't know who he thought was listening to us, but he rushed out and left me alone with my Shirley Temple.

It *did* have to do with fucking, I figured. And it had to do with women. I thought no further . . . that made Armida a *puta*. Things cleared up. I remember thinking: Adults say more when they don't say anything.

Mother finally came down. She looked beautiful. Her hair was up and she wore a white dress that showed the loveliness

of her white skin. She was tall, taller than most of Father's male friends—and prettier than all the other wives. At moments like this I forgave all her silliness.

I compared my brown coloring to hers and wished I had been allowed to wear pants. I felt dumb in a dress.

Mother checked the table. "Who's been picking at the food?" she asked angrily.

"The brown shoes," I answered.

"What?"

"That's what Tony called them. They're outside."

She found Tony in the kitchen. "Tony, who's been at the food?"

"The newspapermen are here, señora. They're out in the yard. You know how they are," he added apologetically.

"Goodness, why did they leave such a mess?"

She rushed back to the dining room and brushed the crumbs off the tablecloth.

The bell rang and Mother jumped up.

It was Chapa, Father's workman, who came to chip the ice blocks.

The doorbell rang again.

Suddenly, as if on cue, all the guests arrived. Tony and the busboys were busy pouring drinks for everyone. Petra and Candelaria bustled in the kitchen, and Mother shook hands with the men and kissed the ladies.

But something was strange; something was very wrong. Families I had known all my life were there; they talked to each other; they talked to me. Yet their voices lacked the party sound. It was as if they were in our house for the first time and they were afraid of saying something wrong. They didn't have their children or maids with them.

There was something else: the food. No one was eating much. The club busboys passed trays around and returned to the kitchen with them more than half full. Everyone had al-

ways loved Mother's American-style hors d'oeuvres before.

They drank their first drink but politely refused Tony's offers for a refill.

"Not for me."

"I've had enough, thank you."

Mother looked sick.

Finally Father arrived in a truck with the band from the club. Things will get better, I thought.

"That's your corner, boys," he said, pointing to a space near the front living-room window. "Mauricio, you can hook up your mike here. I have a special extension."

Mauricio was the club singer. He had made three records on RCA and had sung in Mexico City. He had been born in our town and everyone said he would be famous. He had light brown curly hair—hardly looked Mexican—and he had played with his band throughout Mexico, Venezuela, Brazil, and Argentina.

Whenever Father gave banquets for bullfighters, Mauricio always played. He could sing in three languages, French, English and Spanish, and he had met Frank Sinatra in New York City. That was another thing about Mauricio—he had been to New York. That's what made the party so special. We had two people who had been to New York: Mauricio and my uncle. And here they were in *my* house.

Things should have been special. People should have realized the specialness of the event. But they didn't. They didn't appreciate a damn thing. They didn't eat Mother's food, drink Tony's drinks, or dance.

Even when Mauricio played and sang, the guests only smiled blandly at him. I stood by my parents and heard Father assuring Mother, "Things will pick up once Hugo gets here, I'm sure."

"No one's touched the food—except the reporters," she complained.

"Vultures always eat, Diane. Don't worry."

I suspected he didn't believe it himself. His face was bitter. He walked up to Pablo Guzmán, the banker, and clapped him on the back.

"Pablo, where are your children?"

"At home, Hector, my wife's not feeling well. We won't be staying long. We came to welcome back the doctor."

Pablo Guzmán smiled at Father. "Another time perhaps."

Six-thirty.

The band did a drumroll which started the minute Uncle, Tía Milita and Victor pulled up to the front of the house. As soon as they entered the living room, the cymbals clashed and everyone shouted, "Welcome home!"

My Uncle Hugo was a small, soft-spoken, delicate man. He moved appreciatively among the people who had come to welcome him. The moment he and Daddy saw each other, they embraced warmly. It was the first time they had been together in nearly twelve weeks.

"Son of a bitch, I've missed you," Father said.

My uncle laughed. "Hector, you never change."


*I FOUND* Victor.

"I know what *puta* means," I said.

"You do?"

I whispered, "Armida's a *puta*."

"She is? What's that?"

"Remember those dogs we saw last Easter?"

He pushed me away from him. "Andrea, why are you saying these things right now?"

"Listen to me."

"No. I want to be with my dad."

"No kids came. He's busy with his friends. You might as well talk to me. What did your father bring you?"

"Oh, Andrea, I have boxes and boxes of stuff. He brought things for you too."

"What?"

"You'll see. Mother said you're all coming over for breakfast after Mass Sunday. Daddy's going to surprise you."

"I hope it's not a doll."

He scowled. "Andrea, be a girl." He looked around the house. "It feels weird."

"I know. I told you, we're the only kids here."

"Why?"

"Who cares? Let's go watch Mauricio."

He was in the middle of a song but he waved to us anyway. When he finished people clapped and called out for a few songs. While he was singing, the brown shoes came and took pictures. From Mauricio's vantage I saw our guests standing around like store mannequins—fixed, frozen into poses.

Then the brown shoes cornered my parents and my aunt and uncle and took their picture. They all smiled at the camera and acted as if they were having a wonderful time. But I could see that Mother was miserable. She kept eyeing the untouched food. So much of it was still there!

By ten o'clock our house was nearly empty.

Mauricio and his band played on and on. The last remaining guests left—leaving behind them Candelaria's handmade tamales.

Mother took some of the tamales and put them on platters. She gave them to people as they left. She guaranteed in her Spanish, "They're wonderful for breakfast."

Father stood at the door, a look of disdain and rancor on his face and said nothing to the guests as they filed out. I suspected he was keeping stock of who did what; I felt he was storing up memories as to who left first, noting who had set off the tidal wave of departures. They had arrived in a horde and left the same way.

Mauricio and his band played on for my and Victor's families, Tony, the busboys, and the maids.

Father gave Tony an envelope. "Go home to your family."

"I'm sorry, Don Hector," Tony said. "The liquor was the finest I've served. The food—"

"Good night, Tony."

The waiter said nothing more. He took the liquor out of the study, moved the portable bar, tipped his helpers and went home.

The sweet smell of homemade tamales permeated our senses. It was past my bedtime. Victor nodded sleepily; I kept nudging him awake—I didn't like the way everyone looked. Mother's face was pale, pained; Father's dark features were darker than I had ever seen them, even after the killing of the watchman. Tía Milita sat staring at a wall.

My uncle, the celebrity, walked over to Mauricio and asked, "Will you sing 'I'll Be Seeing You'? No one can do it the way you do."

The curly-haired singer beamed and sang, first the English version and then the Spanish. Uncle sat in front of the musicians sipping his scotch in a tiny crystal glass that we kept in the house just for him and he listened to Mauricio's words. Tears rolled down Uncle's face.

At eleven o'clock Father told the band to go home.

"Señor, we'll play till one. You've paid us," Mauricio said.

"You were very good," said Father, and helped to pack their instruments.

Reluctantly, the musicians left. Candelaria and Petra slowly put away the many leftovers. Father turned to his dearest friend and shrugged helplessly.

"Small town, small people," Uncle said simply.

"They came for you and left because of me," Father said. He reached into the side cabinet and pulled out a short fat bottle. "Napoleon!"

"Napoleon it is!" Uncle answered.

Mother and Tía Milita looked at each other and went upstairs to Mother's study; Victor and I went to my room.

"So do you want to know about *puta?*"

He wasn't listening to me.

"It's like fucking," I continued.

"You're still thinking about Armida and those boys, aren't you?" he asked crossly.

"Yes," I admitted. "Remember when your cousins were here? Remember the dogs?"

He closed his eyes tightly. "That was ugly. You always want to talk about bad things. Mother's right, you're not good for me." He started to curl up and go to sleep.

"Victor, wait! Armida is a *puta*, don't you see?"

"So what?"

"So everything. Now we know what she is. Doesn't that matter?

"No! It doesn't explain anything. You try to make everything dirty. You like dirty things, Andrea. You really do."

"Victor, sometimes I hope Beto gets you."

"Father's home now," he said coolly. "Things are different. I'm not alone."

"You weren't alone before. They still got you."

"Your father doesn't count," he said. He curled into himself and almost immediately I heard his steady breathing.

Downstairs I heard Father's and Uncle's voices—bursts of laughter followed by quiet talk. From Mother's study I could hear nothing.

I decided to go there. I knocked on the delicate glass door.

"What is it, Andrea?" asked Mother.

I opened the door. "Nothing. Victor is asleep." I looked at Mother's red eyes. "What's wrong?"

Tía Milita answered for her. "She's tired."

"What's wrong, Mother? Nobody ate the food. Why did they leave?"

Mother burst out crying. "I hate this town, everything about it, everything in it." She sobbed, sobbed all over her white

dress. Her blonde hair fell loosely over her face. She reminded me of a punctured egg.

"No one stayed to hear Mauricio sing," I said.

Mother sobbed louder.

"Go to sleep," Tía Milita begged me. "Leave us alone."

I left them, checked my room and saw that Victor was sleeping, his mouth open wide. Downstairs I heard the sound of men laughing in Father's study. I crept halfway down the stairs.

"Really?" asked Father.

"I swear it," confirmed Uncle.

"I love *gringas!*" howled Father.

From the stairway I thought I heard Father slap his leg. I envisioned him enjoying one of those jokes that made Mother cringe.

# 20

I SAW the son of a bitch leaving Popeye's the next afternoon when the heat was at its highest, when I knew Don Pancho, Armida's husband was taking his nap. Smelly Hands sauntered out of the store looking satisfied.

Outside were two of his friends leaning lazily against the storefront, hands in their pockets, dressed in black pants and white shirts. They were the boys who had helped Tony serve drinks to our guests the night before. Smelly Hands pranced in front of his friends and made two tight fists and pulled at his groin. They laughed loudly; one of them clapped him on the back.

I wanted Father to bring the car to a stop, but he was suffering from two hangovers: the Napoleon and Mother's endless weeping over the party, which had driven both of us out of the house after breakfast.

Mother had started early. "A town of hypocrites . . . and you getting plastered at the club with the laundress . . . all the work . . . the expense . . . I hate them . . ."

When Father failed to soothe her he asked me, "Want to go to work with me?"

I flew upstairs and dressed.

Father and me at the warehouse—it was like old times. I loved going to work with him. He made things happen; he made laughter—though it was usually outside our home.

"Tell your wife to give your balls a rest," he said to a young workman who was loading a truck too slowly.

The rest of the workers howled at the young man, who had been married a few days earlier. They all worked faster after Father's remark.

And when the August heat became unbearable, Father brought boxes filled with iced beer to his men. He let them play the radio all day; he joined in their singing, his tenor voice rising higher than theirs, his phrasing playful, personal. That day I too sang with them. We listened to Mexican songs which celebrated suffering—always for the love of a woman.

"Mexican songs are the most romantic in the world," I'd heard him say endless times. Candelaria had told me that you could end the songs anytime you wanted to. Did that mean Mexicans could end their love anytime they wanted?

I remembered how Father had left the house with Mother crying upstairs. His last words were "If I hear you one more minute, my head will explode."

That afternoon as he was driving me home for lunch, as we passed Popeye's and I saw the busboy coming out, I was sickened by the thought of love—in song, in practice. I loved no one, suffered for no one, believed in nothing.

I hated myself for squirming in front of Smelly Hands when I had taken him our money to feed his stupid family. I hated my weakness. Victor was right: Smelly Hands didn't deserve the money. I resolved never to give him another cent.

I turned to Father and stated, "A *puta* is a bad woman who lets people touch her for money."

Father turned off the radio.

I thought I saw a smile cross his face. "What happened to the Chinese?"

"Am I right?"

"Who have you been talking to?"

"I heard it at the park."

"Well, you're right—in a way. They let people touch them for money. Some say they're bad ladies. They're poor ladies too. Good people like you and Victor should pray for them. The sisters don't talk about them much, I imagine, but they need prayers."

"I hate them."

"I don't want you to like them. Hate them if you want to, Andrea. I don't want you to talk about them to anyone else but me, understand?"

His voice took a gentle turn. I felt invited to speak to him further. Again I held back.

"I don't want you speaking of this to Victor either."

"Why?"

His voice became deadly serious. "Because I'm telling you not to, and because . . ." He seemed to grope for words. "He's different. He gets hurt easier, feels life in a different place than people like you and me. I don't know. Don't do it, all right?"

There wasn't much I could say. I knew I had just heard something important, one of those things I was supposed to understand later. Still I had to ask.

"Father, is he better than me?"

"No, Andrea. He's just not my son. Love him. He will always need your love."

Upset about Smelly Hands, upset about Father's making me promise not to speak to Victor about *putas*, I went to my room, leaving Father to deal with Mother's hurt feelings.

I didn't want lunch; I wanted revenge. Petra had misunderstood my reluctance to eat as fear of hearing my parents

quarrel and brought me up a peanut butter sandwich with milk.

I threw the sandwich on my bedroom floor and squashed the grape jelly into the rug. "I hate this food."

Petra looked at me and left the room. She reappeared moments later with a bar of soap in her hand. In silence she stepped over the mess I had just made, grabbed me by the braids, and dragged me to the bathroom.

"Take that washcloth."

I took it.

"Wet it and make soap suds with this." She handed me the bar of soap and I did as ordered.

She gave my braids another yank and led me back to the bedroom. "Clean that up."

"You've never hit me before." I was close to tears.

"I should have. Wipe it clean."

I did. She took the cloth and left my room—slamming the door shut.

"Petra! Please come back!" I sobbed. She didn't.

An hour later I was starving. Angry at having been forced to wash the rug, I drank two full glasses of water. I lay down and the water sloshed in my stomach.

I wanted vengeance against Smelly Hands—to hurt him, hit his face, crush his legs. I yearned to do something terrible to him and to Armida for letting him do whatever he did that made him so happy.

I lay there that afternoon and felt myself turn into a monster and I let myself go; I let hate run wild throughout my head, my heart. I wished I were ten feet tall so I could stab or stomp Smelly Hands to death. Armida too—*puta*—dog, bitch.

I heard the phone ring. Mother talked. I had no interest. I sulked in my room until dinner.

The sun had set; outside the insects started their night songs. Our house was an oven. The buzz of electric fans filled the

dining and living rooms. The feel of the house told me Father would not be home for dinner. My sister went to sleep early. Petra served Mother and me without a word; she avoided my eyes.

Mother barely touched her food. Normally I would have asked if anything was wrong; but there was too much turmoil in me to bother with her troubles.

I had nearly finished dinner when Mother said tiredly, "Milita called. She doesn't want you to see Victor again. He's had an attack of some kind . . . didn't really say."

I nearly threw up. "Attack? What kind of attack?"

"Didn't really say."

"You already said that! Tell me *exactly* what she said."

"Don't shout at me. I don't remember. She was upset too. Your uncle is trying to find out what's the matter with him."

I felt sick. "Mother," I pleaded, "you have to take me over there. I can quiet him down. I know how." He's going to tell, I thought.

"That's out of the question. Let his parents worry about him. She said Victor saw some boys outside his house. He thought it was the same ones who beat him up before."

"Did *she* actually *see* them?"

"They were gone by the time she got to the porch. Victor was screaming. Andrea, cooperate—until your Holy Communion. She insists he must have absolute rest if he's to have the Communion ceremony with you."

"I don't care about that. You don't know—"

"We have to do it jointly. The church has been reserved all year. That boy is always upset about something. Milita spoils him too much. That's his problem. Sometimes I wonder why you insist on playing with him so much." She pushed her plate away.

"Do you think they were there?"

"What?" She was barely interested in me.

"The river kids, do you think they were there?"

She looked sadly into my eyes. "If you only knew what it felt like to see people you thought were your friends—just walk out of your house. They could see all the trouble we went to. It's not worth it."

"It already happened, Mother. Forget about it." I thought she was going to start crying any minute.

I folded my napkin in fours and excused myself. I had to plot my revenge against Smelly Hands. I had kept my part of the bargain and he hadn't. Now he was going to be the sorriest busboy in the whole world.

The plan came suddenly—a vision that I could see clearly in front of me. The only thing that kept me from putting it into action right then was that it was night.

# 21

*A*RMIDA *es puta en la tienda.* Armida is a whore in the store.

After hours of trying, that note finally looked adult. It was ready when the time came.

Now that Victor and I were separated, Mother drove me to receive my final religious instruction. I demanded to go in the mornings; if my plan was to work, my afternoons had to be free.

For three days I hid in a doorway across from Popeye's during the peak of the afternoon August heat. My hideout was uncomfortable, cramped. I fought off the sleepiness that came daily by stirring up my hatred against Smelly Hands.

On the third day he came alone at the time of day when most of the town slept, when Don Pancho took his siesta in the bedroom behind the bar.

I knew Smelly Hands would come; he had to. I had waited for him for so long I almost jumped out to greet him as I would an old friend—as I would Victor.

I knew the routine as well as Smelly Hands. There was only one person in Popeye's, a maid, and she left a few minutes after Smelly Hands entered. When I was sure Armida and Smelly Hands were alone, I put my plan into action.

I crossed the empty street to where Don Pancho slept, crept up to the glassless window, and sharply rapped my knuckles against the frame five times; then I threw in my note tied to a rock. It flew easily through the light cotton curtain.

I crossed the street again, stood squarely in front of the store, and waited. The noonday sun baked my head; I welcomed the heat.

She screamed first, a loud "Nooooo!" followed by a pleading nearly choking "*Pancho, por favor!*"

Then out rushed Smelly Hands. His pants were completely off. Something was terribly wrong; the other boys had never been naked; yet there he was—naked from the waist down. I saw all of him.

He tore down the street, hopping on one leg, then the other, trying to jump into his pants. He had no underwear, just his usual black busboy pants and white cotton shirt, which was unbuttoned.

He was halfway down the block before I came to my senses and yelled to him, "*Adiós, Rodrigo!*" I waved my arms wildly at him. *"Buena suerte!"*

He looked back and saw me. Then, as I had seen him do in front of his friends only a few days before, I made two tight fists around my groin.

He stopped, his black hair spread sloppily across his forehead, and he stared at me. And he *knew*. His lips curled back as he finished dressing. He moved toward me.

Armida ran out to the street. She was almost naked except for a dull pink slip—torn in front. A crazed Don Pancho, wielding a leather riding crop, followed her.

Smelly Hands was nearly on me when Armida begged him, "*Rodrigo, ayúdame, por favor!*" Rodrigo, help me, please.

For a moment I thought he was going back to help her, but as he turned away from me and toward her, Don Pancho leaped over the half-fallen Armida and charged at him, shouting, "*Estás muerto, hijo de puta!*" You're dead, son of a whore.

Effortlessly Smelly Hands outdistanced Don Pancho. In seconds the busboy was at the end of the block and out of sight. Fury fully unleashed, Don Pancho turned back to Armida.

Pinning her down by the hair, he struck her with the riding crop across her legs. She too was without underwear. Her screams pierced the afternoon heat.

"*Pancho, no, por favor,*" she begged repeatedly.

"*Puta! Puta!*" he answered, gaining momentum with each stroke.

Suddenly Armida jerked her hair free from his grip and stood up and faced him. She threw herself at him and, in a pitiful gesture of rebellion, tried to kick him with her bare feet. His crop came down hard across the front of her face.

And then I came between them, yelling. "No, Don Pancho, get the busboy, not her! Hit the boy!"

Don Pancho brushed me away. I fell to the ground and saw him start on her again. "It's the wrong person!" I yelled with all my might. "This is wrong!"

Again I tried to pull them apart. The crop whooshed through the air and landed on my shoulder. A hot paralyzing pain shot through my body. The blow knocked me to my knees and I scurried out of the way. The crop whooshed again and landed on the pink slip.

She curled into a ball and let her husband beat her until she passed out. I quickly moved away from them. The pain in my shoulder had spread to the rest of my back. I tried to run; I couldn't. Angry, frustrated that the son-of-a-bitch busboy had

gotten away, I pressed my shoulder into me and limped toward home. I looked back and saw a crowd around the couple.

The welt on my shoulder went unseen. I put myself to bed early and relived the afternoon, the pulsing laceration my only solace. All night Armida was with me. Awake or asleep I saw the beating, her torn slip, her private parts showing for on-lookers to see and for the rest of the town to find out about later.

## 22

MOTHER drove me to catechism the next morning. She waited for me while Sister went over the differences between venial and mortal sins. Mortal sins were the worst. If I were to die with one of them on my soul I would face eternal damnation. Breaking any of the Ten Commandments, we were told—missing Mass on Sundays or Holy Days of Obligation, eating meat on Fridays—were all mortal sins.

I memorized the definition of sin. I learned those words, remembered them, yet failed to see how I could ever be forgiven for the pain I had caused. The good sister was so buried in layers of cloth she could never have understood the sin I had committed against Armida. Dressed in her holy habit, Sister seemed too innocent to know about pink slips, about curtains that snap back in midafternoons to allow old and young bodies to rub against each other. She told me about sin; yet she failed to provide me with a vocabulary that would describe what I had done to Armida. In my heart I knew what

I had to do before I stepped into the confessional for the first time.

I kept to myself when I got home and, when I was sure of privacy, I took a pillowcase and went into my closet, took out all the money that we had left, placed the bills into the pillowcase and with it slung over my shoulder, I walked to Popeye's.

A silent crowd stood in front of Popeye's. Alarmed, I pushed my way to the front and saw that heavy boards had been nailed across the doorway and store windows. Black paint which had run unevenly down the wood announced, CER-RADO. Closed.

"Where are they?" I asked a grown-up standing next to me. She shrugged.

Through a tiny crack between the boards I saw that the store was still full of merchandise. Then I went around to the side entrance to the bar; it too was boarded up. I ran to the window where I had thrown in my note to Don Pancho and found the same.

I struck the boards until my fists throbbed. Then, with the lonely anguish of one who realizes she has committed an act she can never erase, I went home—the money still in the pillowcase.

"Popeye's is closed. Everything is boarded up," I said to Mother. "The store's full of stuff. The people are gone."

"What would you ever want to buy from there?"

"Something."

"I'm going to the other side tomorrow. You can get anything you want from Kress's."

"What happened to the people?"

"Who knows?" she answered. "Andrea, are you crying?"

I sobbed. "I want to know where they went."

She kissed away my tears. I threw my arms around her and wept until hiccups came.

"Petra," called Mother, "Andrea has the hiccups."

Holding my breath, I drank a full glass of water. The two women looked at me to see if Petra's cure worked. It did, as always.

Mother looked at Petra and said, "Don't ask me what it's about. She went to Popeye's, saw that it was closed and burst into tears."

"What did you want, Andrea?" asked Petra. She was being nice to me again.

"To buy something," I lied.

"From what I hear, Popeye's won't open again."

"No great loss," said Mother.

I blurted passionately, "I love Popeye's! I love it more than the club, more than anything in this town!"

I could feel myself unraveling before them. Their eyes told me how much of me they were seeing. Fearful of exposing any more of myself, I picked up the pillowcase that I had heedlessly dropped at my feet and dashed to my room, where I stayed, sometimes crying, sometimes sleeping, until dinnertime.

Later that evening I tried calling Victor, but Petra caught me asking the operator for the number.

"You know you're not to call him."

"I want to tell him about Popeye's. It's important. That's all I'll say. I swear to God—"

"Listen to yourself, Andrea, swearing with God's name."

"Stay and hear for yourself. All I'll say is 'Victor, Popeye's is closed,' and I'll hang up. I sw—"

She put the phone back on its cradle. "No."

Obsessed with wanting to know where Armida was, I spied constantly on the maids.

I heard Candelaria laughing in the kitchen and saying to Petra, ". . . every one of those gold teeth of hers—gone, gone . . ."

Petra said Armida's family had a meat stand in a market in Sonora.

From Father I learned that Sonora was a state several hundred miles away.

*Armida, please forgive me*, I prayed several times a day. I silently reached out to her. I wanted her to know what I had done. I needed her to know everything. I wanted her forgiveness, and if she chose to beat me for what I had done, I would welcome her blows.

Fearing the vengeance of Smelly Hands, I stayed inside the house. I thought little about Victor's safety. It was me Smelly Hands had headed toward. It was me his eyes had marked; I had no doubt that had he been able to get his hands on me, he would have strangled me—at whatever consequence to himself.

I called the club and spoke to Tony. Petra was by my side.

"Tony, this is Andrea. Is Rodrigo there? I don't want to talk to him. I just want to know if he's there."

There was a long silence, then, "Rodrigo is gone, Andrea. I think you already knew that."

"I don't know anything. Where is he?"

"You really don't know what happened?"

I spoke in my most helpless, childish voice. "No. I don't want him to scare us. He's mean to us. He said Beto was going to get us."

"He's gone to the other side," Tony said. "I don't know when he's coming back. I wouldn't worry." He paused, then added, "This wouldn't have anything to do with that certain question you asked me about a certain word—a *bad* word— would it?"

"No. Goodbye, Tony." I hung up.

Petra asked, "Has that watchman's son been teasing you children?"

I kept my childish voice. "He sent those boys to Victor's house."

Petra fumed. "Evil boy! Why didn't you tell me of this sooner, Andrea? I've kept your secrets before."

"I *am* telling you. And it *is* a secret. Tony said he's gone to the other side and won't be back."

"That's what they say."

"Why?"

"Because he's no good and that's all you need to know. If you're afraid to go out and play, I'll go with you—to the park or anywhere else, understand?"

I nodded and she opened her arms to me and I went to her.

By confiding in Petra I had attempted to feel like a little girl again. By day I let myself be coddled and protected by her, and then the nights would come and with them came fear and guilt, and I would wake up in the darkness and feel a terrible, familiar weight on my chest. It was so definite, so solid, that I moved my hands across my chest to verify that no rock was pressing down upon my heart.

I had succeeded in ruining Smelly Hands, but the sound of Don Pancho's crop rang in my head day and night. I lived for my first confession.

# 23

ONCE the invitations for the Holy Communion Mass and banquet were mailed, Mother and Petra fretted over the number of RSVP's, the seating order of the guests and my wardrobe.

My dress.

It lay covered with Armida's money. If the thought of her made me ill, the idea of anyone finding the money paralyzed me. I had to do something with it, something good that would ease the weight I bore. It wasn't a matter of confession; that was out of the question. I felt I had to *do* some act that would repay the harm I had caused Armida.

One Thursday evening I transferred what was left of the cash—there was still a lot of money—into an ordinary shopping bag and buried it in our weekly trash. Then I stood on the balcony and waited until tall blue-eyed Rancho Grande came by. He usually appeared around dinnertime when the sun was close to setting.

Methodical as always, he went through the bin item by item, separating out what he

wanted and setting aside all he found useless. He got to my sack. He picked it up, opened it, peeked and froze. He stuck his entire head in the bag and kept it in there for a long while. Then slowly he pulled his head out and looked around to see if anyone was watching.

Quickly I ducked down and when I figured he was gone, I checked—fully expecting him to have moved on. Instead, he was looking directly where I had been hiding, as if he'd known all along that I was there waiting to show myself.

His blue eyes looked into me for an eternity, then slowly, imperceptibly, he nodded acceptance of the gift. I smiled and waved to him; he held my gaze once more, then he continued working our trash with slow orderliness. That evening he also took some leftovers from my parents' dismal welcome-home party for my uncle: a half-full jar of olives, small glasses with pimiento cheese, crackers, some hardened tamales, and all the newspapers.

The next day Petra took out my Holy Communion dress and hung it to air out. The dress was made of silk and covered with thick white Spanish lace. I felt no desire to wear it; Mother had to beg me to try it on to see if it still fit.


PAULETTE, my American grandmother, arrived from Los Angeles exactly a week after I gave Rancho Grande the money and two days before my Holy Communion. Days before her arrival Mother bought new things for the house. Cristina and I were to become roommates. Grandmother's room was fixed up with new curtains, new pictures on the wall and a bright orange bedspread.

Between the Holy Communion and Grandmother's visit Mother found no time to feel depressed. She had been so despondent since Uncle's reception I was afraid Father would start staying away again. Then one morning a telegram arrived

and everything was different. One small yellow piece of paper had brought Mother and the entire household back to life.

"My God! Hector, listen to this. Mother is flying directly to San Antonio, from there she's taking a small plane to *our* airport. It's all dirt!"

Father grabbed the telegram. He let out a small whistle. "Call her up, Diane. Tell her to come by train. Women her age shouldn't hop around on planes, for Christ's sake."

"It won't do any good."

"She's crazy. She's got to take the Pullman. So what if she misses the Holy Communion?"

Grandmother flew into town.

All that day Mother was restless, nervous. Every time the phone rang she would jump and scream, "Oh no!" Then, because she received no bad news, she would ask herself, "Why did she do this to me?"

I laughed silently at Mother and longed for Grandmother to arrive. I had met her four years before but didn't remember her too well. I only recalled that I had good feelings toward her and that she made me want to be near her.

Father honked and we ran out.

Mother cried, "Thank God you're safe."

In a low husky voice Grandmother said, "Of course I'm safe. Let me look at these girls, these babies of mine!" She crushed me with strong hugs and kisses. "My Andrea and her braids. And this is Cristina! Oh my, Diane, she is beautiful!" She reached for my sister.

Mother screamed, "Don't do that!"

Too late. As soon as Grandmother reached out, Cristina started howling hysterically.

"What's wrong with her?" asked Grandmother, alarmed.

Mother smiled nervously. "It's your sunglasses and hat. Take them off. She's afraid of them."

Cristina's cries filled the street.

Grandmother laughed. "A fine how-do-you-do. What do you feed this creature?"

Mother promised, "She'll calm down in a while—then you won't be able to keep her off you."

Grandmother stood in front of the crying Cristina and took off her sunglasses and large floppy hat. She was blonder than Mother, her eyes bluer. I wanted her to stand still so I could look at her closely. She was busy fluffing out her hair. Cristina had clamored herself purple; Mother was unable to calm her down.

Suddenly Father bellowed, "Women, get inside!" He was loaded down with luggage and boxes. He plowed through us, trudged upstairs to Grandmother's room and dropped everything in the center.

Grandmother sat on the orange bedspread. Her husky voice and rich laughter filling the room, she distributed her presents without ceremony, without waiting to see how grateful we were. She had brought something for everyone. Petra got a new purse and a black sweater; Candelaria a shawl for Mass.

Whenever something was for me, Grandmother would say, "This is for the party girl."

I received the most gifts—a bracelet, a book, Snow White and the Seven Dwarfs, and a Tonto bow-and-arrow set. Thank God Grandmother hadn't believed that I was a savage as I had heard Mother say to her weeks ago. It bothered me being called "party girl." Grandmother wasn't Catholic; she couldn't possibly know how serious a Holy Communion was. I found it easy to forgive her.

As Mother predicted, Cristina overcame her distrust of Grandmother and crept close to her. Grandmother sat still while my sister looked at her and then back at Mother. Cristina compared the hair, eyes, faces. "Don't count the lines," said Grandmother.

"That's your grandmother," Mother explained to Cristina. "Say 'Grandma.' "

Grandmother looked at Mother and raised her eyebrows. "Oh no you don't. The word 'grandmother' adds decades to a woman." Grandmother pointed to herself and slowly enunciated, "Paulette. My name is Paulette."

Mother shook her head and smiled. "What are you doing?"

"Telling my grandchildren my name. I want them to call me by my name. What's wrong with that?"

"It's impolite." Mother wrinkled her nose.

"Nonsense. You'll call me Paulette, won't you, Andrea?"

"I will if you want me to—and if you don't call me 'party girl' anymore."

"It's a deal." She laughed and repeated to Cristina, "Say Paulette. Paaaul-e-tt."

Cristina stared into her mouth.

Paulette asked Mother, "Does she understand English?"

"She understands some things, but what few words or phrases she says are in Spanish. She's a lazy talker, not like Andrea."

"Well, she'll learn some things while I'm here. Yes sirree, Paulette from Hollywood is here and we're going to have fun, right, Andrea?" She pinched my cheek. "Kiss my dimple."

I did immediately. Cristina took a little more prodding.

Mother brought in my Communion dress and veil and showed it to Paulette, who studied it with great care. "Good thing I brought her a skirt and blouse. She can change after the church ceremony."

Mother seemed displeased. "It won't kill her to wear it for a day. Do you know how much it cost?"

"It's constricting *and* beautiful. But she's still a child and if it's her special day she should be comfortable too. It's damn hot. What do you think, Andrea?"

"I want to wear a skirt and blouse. I've never worn them

before." I was speaking the truth. I had school uniforms, pants, shorts and dresses. Not one skirt and blouse.

Mother was unconvinced. "Victor's keeping his gown on all day."

"A dress?" scoffed Paulette.

Mother said softly, "His parents are dressing him as a cardinal. He's wearing a long taffeta gown with a lace slip over it."

Grandmother laughed and laughed. "A bride and a cardinal—age nine! We wouldn't do that even in Hollywood."

Mother laughed too. "All right, Paulette, you win. You too, Andrea. I can't fight both of you. I won't need to ask Hector what he thinks."

"Good," said Paulette. "Now let me finish unpacking and get into something cool. I need to change out of these soggy clothes."

A while later Paulette came downstairs dressed in light blue slacks and a matching sleeveless blouse. She wore sandals; her toenails were painted red. She had washed her face and combed back her hair. She looked prettier and younger than when she arrived.

Father cried out, "My God, I have the sexiest mother-in-law in the whole world."

"And the thirstiest. How about a nice cool gin rickey, lots of lime, please, son-in-law."

"You got it. I'm having a Tom Collins. What about you, Diane?"

"Ah, ah," stammered Mother, "I'm not sure if I—"

Paulette interrupted her, "Give her a rickey—light on the gin."

Father walked over and kissed Mother lightly. "A rickey okay, honey? It's time to celebrate."

Mother shrugged helplessly. "I can see I have no choice—not in this crowd."

They drank until dinnertime, when Father suggested letting Petra feed us and put us to bed. "We'll go out to dinner, the club, anywhere you like."

"I want to eat right here with my babies, thanks, Hector. I want to relax. Besides, another one of these and I won't be able to walk."

"It's air-conditioned," said Mother.

"A sandwich will be fine. If you two want to go out, it's fine with me. I don't want to budge."

We ate sandwiches. It was fun watching Mother obey her mother. Paulette talked constantly. "The flight to San Antonio was wonderful. Though I must admit transferring to the lighter plane did make me nervous."

I asked, "Why?"

"Well, for one thing, the damn thing wouldn't start."

"Wouldn't start?" echoed Mother.

Paulette continued, "There were four of us and we were roasting. Anyway, the kid finally got the plane in the air. Once we got up everything was fine. The landing was something else. We hit the ground so hard I thought the wings would fall off. Great airport, Hector. You have to do something about that."

"How old was the pilot? You said he was a kid," said Mother.

"Well, at fifty-two, anyone under thirty is a kid. He did claim to have flown in the war. Don't look so worried, Diane. I'm here and I'm safe."

Mother sighed loudly. "I hope you'll take the train home. Do it for me."

"Another rickey for my daughter, Hector. No promises."

Grandmother can get out of anything, I marveled.

Grandmother-Paulette, Grandmother-Paulette. I couldn't decide what to call her inside myself. I wanted to own her, but the name Paulette didn't let me lay claim upon her. Grand-

mother did. But the red toenails and blonde hair didn't go with the word "grandmother."

"Paulette," I asked, "why can't I call you Grandmother at home and Paulette around people?"

"Paulette? Isn't it *Paula*?" asked Father.

Mother took a sip from her drink. "Oh, Hector."

Father seemed confused. "What did I say?"

Paulette raised her hands as if to calm everyone down. She turned to me and explained, "Andrea, your father is right. My name is Paula. But that's so plain, dear. I now prefer Paulette, as in Goddard. The woman's changed my entire life."

"I'll just call you Paulette," I offered.

Paulette persisted, "You see, Paulette Goddard is a beautiful lady actress, red hair, porcelain skin, love, excitement, passion. Paula is Paula. No strings attached. I want a few strings, Andrea. If you want to call me Grandmother, that's okay. But if I frown, call me Paulette. That's our signal."

"Paulette's fine," I agreed.

Mother rattled an empty glass at Father. He refilled it. Mother drank, and pretty soon she was giggling along with Paulette and Father.

That night was the happiest we'd had in weeks. It was a party listening to Paulette, a pretty lady whose graceful white hands never stopped caressing Cristina and me. She drank like Father and she smoked Pall Malls and I came to love her swiftly and completely.

That was a Thursday night. It was August 28, 1947. After dinner I went outside to check our trash. It was exactly as Petra had left it. Rancho Grande had not come by. He didn't need our trash anymore. I felt happy about that.

That night I went to sleep to the sounds of laughter downstairs. Father's was the loudest of all.

# 24

THE following afternoon Mother supervised my bath. She took out a pastel-blue dress with puffy sleeves and I wore it with excitement. The dress had a belt instead of a sash. Petra braided my hair tightly. I looked into the mirror and saw that although I looked nice, I had a rabbit look to my face, that of a frightened young hare. As if by written agreement, no one talked to me. That was good. Tomorrow would be my Holy Communion.

Paulette stayed out of sight. Candelaria peered at me but said nothing, Petra cared for me in silence. Mother drove me to the church and said only what was necessary. A call had come in for Father at nine o'clock that morning and he had been gone since.

Victor and Tía Milita were waiting for us outside the church. He wore black pants and a white shirt. Bad choice of colors, I thought. I was surprised that Victor would allow himself to be dressed like a busboy. He seemed heavier and his curls were all gone. Tía Milita loved to cut his hair.

Everything that had happened to my life since the party flashed through my mind the moment I saw him. My note to Don Pancho—how easily it had sailed through the window— seeing Smelly Hands trying to hop into his trousers, the beating of Armida, the closing of Popeye's, and my giving Armida's money to Rancho Grande—all this in less than eleven days. Victor seemed so innocent to me.

The women kissed each other lightly on both cheeks.

"Finally!" said one.

"At last!" said the other.

Victor and I walked slowly behind our mothers. His face was glowing with anticipation.

"I've tried calling you," I whispered.

"Tried calling you too."

I was relieved to hear that. The bond still existed. "Are you still sick?" I asked.

"I got scared when Beto and them came to my house. I think Mother was more upset than me."

I didn't believe him. "I thought you were mad at me."

"It wasn't your fault. Besides, they didn't come back. They knew Father was home. Did you see his pictures in the paper?"

I lied, "Yes. They were nice."

We entered the church. Padre Lozano and Sister Angelica were waiting for us in front of the altar. The padre nodded to us and went into the confessional, a dark wooden structure with maroon curtains. Sister scurried over to us and pressed our mothers' hands. She seemed so anxious; they all did.

"Andrea, go to that side. Victor, go to the other." Sister said to our mothers, "Wait up front for them."

I asked, "Why can't we sit together?"

She didn't bother to answer. She took Victor by the hand and led him away from me.

"Let me ask him something first," I pleaded.

He looked at me, a question in his eyes.

Sister said firmly, "It's time to examine your consciences. Do it carefully."

Not caring who heard, I called to Victor, "Are you going to tell?"

Sister scolded me. "Andrea, you're in church."

Disregarding her, I again asked Victor, "Are you?"

Vehemently he nodded his head. Then he knelt, folded his hands in prayer and bowed his head. I knelt too and waited in vain for him to lift his head and look at me. I didn't examine my conscience. All I could think about was that he didn't know. Here he was about to confess everything and we didn't have the money anymore. Something good had been done with it. Maybe our sin had been absolved and we were about to do penance for nothing.

Then I heard Sister whisper his name. That startled me. Somehow I had expected to be first. Victor walked toward the confessional. I waited, counting on him to give me one last look, but he didn't. Mother and Tía Milita were sitting in the front row. As soon as Victor closed the curtain behind him, Mother looked back at me, waved and smiled. I scowled at her, lowered my head and prayed.

"God, You know everything, so don't get mad at me if I don't tell the priest everything. I'll try, God, but don't punish me if the words don't come out. You know I went back and tried to fix things with Armida. You know I gave her money to Rancho Grande and that was a good deed because he saved us from the river kids. And You gave our house a lot of trouble this summer and so in a way, we're even."

I remembered Candelaria's warning about making bargains with God and added, "I'm not making a bargain. I'm just reminding You that things are even now."

I blessed myself and sat back and waited for Victor to come out. It was cool in the church and I grew goose pimples on my arms. I felt the cold inch down to my legs and pretty soon I was very cold. Victor was talking a long time. I saw Mother

and Tía Milita whisper to each other. Sister Angelica seemed unconcerned about the length of time Victor was taking. I saw Sister's head drop forward; soon a light snoring filled the empty church. The four of us waited for what must surely have been an hour.

Feeling betrayed, angry, I thought, Victor, you're really confessing. I wondered if maybe he had some sins I didn't know about, but threw out that possibility. I had come to believe that Victor only sinned when he was around me.

He emerged drenched in sweat, hands folded across his chest, head bowed. He stood in front of Sister and coughed lightly. She jerked her head up and led him back up the aisle so he could say his penance.

Victor looked at no one. He buried his head in his hands and stayed that way. I didn't bother to wait for Sister to give me the sign; I stepped forward and entered the cubicle. The space was tighter than I had expected and it was extremely hot, not from the summer heat but from Victor. Some part of him was still there.

All summer I had moved toward this moment, the moment when I could confess my sins to Padre Lozano, and now that I was there it seemed as if someone else was kneeling in the confessional. It certainly wasn't me.

"Bless me, Father, for I have sinned. This is my First Confession . . ." And I enumerated my sins. "I take money from my mother's purse, I tell lies, I use God's name in vain, I'm rude to my parents, I hit kids at school . . ." I recited, catalogued, then brought it to a close. "For these and those sins I can't remember, Father, I am heartily sorry."

"You have examined your conscience?"

"Yes, Padre."

"These are *all* your sins?"

Why did he lean on the word *all*? I suspected Victor had told on himself and me too.

I answered, "They're the ones I can remember."

"Examine your conscience once again. Remember that to-morrow you will receive Jesus for the first time. Say a prayer to the Blessed Mother asking her to grant you the courage to make a good confession."

A square of lace separated me from the priest. My eyes had grown accustomed to the dark and I was able to see his profile clearly. I leaned my head against the cloth and from the core of my being spoke in silence.

*Padre, I saw a* puta *let boys touch her and I liked it. I stole her money and then I told her husband on her. He beat her in front of everybody. But it was a mistake. I really wanted to pay back Smelly Hands. The wrong person suffered. Now I can't find her and beg her forgiveness. I didn't keep her money. Rancho Grande has it. He's good. He saved us once. Forgive me, Padre, I've ruined a life.*

"Padre."

"Are you ready?"

"I nearly took out my sister's eye trying to cut her eyelashes. I was jealous of them. Also at the club, I break things like glasses for no reason at all. Sometimes I say dirty words to myself and sometimes I yell them at people I don't know."

"That's all you can remember?"

"Yes."

"You feel ready to receive the Body and Blood of Jesus Christ our Savior?"

"Yes."

"For your penance say two rosaries to the Blessed Virgin asking her to guide you and be with you at all times. Begin your Act of Contrition."

"Oh my God I am heartily sorry for having offended Thee . . ." Angry, disgusted, I finished before he had completed his prayers of absolution.

"Go with God."

"Thank you, Padre."

A dizziness came over me as I left the confessional. I took

several deep breaths to steady myself. I was so mad even breathing was difficult. Two rosaries! Two whole rosaries! Damn Victor. What had he said to Padre Lozano? And where had Padre Lozano gotten the idea I wasn't telling the truth?

The chill of the church brought back my goose pimples. I looked around and saw only Sister Angelica.

"Where's everybody?" I asked.

"Shhh. Outside, waiting. Say your penance."

"Is Victor finished with his?" I asked as I knelt down.

"Shhh. Yes."

Damn Victor. Damn snitcher. I hadn't been in the confessional twenty minutes and had received two rosaries. He had been there an hour and had already finished his penance. I didn't even have a rosary with me and I wasn't about to start counting my fingers either. If I stayed and said all my prayers, everyone would know I had received a worse penance than what Victor got.

I saw Padre Lozano leave the confessional and I quickly bowed my head. I said five Our Fathers and twenty Hail Marys. God, I'll finish the rest later, I promised.

The sun was setting. At the bottom of the church steps Victor hopped like a rabbit. He saw me and smiled happily.

"Don't you feel good?" he asked.

I wondered where to hit him. He was beaming from inside out.

"Just think," he said dreamily, "right now our souls are pure. If we died this minute we'd go straight up to heaven— no purgatory, nothing."

*Maybe I should kill him. God forgive me quick.*

I cleared my throat. "Why didn't you wait for me?"

"I finished my penance and then my mom and yours saw me and we all came outside. They're sitting in the car, see?" He narrowed his eyes in suspicion. "Andrea, how come you came out so fast?"

"How much penance did you get?" I asked.

"Twenty Our Fathers and twenty Hail Marys." He studied my face closely. "Andrea, you didn't tell everything, did you?"

"You told Padre Lozano about me, didn't you?" I raised my arm as if to strike him. "I could tell by what he asked me."

His voice shook. "What did he ask you?"

"Shit, Victor, you told." I felt sick.

He lowered his head. "I confessed everything, Andrea, and I'm glad." He raised his head, challenging me to hit him.

"Well, I confessed everything too," I lied. "I confessed more than you because I know more than you. You don't know anything. You just hide out with your mother and don't know a damn thing."

His eyes opened in horror. "You're cursing! You just went to confession."

I smiled at him and said, "Victor, we don't have any more money. I gave it away to Rancho Grande."

All the joy left his face. "What?"

"I had to. It was in the trunk with my dress. I couldn't let them find it."

He could barely ask, "Why him? Why not beggars or the poor box? I already confessed. In a way I paid for it."

"He saved us."

He sat down on one of the church steps. "Andrea, you gave it to Smelly Hands, didn't you? You used our money to get rid of the curse on your house. You stole our money from us! That dirty boy has our money!" He shook his head in disbelief.

I made the sign of the cross. "I swear to God, Rancho Grande has our money. Now we know for sure he has a treasure." I tried to make my voice sound happy, but the attempt fell flat. "Maybe we can try to steal it back next summer."

"*All* gone?"

"Every bill." Now I was glowing.

"You could have kept some—just to play with." He thought for a while, then announced solemnly, "I don't want to get

that money back from Rancho Grande. He lives at the river. I hate that place."

I gloated and cautioned, "Don't hate, Victor. That's worse than cursing."

He made a fast sign of the cross. "Don't talk about this anymore."

I pressed. "One more thing."

Pain crossed his face.

"Smelly Hands ran away to the other side."

"How do you know?"

"Tony told me. And Popeye's is closed. Big boards are nailed across the windows and doors. Petra said they moved away forever."

"All that money . . . gone," he said sadly.

I reveled at the power I had over him. In a few minutes I had taken him from ecstasy to wretchedness.

A cheerful voice pierced me. "How was it, Andrea?" It was Mother.

I answered sullenly, "I don't want to talk."

Mother sighed tiredly. "Come on, Milita," They took envelopes out of their purses and returned to the church.

The ride home was long and silent. Our mothers tried to brighten the silence by taking us to an ice cream parlor on the way home. I savored the gloom of Victor's mood.

I never told him about the note I had sent Don Pancho, because I knew he would have applauded Don Pancho's beating Armida.

I looked over at him and felt no sadness at his depression. He had lost our money because of me and I imagine he felt I had betrayed him. But I knew that somewhere on the planet, for the remainder of her days, a *puta* would be asking herself, *What went wrong with my life?*

Mother parked the car to let out Victor and me. Tía Milita pulled up behind her. Dinner was scheduled to take place at

our house that evening. Our parents had designed a symbolic night-before-the-event feast. Paulette was to be the center of the evening.

I had lied at my First Confession, lied without remorse. My major sin was to Armida; that was my greatest sin and I deposited it in the vessel we carry inside our souls, the cold lonely vessel that holds pain and secrets that cannot be shared with anyone—for even in the telling the weight does not diminish. At an early age I learned what it was to be condemned to silence, to spiritual solitude.

I had also lied to my accomplice in sin and in doing so I lost him, threw him away and received nothing in exchange. Something had separated Victor and me that afternoon. This time it wasn't parents. It was something bigger. He had betrayed me, I felt, and so I paid him back and won something, but lost him.

Yes, we saw each other and played and laughed, but those special secrets that bind people's souls were never exchanged between us again. I remembered Father's advice of a few days earlier. "Love him. He will always need your love."

I was committed to love him.

## 25

PAULETTE stood on our front steps dressed in white slacks and white blouse, and hollered at Mother and my aunt as they got out of their cars, "Sure you want to come in?"

Good, I hope something terrible has happened, I thought.

Mother and Tía Milita froze in their tracks. Victor asked me, "Who's that?"

"My grandmother."

"No she's not."

I smelled a roast cooking.

Mother's face was rigid. "What's wrong?"

"Beats me. Come on in. I'll tell you the details," said Paulette.

Paulette introduced herself, "I'm Paulette, Diane's mother. You must be Milita. We missed each other last time I was here."

My aunt's English, which was usually quite good, was somewhere else. She answered, "*Mucho gusto.*"

She's frightened, I thought. I took back my wish for a catastrophe.

Mother took control. "Mother, what's gone wrong? Where's Hector? And Hugo?"

Paulette explained, "Both men were here waiting for you. They seemed restless. They had a drink, talked awhile. Hector asked Petra if someone from the newspaper had called. She said no." Paulette lit a Pall Mall and sipped at her drink. "Then the phone rang and Hector jumped to answer, heard the message and hung up. He embraced the doctor and sobbed, "He's dead.""

We all jumped from our seats and asked, "Who's dead?"

Paulette waved us down. Her face was serious. "This is where the plot thickens, people. From what I was able to make out, some matador—"

In chorus Mother and Milita asked, "Not Manolete . . ."

"Exactly. He was killed, gored in Spain yesterday." She turned to Mother and asked, "Remember how he raced out of here this morning? That's what all that was about."

"Hugo went away too," said Tía Milita.

Paulette said, "Apparently they've been across the border trying to get confirmation. They've received it more than once, I suspect, because after they raced out of here other newspapers called Hector. One from Houston, another from Dallas."

"Same message?" asked Mother.

Paulette nodded. "Can I fix you girls something? Milita?"

My aunt stood up, keys in hand. "We'd better go home. I'm sorry, Diane. I don't think the evening will work out."

"Dinner's already cooking," said Mother. "What's the difference?" She said this halfheartedly and seemed relieved when my aunt turned to Victor and waved him toward the car.

"There's too much to do tomorrow. The kids need their rest. Manolete's dead, but the First Communion has to go on." My aunt's voice was bitter. She added, "I dread thinking what condition they'll be in tomorrow morning."

"What a summer," said Mother, walking Victor and Tía Milita to the door.

"Nice meeting you," said my aunt. Victor waved goodbye not to anyone specifically; he just waved.

I don't know if Victor looked back at me. I too loved Manolete and knew that my father's adoration for the long-faced matador was not an idle fancy. I had come to love him too, perhaps because of Father's love, but also because I had witnessed the tall, thin-framed Manolete summon the bull to his territory and never recoil to avoid collision.

From Father I had learned what was taking place in the bullring. Killing the animal was not the issue. The bull was supposed to die. All that counted was *how* the matador lived that moment and *how* the matador brought the powerful bull to an honorable death. Sorrowfully I realized that my father would be changed forever. The purest of matadors was dead.

I suppose we ate something that night. Paulette was all I remember of the evening, other than the news of Manolete's death. I vowed to speak to no one but Father about the death.

After Milita and Victor left, Paulette asked me in her husky voice, "Well, Andrea, did you get all those sins off your chest?"

"Guess so."

"Good." She chuckled. "Nine-year-olds must be full of sins, huh?" She jerked my chin up to her face and looked into my eyes. I held nothing back. I let her see me. Paulette grew serious and said to me in a half-whisper, "Well, maybe there's something to that arrogant chin of yours." She placed her face parallel to mine and whispered, "Don't be too sorry for what you've done, Andrea. Your whole life has yet to be lived."

Mother was in a mood. Paulette was intolerant. "I didn't risk my life on a plane to come here and mourn," she said.

Mother snapped at Paulette, "Someone very important to my husband just died. This is no time for levity."

"What about tomorrow, kiddo? What about Andrea?"

"I'm all right," I said. "Bullfighters often die."

"Kids make their First Communion all the time too, but for each it's the first time," said Paulette, her voice laced with

sadness. "Andrea, want your hair cut? Or do you want to wear it in braids tomorrow?"

"Father said my hair was to be long until I'm fifteen."

"He's out of town. Want me to cut your hair?" she asked me.

Mother looked up, her face paling to blue. "Mother, I don't have enough problems, you have to redo my daughter? Girls here cut their hair much later in life. It's a whole big deal."

"I'll handle Hector. Tomorrow's a big deal."

I followed Paulette upstairs and stood with her before the bathroom mirror and watched her snip off my braids. My hair length came down only to my shoulders. It was stick-straight.

"I look like Tarzan, Grandmother."

Paulette looked into the mirror and admitted, "So you do. We have to make pin curls."

She took bobby pins and went to work. Soon all my hair was fastened in circular units. "You'll look great in the morning," she promised.

"Father's not really out of town, is he?" I asked.

"No," Paulette said. "He's just out mourning. Same thing. Tomorrow he'll feel so lousy he'll be asking that we ship him anywhere."

Paulette went to her room and returned with a long white scarf. "We'll tie your head up in this for tonight. You'll sleep more comfortably." She wrapped it around my head and made a bow at the top.

I looked at myself. Never—not even after the river kids had beaten me up—had I looked so plain and homely. I looked like a meatball sealed in a flour tortilla. I swallowed hard to keep the tears away.

"No, baby," said Paulette. "Don't feel bad. In the morning I'll comb it out and it will look fluffy and beautiful. Will you trust me?"

Mother came in and screamed. "My God! You did it!" Then my tears did come down—in a flood.

"The hair's still there, Diane. Andrea darling, don't. Please. Both of you stop this. It will be fine. The hair is still long enough to braid if braids are a must. They'll be a tad shorter, that's all."

Mother put her hands around her face. She looked as if she were trying to keep her head on. "What am I going to tell Hector? He loved her braids."

"That your crazy mother did it to make his daughter look like a beautiful young bride. You're dressing her up as one. Who ever went to a wedding where the bride wore braids?"

"Mom, you are crazy."

"I don't care what I look like," I sobbed. "I'm ugly and I'm going to hell anyway."

"What a fun household," scoffed Paulette. "No wonder Hector stays out so much."

"That's uncalled-for, Mother," said Mother.

Paulette left the bathroom and slammed the door to her bedroom.

I said to Mother, "I'm sorry. I didn't know how to stop her. She's trying to make us happy, I think. Now we've made her unhappy. She was happy when she got here. What's wrong with us?"

Mother hugged my head and kissed both my cheeks. "Come on, let's go make up with Grandma."

"I like calling her that better," I confided.

"Don't blame you," said Mother and winked. "Blow your nose."

Mother tapped lightly on the door. "Mom, I'm sorry. We both are. Can I come in?"

Paulette opened the door and stepped back to let us in. "I think we're a bit tired. Let's go on from here." She embraced Mother and hugged me tightly. "I promise you, my baby, you'll look like a million bucks tomorrow."

"Andrea, it's getting late," said Mother. "You have to wake up early."

I remembered my unsaid penance. I still owed two rosaries minus the five Our Fathers and twenty Hail Marys. "I'll put on my pajamas," I said. "Are you going to bed soon?"

"We'll probably talk awhile first," Mother said. "But we won't go anywhere. We'll chat right here. Are you okay?"

"I don't want to be by myself. I want it to be the day after tomorrow," I said. "I still owe some prayers."

"Penance?" asked Mother.

I nodded.

"Oh, Andrea. Scoot to your room and get that penance said."

Paulette said, "Somehow the word 'penance' doesn't belong in the mouths of babes."

I undressed and knelt by my bed, rosary in hand. I could hear Mother and Grandmother talking in the next room. Cristina slept soundly in her bed. I wondered about Father. I started my rosary and halfway through the first one my head dropped on the bed. I lost my place on the beads and started in the middle. I raced against sleep, whispered my prayers to keep myself from drifting into the following morning. It didn't matter to me if I hadn't told all my sins. I had to do this penance for God's sake.

I rambled, sputtered the Hail Marys; my count was off. I kept losing my place but I was convinced I had said more than enough. I crawled into bed exhausted. My head felt heavy from the bobby pins. I realized my braids were gone. What would Father say? Manolete dies and my braids are cut off—both on the same day. I found myself fully awake. Afraid to be alone, I left my room and moved toward the voices.

"I'm scared," I told Mother and Grandmother.

Mother asked, "Why are you still up? The door's open and the hall light is on. Is this something new?"

"It's the old Communion jitters," said Paulette. "Come get in bed with Grandmother."

"Mother, she kicks."

"I kick back."

I climbed onto the orange bedspread. Paulette had propped the pillows against the headboard and was resting casually on them. An ashtray was on her lap; a smoldering Pall Mall filled the room with smoke. Mother was lying down at the foot of the bed. I liked the way they looked together; it felt friendly. Everyone had someone.

"Let me pull down the bedspread, Andrea," Paulette said. "And here's a pillow. How's your head?"

"Heavy."

They both laughed. I got in between the sheets. They were new, smooth, cool. I still had my rosary with me. Mother saw it.

I quickly explained, "I finished my penance. I'm sleeping with it just for luck." I stuffed it under the pillow and turned over on my side. "Good night."

Paulette leaned over and kissed the top of my head. Mother took one of my feet and held it between her hands and kissed it. I am loved, I thought. *Love me too, God*, I prayed.

The room was silent. My breathing slowed down and I let my body rest comfortably in Paulette's bed. My eyelids were getting heavy when I heard my name. Their voices were low, subdued.

". . . open the world to her, Diane. Talk it over with Hector. Enough of that. Tell me why you abandoned your art. You studied for so long."

"I can't paint in this town."

"You can't blame Hector for that. Your studio is beautiful."

Mother's voice quavered. "He drains me. I can't explain."

"He adores you. Perhaps you married too young. The heat got to you at a dangerous time."

"He desires me—constantly."

Paulette chuckled. "Don't complain."

"There's more to marriage than that, Mother. You know that."

"After three marriages I know the importance of desire."

"You don't believe in spiritual or intellectual bonds?"

"Of course I do, Diane. But that wasn't why you married him. You were drunk with lust when you called me long-distance and announced your marriage. Let's not cloud the issue with talk of spirituality and all that other stuff. Now if the bonfire's turned to embers that's another story."

"I won't let my marriage fail."

"I'm afraid I haven't set a good example for you, have I?"

"I'm not resentful, if that's what you mean," Mother said softly.

"Thank you."

"Have you planned ahead?"

"Are you hinting at my age?" Paulette laughed quietly.

"I worry about you."

"To be truthful, I can't decide whether to spend my energies fanning the flames or putting them out."

They burst out laughing. The bed shook. I could tell they were laughing with their hands over their mouths.

# 26

WHEN I saw the orange bedspread I realized I had been allowed to sleep all night with Paulette. The bed was empty, the door closed.

I yelled out, "Where's somebody?"

Moments later, Father, unshaven and bleary-eyed, opened the door. "I'm right here, baby."

"When did you get home?"

"You were asleep."

"You got drunk."

He sat on the bed and looked at my head. "What's all that?"

"Paulette cut some of my braids to make curls."

He put a hand to his forehead. "She what?"

"It's all right. I wanted her to." My Holy Communion day and I had already told a lie.

He was speechless.

"Don't get mad, please. I have to have a good day." I held his hand. "I'm sorry about Manolete."

He swallowed, and squeezed my hand. "You know, he was going to retire after this season." He sighed. "Thirty years old, just thirty . . ."

He could hardly breathe. There is nothing anyone can do to help him with his pain, I realized. It has to lie there forever—like mine about Armida.

Petra came in. "Let's get ready, Andrea." To Father she said, "Let me bathe her first, señor. It won't take long."

Father said, "Tell me about her hair."

"I had nothing to do with it," Petra said quickly.

Father got up to leave the room. "Daddy," I said, "I'll offer up my First Communion for Manolete."

He looked at my face and at the scarf around my head. His face twisted in pain. "God love you," he said, his voice close to breaking.

Petra gave me a quick bath, reminding me constantly that I must not allow one drop of water to enter my mouth. She didn't even let me brush my teeth. "God must be the first and only thing that enters your body."

Grandmother's been married three times, I remembered. That meant she had loved, and stopped loving, someone three times. Did I have a grandfather? No one ever talked about him. Mother never talked about a father.

Americans are strange. They let go of things. I'm half American, I mused. I'm half of what Paulette is. I liked that. What was her world like?

Petra put on my dress. There were endless buttons in the back and around the wrists. The dress swished when I walked.

Petra said, "Put on your shoes and socks. I'll tell your grand-mother to come do your hair."

I went to the bathroom and waited for Paulette. I looked in the mirror and saw that I still looked horrible.

"You're still in doubt. I can tell," Paulette said. She was dressed in a cream-colored linen suit. Her blonde hair was combed back and held with a tortoiseshell clasp. She looked beautiful.

"Hurry," I urged. "I want these wires out."

She lowered the toilet seat and I sat on it. Paulette pulled out the pins with both hands. Her face was close to mine. I could see small lines around her eyes and mouth. Her nose was thin like Mother's. She put the pins in a small bag and then brushed my hair back. She brushed a long time and ran her fingers through my hair.

"Hmmmm. Better than I hoped for."

"I want to see."

She kept me down. "Not yet."

She took a comb and parted my hair on the side and brushed some more. Then she took white barrettes and placed them along the side of my head. With her fingers she brought some of the hair around my face. She stepped back and smiled.

Again I asked, "Now can I see?"

"One more second." She smiled and winked at me. "Don't get upset now." She took out a tube of lipstick from her suit pocket.

"I can't wear paint!" I said loudly. "This isn't a party. It's a holy day."

"Shhh. I know that. I know what I'm doing." She made a few light strokes across my cheeks with the lipstick and then rubbed in some Jergens lotion. "Now you can look."

Maybe it was the part on the side that made the biggest difference. I had always parted my hair in the middle. My cheeks weren't red as I had feared, but were a faint pink. The curls fell softly around my face. I liked myself very much.

"Tell me how you look," Paulette said.

"Okay."

"Tell me how you look," she repeated. "I won't tell anyone."

"I don't look like me, do I?"

"Of course you do. It's magic to move hair around and sneak in a little color here and there. No one will know the difference."

"I look older."

"Nine-year-olds dressed as brides look older. Let me put on the veil." She fastened it back on my head so that the tulle did not cover my face and curls. "You look beautiful, my baby. Even Hector will have to agree."

We marched downstairs. My parents were still at the dining-room table. Father was still unshaven.

"Behold the most gorgeous nine-year-old in the world," Paulette announced.

They looked and looked at me. Mother was the first to nod in agreement. "Absolutely marvelous," said Mother under her breath.

I waited to hear from Father. He stared at me with sad eyes. "You don't look like my little girl."

Close to crying, I begged him, "Don't say that. It is me."

"Hector, go shave," Paulette urged. "You don't look like yourself either."

Reluctantly he left the room. Mother excused herself and followed.

Paulette and I watched my parents climb the stairs.

"Don't worry about your daddy, Andrea. He'll come around."

"He's so sad. It's Manolete more than me."

"He's a big boy. Today's your day. Worry only about yourself."

"This dress is beginning to choke me already." The collar was stiff and rubbed harshly against my throat.

Paulette took my hand. "See that bag over there? Go look inside."

I walked over, the long dress threatening to tie itself around my ankles and send me to the floor. Inside the bag was a skirt, blouse, and light jacket. "They're the same color you're wearing," I said, pleased.

"You'll change after Mass and before breakfast," Paulette whispered. "No need to have you suffer in *that*."

"Did Mother say it was all right?"

"We'll surprise her. Put the things back in now."

"You mean it's a secret?" My spirits lifted. "It's just between us?"

"I guess it is. Do you like secrets?"

"I've got some," I admitted. "Do you?"

She smiled and reached for a Pall Mall. "A few."

"Grandmother, can I tell you one?" I didn't wait for her to answer. "I was pretending to be asleep last night. I heard you and Mother talking about me."

Paulette leaned over and fluffed my curls. "How would you like to come stay with me for a while?"

"You've been married three times," I reminded her.

"That's no secret, darling."

"I didn't know it. Does Mother have a father?"

"Of course she does. He's never kept in touch with us. He left when Diane was barely Cristina's age."

"Where is he?"

"Back East somewhere. It's been over thirty years, Andrea."

"He just left Mother and never saw her again? He left her when she was a baby?"

Paulette nodded. "I was a baby too, come to think of it."

"My father would never leave me. Why do you want me to leave him?"

"I don't, my love. Hector *loves* his women."

"Is Mother going to leave him?" I asked nervously and quickly added, "I heard her talk to you on the phone."

"I can't answer that. What goes on between a husband and wife is a *real* secret, a mystery." Her husky voice was lower than usual. She was talking to herself—not to me.

"Candelaria said to me that nothing lasts forever, and it's a long time till we die," I said loudly. I wanted Paulette to keep giving me attention.

"The old woman said that?"

I nodded.

"I like that," she said to herself.

"It scares me," I confessed. "I want to be with my father always. And I always want to be with Victor and—"

"Leave yourself room for change, Andrea. Don't hold on to things. People, places . . ."

I remembered Rancho Grande. "I get rid of things too. I give things away. But I don't want to be married three times."

Paulette laughed out loud. "I'll buy that!"

A LARGE congregation was gathered outside the church. Everyone was dressed in suits, hats, gloves. Cristina started howling immediately.

"Take her in around the side," Mother told Petra.

Once my sister was out of sight, Paulette and Mother put on their hats. I got out of the car and waved to my family's friends. Several women came forward to help me step onto the sidewalk. My heart beat rapidly and my hands shook.

"You look like an angel."

"She has curls."

"Diane, she looks beautiful."

Victor and his parents arrived. He was dressed as a cardinal and moved solemnly toward my family and me. "Now I've seen everything," Paulette murmured.

Victor heard his share of praises. He saw me and his eyes opened wide; he said nothing.

Swallowing my pride I asked, "Do you like my hair?"

"It's short."

Padre Lozano and four altar boys waited for us at the church entrance. Victor's parents gave me my candle and my parents gave him his. Victor's parents were now my godparents; my parents were now his.

The priest led the way to the altar. Before giving us the

Eucharist Padre Lozano spoke to us. "This is the most important moment of your lives. It is the end of childhood and the
beginning of adulthood . . ." He didn't look at us. He spoke
to the entire congregation. "The acts that you commit from
this day forward are not the acts of children . . ."

My chest felt constricted. *God I'm sorry. God forgive me.*

The Host felt dry in my mouth. Padre's fingers were thick
and forced me to open my mouth wider. I moved my tongue
and created enough saliva to allow the Host to dissolve; then
it just sort of slid down. I bowed my head, waiting for Victor
to receive his Host. Then Padre distributed Communion to
several people lining the altar rail. I looked back and noticed
Father was not receiving Communion.

My heart went out to Father. He had had no time to make
a confession. I decided he would receive my First Communion
kiss. Petra had told Victor and me that whoever received a
First Communion kiss would never die with a mortal sin on
his soul.

The thought was fascinating and the anticipation of kissing
Father and saving his soul made the rest of the ceremony go
by faster. I did pray for Paulette and Manolete, for Petra,
Mother, Cristina, Candelaria and Armida.

Mass ended and photographers blinded us with flashbulbs.
Our godparents led us back up the aisle and out to the church
steps, where more photos were choreographed. Victor and I
were pulled here and there, separated, united.

Then someone called out, "*El primer beso de comunión.*"
The First Communion kiss.

People stepped back and suddenly Victor and I were again
the center of attention.

I looked around and called, "Daddy, it's for you," and held
my arms out to him. The crowd clapped as I kissed him. He
held me tightly, his eyes moist. We posed for pictures. Father's
lower lip shook.

Then came Victor's turn. Father and I stepped back. In a strong clear voice I heard him call, "Andrea, it's for you," and he held his arms out to me. He kissed my mouth twice.

*THE* banquet was noisy with the laughter of guests. I noticed that Tony was not among the waiters serving us. He and his wife sat with our friends. A large table held numerous presents. I was still tasting the sweetness of Victor's mouth, the wonder of his gift.

I wanted to ask when he had decided to do this for me, but I dared not speak to him of it. I left it alone, locked it in my heart—and felt the charity of his kiss magically absorb the bitterness that only a few days before had nearly killed me. The collar around my neck itched and I had scratched myself raw. Both Victor and I were sweating. I undid the buttons around my wrists. That gave me the freedom to reach for as much sweet bread as I wanted. Victor and I ate with pleasure, throwing table manners out the window.

I felt a light tap on my shoulder. It was Paulette. She had the small bag with her. "Ready to change, Andrea?"

I followed her. Victor looked at me, his face shiny with sweat. I sat back down. "Thank you, Grandmother. I'll wear this. It's just one day. It won't be forever."

# 27

I WAS with Paulette every possible moment until she left. Victor was unable to be with her for even a few minutes.

Playfully, she teased him. "Come here, you beautiful cardinal. Let me kiss those eyes, those long lashes."

Victor froze; Paulette held her arms out to him and beckoned. I shoved him forward, and explained to him, "She's just playing, Victor."

Paulette's voice softened. She lowered her arms. "I don't want to frighten you. You are one of the most beautiful children I have ever seen." She smiled coyly at Victor. "Old as I am, I still admire a handsome man."

Victor stood there. I laughed out loud, trying to make up for my friend's silence. "He's shy around people he doesn't know."

Paulette tousled his hair lightly. "A sign of sensitivity. I've got news for you, young man, you are going to have women draped all over you someday. Grab him while you can, Andrea." She winked at us, lit a Pall Mall and went upstairs.

Victor waited until she was totally out of sight before saying, "I don't know what to say to her. She's strange." He scratched his leg vehemently.

"Stop scratching. She's gone now. You're stupid. Don't you think she's funny? I want to be just like her."

"Your hair is dark."

"I'll paint it."

"When is she leaving?"

His question reminded me that Paulette would not always be with me. "I hope she stays forever," I said.

"Well, she can't, and after she leaves you're going to want me to play with you and maybe I won't."

I stayed with Paulette and was consoled by her promise: "This Christmas you'll all be with me. I'll get the biggest tree and maybe your mother will play the piano for us and we'll sing. Do you like to sing, Andrea?"

"Grandmother, it's my favorite thing."

"That settles it, then."

The day she left, she moved around too quickly for me to cling to her and cry. Father loaded up the car and then I was being kissed—not in a special way—I was kissed with the kind of kisses you get when there are lots of people to kiss. Paulette even kissed Candelaria and Petra.

As soon as the car pulled away, I felt alone and fearful again. I had hidden my shame, my pain about Armida, by nestling in Grandmother's arms. I thought of Victor with his solemn promises never to sin again, and was glad that I had dived into Paulette's happy noise.

Yes, I chose Paulette over Victor, and after she left I avoided Victor and took to waiting around outside the still-boarded-up Popeye's. I longed for another chance to stand before Armida and tell her what I had done to her life. My plea for forgiveness remained unsaid, my sin unredeemed.

One evening Petra came for me as I sat outside the store. "It's no good, Andrea. The store will never open."

"You don't know."

"I do know." She took me by the hand.

"They have to come back for the things in the store. They can't leave all that stuff in there." I thought of the hidden money that was probably somewhere up in the loft.

Petra pressed my hand. "Don Pancho sold the store. He has moved to another town."

"Does he have a lot of money now?"

"Why do you care about those people?"

"The lady was my friend. Don Pancho was mean to her. I hate him."

"Think of other things, Andrea," she said. "The lives of those people are none of your business."

I argued, "But he hit her in front of everyone. And why did Candelaria laugh when Armida's teeth got knocked out?"

"She meant no harm. What happened to that lady was very sad."

"Petra, did everyone think it was sad?" I trembled inside. What if I told Petra I had done it all?

"People are cruel. Some laughed."

"Victor would have laughed. He thinks he's so good."

"He wouldn't laugh now. No one laughs about Armida anymore."

I heard something dark in Petra's voice. I pulled at her and asked, "Did Don Pancho kill her?"

"No, my Andrea," she whispered. "Not Don Pancho." She drew in her breath as if to take back what she uttered. It was too late. She had said the words I feared most hearing.

My legs felt it first. I hit the sidewalk, falling completely, wishing the ground were soft enough for me to burrow into—and to let the earth cover me forever.

Petra tried to lift me. I was too heavy. "What have I said, dear God," she cried. "My baby girl, my baby girl. No, please." She knelt beside me, took me in her arms and asked, "What have I said? Andrea, tell me."

My mouth flooded with a bitter yellow liquid and I vomited on the ground and over Petra and myself. My stomach moved in endless spasms. With the hem of her dress, Petra cleaned my mouth. Carefully, she worked the black material across my lips and chin.

Although Petra's face was right in front of me, I could barely see it. I felt that whatever was me, whatever was inside of me that told me I was alive, was getting smaller and smaller.

When I was able to take a full breath, I begged, "Petra, listen to me. If Armida's dead, I killed her."

"Shhh. Stand up. Come up." She put both arms around my waist and lifted me. "Don't even think that," she ordered. "Come on, walk."

"Petra, it's true. I did it—not on purpose. It's like the watchman. It was an accident."

"Andrea, no one killed Armida. No one *killed* her. Do you understand?"

I felt myself going limp again. "She's dead, Petra. Right now, she's in the ground—dead, isn't she? If no one killed her, that means she did it to herself, doesn't it?"

She nodded.

"How?"

"They say she used a rope."

I screamed, "She's burning in hell! You can't do it. You can't kill yourself. She's in hell! Petra, help me!"

I hit her arm countless times, hoping to shake some new, less horrid words from her. She found the strength to carry me home and put me to bed without Mother hearing my cries. I cupped my hands across my mouth and howled silently, forcefully, into them. I struck my thighs, scratched my legs, and tore at the inside of my mouth, but I felt nothing.

Mother came in, worried. She took my temperature and decided that I was overtired. Father followed, trying to talk to me. I feigned a sleepy weariness.

Finally, Petra brought up some dinner. She looked frightened. "I'm not going to say one word to you," she said.

"She's burning in hell, isn't she?"

"No one knows what God does. There are rules, but He is merciful. He can forgive anyone. No one, do you understand, no one can speak for Him. The woman suffered enough in this life."

I asked, "Did you know she was a *puta*?"

"Who tells you these things?" She was angry. "Where do you learn these words? Is this what you and Victor do? Talk trash?"

I asked again. "Did you know she was a *puta*?"

She put the tray of food next to my bed. "In a small town like ours, we look into each other's lives every day. We know." She left the room.

I wished with all my heart that Petra was right. I yearned to be high up somewhere and let people look up and see me, see *into* me. I wanted them to see me reaching into the coiled rope and taking Armida's stockings full of money. I wanted them to see me throw the note and rock through the window. Such a little rock.

*The note, the beating, the rope.*

I sat up in my bed, wrapped my hands around my neck and squeezed. My thumbs pushed back my throat. I felt my eyes swell. The room blurred. A hum rang in my ears and traveled to the top of my head. I pressed harder, dug my thumbs deeper into me. My right thumb ripped something. The blur became gray, then black. Next it seemed as if I were exploding inside. Desperate to breathe, I coughed—a painful gagging cough. My stomach quivered and again, bitter yellow liquid filled my mouth and spewed onto my covers.

Father raced into the room and I clung to him; in what sounds I could manage, I implored, "Take me with you, Daddy."

He carried me into his and Mother's bedroom. My coughing had become uncontrollable spasms, broken by hoarse, mournful cries that begged forgiveness from no one my terrorized parents could see.

I slept between Mother and Father that night and many nights thereafter. Only when their bodies pressed next to mine would I allow my eyes to close.

# 28

**M**Y convalescence lasted a week, but the damage to my larynx was permanent. My voice remained hard, raspy, hoarse. It was lower than Paulette's, so she teased me when we spoke long distance.

Victor came to see me twice a day—whenever his father came to check my throat. Uncle asked me several times about the bruises on the outside and how it happened. Every time he asked, I merely replied, "I fell."

Victor said he liked my new voice and treated me with a gentle, motherly kindness that allowed me to forgive his resolution to "never commit a mortal sin again."

School brought us together. Our classmates moved ahead; we stayed behind with the same nun. We laughed together again, our laughter always receiving an extra boost when a manly croak escaped my throat. Our games were played indoors. Victor played cautiously, holding every move, every act to a religious measure.

I went along and I saw that in his own pru-

dent manner, he was trying to connect with me in the same places where our lives had once meshed. Impatient, I finally lashed out at him, "Do you know that Armida killed herself?"

Apparently he hadn't heard. His face paled and he looked at me with violent crazy eyes. He covered his ears and shook his head. "That's from *before*. Don't talk about *before*, Andrea!"

I asked, "Before what?"

He reached toward me and grabbed my forearm and dug his nails into it. "Before we confessed."

I put the palm of my hand across his face and shoved him away. "Don't do that to me."

"I'm sorry," he added quickly. "You've been sick. I'm sorry."

He patted the same forearm he had just punctured, then rubbed softly at the broken skin as if he could erase the four half-moon incisions he had carved into me. His face looked sickened by what he had done. I stared at him and sensed fragile, tender cracks inside him.

I said, "All right, we won't talk about her anymore."

"Andrea, she went to hell."

I kept inside my private, painful mourning about Armida. "We can't say what God will do, Victor."

With certainty, he said, "We can about this."

I looked at my friend and felt superior. I visualized his horror if he knew of my connection with Armida's death. I experienced almost a drunken rapture knowing that with a few words I could cripple him.

Looking at the face of beautiful Victor, I dipped into that dark, deep chamber where I had learned to deposit my personal despair and this time, instead of grief, I tasted consolation and pleasure. I judged Victor to be an innocent who would never in his life come to know the pain I had already known.

Briefly I wondered if he had such a place, a cold, lonely room where he hid what he could never share with the world, with anyone at all. No words could capture what is in that

place, I had decided. Once the pain is sealed in there, it changes and so do you.

I envisioned my secrets as knots that swelled and shifted color—from orange to purple. They waited for me to summon them. One was always in the center. Armida was my biggest knot.

No, Victor has no such place, I thought.


CHRISTMAS was coming and Father was driving the family to be with Paulette. Victor wasn't happy with our plans, and I was flattered to see that for a change he would be the lonely one, he would be the one to miss me.

"What if we have to tell each other something important?"

"Like what?" I asked.

"Something. We can't call."

"Write it on paper and we'll read it when I come back."

"That's no good," he said.

Two weeks before we left, he came up with a solution of how we were to maintain contact while we were separated. Every day after school we unraveled balls of twine and tied them together. Eventually, each of us had hundreds of feet which we then rewound into two large separate spheres.

Victor worked out the communication system for when I would be in Los Angeles. One pull was a simple hello. Two pulls meant everything was fine. Three meant everything was terrible. Our code went up to ten. We tested it between his house and mine and it worked.

The day finally arrived. Father and Petra piled suitcases on top of the car and tied them down. The return date was uncertain, and as I saw them squeeze more of our belongings into the brown car, I realized I was going to be separated from Victor for the longest time ever. Mother had chosen all I was to take; but feeling that I needed some tangible keepsake of

what I was leaving behind, I demanded that I be allowed to take the straw hat Victor had bought me in the plaza on the day we went on our glorious spending spree.

Father called, "All aboard!"

Hurriedly, Victor and I united our twine with coarse knots. I hugged him before climbing into the backseat. He gave me a teary smile. I waved to him from inside the car. My friend stood on the sidewalk in front of my house, his face pale, and he clutched his ball of string tightly to his chest.

The car took off and the twine unraveled—as planned. Shocked, I shouted, "It's working!"

Victor jumped up and down and laughed. He was elated, proud of his invention.

Then the car turned the corner and the string snapped. I begged Father to stop.

"I can't, Andrea," he said impatiently. "We have to be in Del Rio by tonight."

# 29

TRUE to her word, Paulette did get the biggest
Christmas tree, and Mother did play the piano
and Father and I sang in English. I fell easily
into Paulette's world—once she reassured me
that the nickname Tallulah was not the name
of a savage.

Christmas morning Victor's family called.
Father and Uncle talked for a long time. Impatient, I pulled on the telephone cord. "Put
your son on the line," Father said. "Someone
here wants to talk to him."

Despite the static on the line, I started crying
the moment I heard him say, "Andrea, our
string broke."

My voice shook. "I still have my half."

"Me too. Did you get a lot of stuff?"

"Clothes. Grandmother has a store."

"Andrea, this is my first Christmas without
you."

I burst into loud moans. "Don't be mad. I'll
tell Mother what to write to you and you tell
your mother what to write to me. Okay?"

There was a barely audible "Yes," and the line went dead. He had hung up.

I looked at my family and yelled, "I want home. I want Victor. I don't want to be here anymore."

I ran into Paulette's room—my room as well—and cried. She followed and threw her soft white robe over me and cradled me in her arms. She was skinny, but strong and hard. I trusted myself with her.

"Crying for friends is all right, kiddo."

I let go with renewed energy at the thought of Victor's and my balls of twine lying separated so many miles away.

"But you know what, Grandmother?" I asked, not caring that my nose was running. "He said this was his first Christmas without me and I hadn't even thought of that."

She stood with me in her arms and dropped me onto the bed. "Nothing like the glooms to flatten a holiday. Enough of this, Andrea. Wash your face. Get pretty. I'll help you write your little cardinal tonight. By tomorrow a letter will be on its way to him."

I wrote Victor that day and then again after New Year's Day. I received a card from him with Jesus in a manger surrounded by shepherds. His mother had written, "May you enjoy all the blessings of this holy season." In his tiny, squared-off writing, Victor had signed his name, *Victor Escalante*.

Once the excitement of the holidays was over my parents took me to a throat specialist, Dr. Davies, a plump pink man with rosy cheeks and neatly trimmed fingernails. Mother and Paulette stood by me as he gently placed a tongue depressor in my mouth and made me go "Aahhhgh." He did this several times, until I gagged.

"There is some scar tissue there," he said. He looked at me and asked, "Tell me again how it happened."

"I fell."

"I know. But against what? It wasn't a sharp object. There is no puncture anywhere. Can't you remember?"

"No. I don't remember," I said angrily. I got off the table and told Mother, "I'm going outside with Father."

Mother and Paulette stayed to talk with Dr. Davies for a while, long enough for Father and me to go buy some ice cream and take our time walking back to the office. I heard nothing else about the visit to the doctor until later that night when Paulette and I were in bed.

"The doctor said time will heal your throat," she said. "But your voice will stay lower than normal. You may need an operation someday."

"I don't care. I like the way I sound."

"Andrea, did you do it to yourself?" Her voice was low like mine, and lying there next to each other in the darkness, the tones of our speech circling around us, bound me to her more than ever.

I told her, "It was something I had to do. Don't ask me more."

"Are you glad you did it?"

"Yes. I had to do it. Don't ask me more."


FATHER was getting restless. He called his business frequently, and there were long conferences between my parents and Paulette. One evening after dinner Paulette took me by the hand and asked, "Have you thought further about staying with me? Would you like to go to school here?"

"You mean all the time?"

Mother said, "We found a wonderful school for you."

That angered me. "When did you go look for it? You never said anything to me." I looked accusingly at Father. He avoided my eyes. I asked Mother, "Are you leaving him?"

Everyone said, "No."

"You mean I would stay here all by myself?"

Paulette said, "With me and with all the new friends you'll make."

I looked at my beautiful Paulette and thought of her world.

"What about Victor? He'd be alone. I'd be alone. I don't want new friends."

Father cut in. "Andrea, your uncle is moving his family to Mexico City. Victor won't be there when we go back. In a few months we'll be moving to Mexico City ourselves."

"Are you running away because you ran over the watch-man?" I asked. "We don't have any more friends—is that why you're making us move?"

Father reached out to grab me, but Paulette stepped in front of me. "Andrea," she said, taking me by the shoulders, "don't say anything you'll regret. Your parents are going to be very busy making that big move. And I want you here. I asked them to please let you stay here with me. You can attend a beautiful school for girls and you'll come home to me on week-ends and we'll go to all sorts of places. I thought you'd like that."

I pulled away from her, from all three of them. "Live at a school by myself? Why do you want to do this to me?"

Mother said, "Your grandmother works. You can't stay here alone. It will be good for you. You'll learn other ways, new things."

I looked only at my father and asked, "Do you want me to change?"

He shook his head. "Not change, baby. We want you to get a better education, learn another way of looking at things. You'll always be my special girl."

"Not if you leave me here, I won't. I think you're doing this so she won't leave you."

"Why are you so cruel, Andrea?" he asked. "Do you think I want to leave you? Do you? You're afraid. Don't be. I know you can be tough, baby. Be tough now."

"Daddy, if you leave me here, I swear to God I'll never go back to you. Never."

His eyes full of tears, he pleaded, "Shhh. Don't say that to me."

Paulette put her arms around him. "She's feeling betrayed, Hector—she's right. That's enough, Andrea. No one wants to hurt you."

"I already swore to God. Remember that, Daddy."

# *Epilogue*

❧

## 1968—Venice, California

WE wrote; my letters were always longer, more frequent; and, as time passed, we sent each other our annual school pictures. Paulette had been right: Victor was becoming a poetically beautiful young man. When we were fifteen, I took to proudly carrying his picture in my wallet and bragging that he was my boyfriend. I enjoyed posing as a bereaved woman separated from the man in her life. I wrote and told him so because I still needed him to measure my actions.

*Dear Andrea,*

*Don't show my picture and don't tell your friends that I'm your boyfriend. I am really mad. I have your pictures and I tell people you are my cousin and that's how I think of you. I am not sending you any more pictures.*

*Victor*

Stunned, angry, bewildered, I took his picture and tore it into as many fragments as possible and mailed them back to him.

*Keep your pictures, jerk. I wish you could have felt every tear I made. Who needs you anyway?*

*Andrea*

The letter was a lie. I needed him. When Mother brought photos of him, I would take them from her, absorbed by the changes in him and I would fight with myself to keep from writing and asking that we forgive and forget.

I placed his pictures with all the other mementos of my early life with him: the ball of twine, my straw hat, our First Communion pictures, and his short boring letters etched out in rigid penmanship that had never changed.

No, I never stopped wishing for Victor. I carried him inside, and lived my life as if I had a second set of eyes, the ones I used for myself and the ones I used for him. I needed my life to be witnessed by him. No new friend ever replaced him.

Hungrily, I turned to music. That filled the emptiness—somewhat. I had always wondered what it was that I could do with ease and feeling, and with Paulette's help, I found music. I wanted Victor to hear my guitar, and I imagined his surprise when he heard me play. I knew he would criticize my still husky voice, and disapprove of my choice of song—I liked blues, especially rough and biting Bessie Smith. I fantasized arguments with Victor in which I would chide him for his narrow-minded priggishness. I waited in vain for his letters but I too refused to yield.

I also refused to yield to Father's invitations to come home to Mexico City, that unknown place where my parents forged new lives. Father's realm seemed small compared to the breadth of Paulette's. She housed me in a place that gave me direct access to my self; Father's world required a narrow passage before I got to me.

Nevertheless, my family's visits to Los Angeles were frequent and not limited to holidays. Although our reunions were

cordial, joyful times, efforts to lure me back failed. The unspoken conspiracy between Paulette and me was to keep me busy with "crucial projects" that could not be interrupted. Mother beamed at my love for music; Father listened to my Bessie Smith songs and nodded in vague approval. Little by little, their requests that I return became less insistent. It was clear that Father had abdicated to Paulette. His visits were marked by a docility foreign to me. He acquiesced to whatever Paulette, Mother, Cristina, and I wanted to do.

IN 1958 I finally flew to Mexico City. Father had promised me a big surprise. Victor was it.

Tall, slender, pale, he smiled broadly as I threw away all resentment of the past five years and embraced him with all the strength I had.

I yelled in English, "It's you! Let me look at you. Are we made up, Victor?"

He waved away my question. "We were pretty silly." He looked closely at me and shook his head and laughed.

I stepped back to get a fuller view of him. His face was lean, the shape of his chin and nose was fine, delicate. His eyes were the same: dark, deeply set in their thick lashes.

He and Father carried my luggage to the car, Victor's car a light blue Opel that barely accommodated the three of us because of all the presents Paulette had sent.

Father complained, "He insisted on driving this little rat of his. I feel like my ass is dragging over the road."

Victor made a gesture of helplessness at Father's nagging and started his car. Gracefully, he weaved in and out of Mexico City traffic. I noticed his expensive watch, his blue sapphire ring, and thought, He's a bourgeois.

But despite what my San Francisco Underground poets would have said of a young man like Victor, I found him lovely, smooth, worth many hours of gazing.

His smile was particularly engaging. I had never seen Victor with his adult teeth—all his school pictures had been serious, studious, ardent. His eyes had had a faraway look, his mouth was always closed, the lips brought together with a sealed certainty that denied frivolity.

Riding home from the airport I stared, marveled at the even whiteness of his smile and I noticed that when he was forced to laugh at Father's uninvited constant navigating, Victor would offset his chuckles with a furrowed brow, never wholly surrendering himself to mirth.

When we arrived home, Cristina bounded out of the house, followed by Petra, only slightly grayer than the last time I had seen her—eleven years ago. She quickly asked, *"Por qué de luto?"* Why are you dressed in mourning?

Cristina exclaimed, "You're a beatnik!" She had discovered makeup and tight sweaters and she was pretty, prettier than I would ever be.

Then the family chaos took over. Mother gave me a foot-by-foot tour of their house, a long, proud tour which detailed cost and labor. Petra followed us closely and finally felt my entire body. She decided I was ill. She claimed my eyes told her so. Father put a new guitar in my hands and suddenly we were singing. Victor disappeared.

I called him for two days but couldn't reach him. Tía Milita was evasive as to his whereabouts. Then one afternoon as I was talking to Petra, he rang the doorbell.

Petra scolded him. "She's been looking for you. Where have you been?"

I added testily, "Didn't you get my messages? I left at least half a dozen with your mother."

Casually, he answered, "I've been getting my passport ready. I leave for Europe on the fifteenth."

"Forget it," I said. "Sit down. I'm getting caught up on old news. Remember Candelaria? She's still alive and working. Tell him, Petra."

Victor waved her to silence.

"Well, anyway, Tony is still at the club," I continued. "We should have our pictures taken and mail them to him. He'd still remember us. What do you think?"

Softly, flatly, he said, "No. There's no point in looking back. Let's go for a drink."

"Good, let's go."

He looked at my casual attire, sized it up, and I figured he decided to let it go. He led me to his Opel.

"I like hearing about the past from Petra. Why didn't you let her talk?"

He brushed his fingers through his hair and sighed heavily. "I've heard it all. Small-town news. Who cares?"

He disturbed me. "Don't you think those days mattered? I think of them all the time." He ignored me, drove in silence. I pulled at his sleeve and demanded, "Shit, talk to me."

He flung off my hand. "Stop that. Those days are over. Everything seemed big then. Can you imagine Candelaria walking around here barefoot with her pipe?" He laughed hollowly, changing the pitch in his voice to alter the course of our conversation.

He smiled and said, "All I can think of is my trip to Europe. I've been studying languages for the past three years. This summer will be my chance to test them out. I love Italian."

"French too?" I asked sarcastically. "And maybe German? But with an Austrian accent—keep it clean and all that?"

"Andrea, you're so predictable. Don't try to bait me. You know nothing about me."

I wiggled around restlessly in his tiny car. "So fill me in. I want to know everything. I'm going to tell you all about me. I don't mind."

I wanted to pierce him, but he seemed only mildly uncomfortable with my blunt declarations.

Deftly he squeezed his tiny car into a parking space that

would barely hold a refrigerator and I followed him into an Irish pub. Oak, brass and copper everywhere. The patrons were Americans, for the most part, plus a few young Mexicans as fashionably dressed as Victor. Apparently the establishment knew him; all he had to do was hold up two fingers and they brought us two Irish coffees.

Seated at a tiny round table, I held my cup up to him and toasted, "To our reunion."

He clinked my cup and drank carefully. I failed to guard myself and the hot liquid scorched the tip of my tongue.

"Jesus! Shit! Fuck!"

He laughed. "Well, now that you've met everyone, are you comfortable?"

I looked around and saw everyone was looking at us. "Sorry, that hurt. I hope I didn't spoil your image or anything." I wiped my mouth and blotted specks of whipped cream off my skirt. "This isn't going very well, is it?"

"Don't try so hard. What did you expect?"

My eyes filled with tears. "Something wonderful. I'm going to embarrass myself and maybe you too. But Victor, I haven't stopped thinking of you in all these years. I'm not in love with you. It's nothing like that. Thank God. But in a way it's more. I've never been as close to anyone." I hiccuped. "I'm talking too much, aren't I?"

Gently, he placed his hand over mine. "We're still best friends, Andrea. No one has taken your place. But you're tearing at me and I won't have that. You want to take me back to that smelly town we grew up in and I won't go. I was miserable there. Don't you see?"

Sometimes a simple question is all it takes to drive a point clear to the core of oneself. I saw that he was right. I had been wanting to tear him bare, had been wanting to regain my place in his life, and so I pulled back, and in doing so, I let him slip away from me—I didn't know how far. That day, the message

that I received and accepted was that if we were to continue to be friends, we were going to start from scratch.

I never asked myself, What's he hiding?

I returned to Los Angeles and almost at once the letters started coming. Once, after he returned from Europe, I complained to him, "I like getting your letters, but you're not telling me any good stuff. All I know is what movies you see and where you intend to go next. Shit, Victor, I don't even know if and how you got laid yet."

I was punished for that. I didn't hear from him for two months. I swallowed my pride, wrote, apologized. His letters resumed. I learned to accept his privacy and left him alone.

My letters to him were confessional journals. I told him every lurid detail of my college years, my romantic, at times miasmic, involvements that left me exhausted, torn. Throughout my twenties, I related to him how Paulette would put me back together, always with kindness despite her weariness over the recklessness with which I pursued experiences. My music, Paulette, and my outpourings to Victor kept me clean.

His letters were tolerant, soft in their admonishment: "I don't understand why you do this to yourself. Do you ever wonder where it's going to lead? Is there something at the end that is worth all you do?"

I was blind. I settled for those words from him. I should have hounded him, cornered him, if necessary, beaten my way into him.

I am haunted by my paucity of energy, by the ease with which the wit in his letters deceived me. When I decided to go into business, he sent merchandise from all over the world to help me stock my boutique. His letters with their beautiful foreign stamps I mistook for worldliness. As time passed, the tone in his writing changed, grew tired. This affected boredom I mistook for sophistication.

The last time I saw him was five months ago, December 15, 1967. I arrived in Mexico City late in the evening. Holidays were the only times I visited family—beginning and ending dates are so set, there's never a need to explain a return time. I wasn't surprised to find Victor waiting for me at the airport.

I asked, "Hector and Diane suckered you into it, huh?"

His hug was a tight squeeze. "Actually I volunteered. When I went by a couple of days ago, they weren't speaking to each other."

"They're back to that again. Maybe they're trying to put passion back in their lives."

He threw his head back and laughed. "Don't tell me. You're still in therapy, right?"

Angrily I snapped, "Is that wrong?"

"It's just that you go around knowing and understanding so much. It's boring."

"Victor, let's not fight so soon, okay?"

We hugged and I followed him to the car.

"Auntie said your singing is taking off."

"Don't believe her. She exaggerates. Last month three clubs let me sing for free."

"What about the demo you made?"

"They thought it was interesting. I hate that word. I've been more successful selling songs than singing them."

"Is that enough for you?" he asked tenderly.

I fumbled for a Kleenex. "Hell no, Victor. I want to perform so badly I can taste it. I want to be the one singing my songs. Time's passing me by."

He drew me to him. "Sorry I mentioned it. Listen, I have good news. There's a new singer in town. I saw him last time I was in Barcelona. He was ousted from Spain for his anti-Franco songs."

"I want to hear him. Take me."

"Of course. Tonight, tomorrow night, every night you're

here if you want. He's fantastic, Andrea." His eyes glowed with excitement.

"If you tell me he's young, I'm going to cry again."

He gave me a gentle nudge. "Sorry, early twenties. Andrea, don't give up. You've worked so long." He lowered his voice in imitation of me. "I like your singing."

I laughed. His clowning always surprised me. "It's easy for you to say," I countered, "You're so goddam rich. Every time I come you have a new car."

"Accounting pays, but it's boring. Hey, listen, if things don't get better, you can always marry for money."

"That does it!" I yelled and pulled at his ear until he screamed.

Victor was right. Alejandro the singer was wonderful. On a rough wooden stage was a straight-back chair. The announcer simply said, "Ladies and gentlemen, Alejandro." The singer moved quickly to the chair and sang. He was there to deliver a message and that he did with anger, sadness and rebellion.

He sang in Catalan and in Spanish. He had long sideburns and he handled his guitar with a caressing sensuality that took my breath away. Some songs were angry calls for revolt; some were mournful, plaintive ballads to dead heroes. He sang with his eyes closed, unaware of the audience. Sweat saturated his white silk shirt. After each song, the applause seemed to shock him out of a private world, and he would stand before us, tall and frail-looking and bow shyly. When he smiled, I was struck by the similarity between Victor and him. Both had an androgynous quality, a beauty that draped uneasily in men of such height.

We stayed for the second show and Alejandro's performance had the same concentrated intensity I had witnessed earlier. I watched, made mental notes and saw how great the distance was between a singer like him and myself. I clapped wildly and made sure he heard me. He wiped his forehead with a

white handkerchief and nodded to where Victor and I were seated.

"Victor," I said, "he's looking right at me. Look! He's staring at me."

"Don't get too excited," Victor whispered. "From what I hear, women aren't his first priority."

"Bullshit."

I asked Victor to wait in the car, then I went backstage and introduced myself to Alejandro. I elbowed my way into his dressing room and made myself the center of his attention. If women weren't his first priority, I could not tell. We talked. He liked my politics. I told him I also sang, and he insisted that I sing for him.

I promised, "I will—tomorrow."

The next night I went to the club alone. I arrived early to ensure I had a ringside table. Alejandro had been packing the small house to capacity. The club sat maybe a hundred patrons—most of them young and politically conscious. I asked myself how it was that Victor came to discover a singer with leftist leanings, but didn't press the thought further.

Halfway through the performance I noticed Victor at a table on the other side of the stage. I waved at him. He looked away and lit a cigarette. Both of us stayed until the end of the evening.

I walked to Victor's table and said, "He's expecting me."

"I'll wait, Andrea. You may need a ride home."

I went backstage and went home with Alejandro. I never thought of looking out front to see if Victor was still waiting. I was too involved being close to someone who could find two countries to listen to his music.

For me Alejandro was a simple stop, a quick stop made on a two-week visit. That was all. We both understood the exchange and took pleasure from the encounter. It was a soft night of romance and song. I sang for him, translated my lyrics.

"Why do you sell things? You should just sing."

"I need to live," I explained. "No one will support me just singing."

"When people know that all you do is sing, they will help you."

"Sure," I said.

I didn't see Victor for the rest of the time I was home. I couldn't reach him by phone or find him anywhere. I went to the club, combed through the audience, but he wasn't to be found. So I turned to my family.

I spent a Christmas and New Year's with them, and even though, as always, I craved Victor, I discovered a new perspective toward that cluster that had once seemed so vital to my existence.

Diane and Hector had reached that state in their marriage where they no longer worked at changing each other, and what they had lost in fervor they gained in peace. When Father stayed out late, Mother read and turned out the light early. Her shopping went unquestioned; her constant redecorating met the approval of Father and friends. My parents entertained; they laughed as a couple; they dressed in unconscious color harmonies.

But it was Cristina who intrigued me most of all. She had married early and her Reymundo was a writer, a scholarly man who taught Spanish literature at the University of Mexico City. They had a daughter, a two-year old devil child who won my heart. Her name was Zaloren.

Reymundo explained briefly, "I chose the name because it had no meaning. She will have to give it some. I liked the sound, don't you?"

I agreed and spent the days with my family teaching the dark-eyed Zaloren how to stroke a guitar, how to break strings, how to howl melodically to please herself. She loved the power of pulling strings, making them hers, and I reveled in the power

of her choosing to be with me and let her test new boundaries of sound and strength. She tested me and pulled violently on my long hair and I loved the vehemence of her tugs.

I looked at Cristina and Reymundo and said, "Someday, I'll be her Paulette." Only Petra and Mother seemed slightly amused by my announcement.

New Year's Eve the family dined with a few of their friends. I was sure Victor's family would be among them. Mother told me that Tía Milita had not been feeling well for some time.

The evening was quiet, once Zaloren had collapsed exhausted on my lap. I accompanied Father as he sang some of his old favorite songs, and together with the warmth of Napoleon brandy we sang a teary version of his and my favorite duet, "Amorcito Corazón." The song touched a vulnerable center in several of the guests and Father and I gladly encored.

Mother broke the nostalgic moment. With a clear strong voice she announced, "I miss nothing of those good old days. You can have every damn one of them."

Finally I understood. I walked over, clasped her tightly against me and whispered, "I don't know how you did it. I couldn't have."

"Andrea, do you mean it?"

"I swear it, Mother."

She gazed calmly at me. "I never thought I'd hear you say that."

Not wanting to lose that moment, I begged off Father's offers of another Napoleon to "welcome in 1968," refused requests to sing more songs, and politely thanked the guests, who assured me that I was surely going to succeed with my music. My flight was scheduled for the next day. I lay in bed and ran the evening through my head. The din in the house died down and the door to my room opened slowly. It was Petra.

Automatically, I held my arms out to her.

She whispered, "I wanted to say my special goodbye. Thank you for my present."

"Petra, you're more my mother than my family, more than all I know. You formed me."

She shook her head. "I did as your father ordered."

"But you understood him. Who else?"

She smiled. "No one except maybe Candelaria."

The name brought me out of my sleepiness. "What do you know about her? If it's bad, I don't want to know."

"You're the only one besides your father who wants to remember those early days. Maybe because you live in another country now, I don't know. Your friend never wants to hear of those times."

"Tell me about Candelaria."

"One day she disappeared. The family she worked for tried to find her. They never could. That is all I know."

"She's dead."

"She was old. But she never allowed herself to become part of a family. We used to talk about things like that. I am fortunate, your family treats me like one of their own."

"You are."

"Candelaria once asked me, 'Where do birds go to die?' I said I didn't know. She laughed at me and warned, 'You'll want to know the answer when your time comes.' "

"That's a riddle, isn't it? I will write a song of it."

Petra leaned over and kissed me. I watched as she padded softly out of my room, the room Mother had designated as mine during my visits to them. I thought of the tiny apartment I lived in; it was above my little boutique. I loved my own home and felt relieved to know that I would leave the next day. Before I fell asleep, I reached out for Victor, who had failed to be with me on my last night.

Early the next morning, I was ready to leave. My luggage was bulging with presents for me and Paulette and goods for

my store. My bleary-eyed father was shouting angrily over my "excesses."

Victor appeared. "I borrowed a van from a friend. I'll take her."

Relieved, Father handed me over to him and pecked me uneasily on the cheek. "My head's killing me, baby."

Victor and I rode in silence. I had had time to figure things out by then.

I waited until the airport lights beamed ahead of us before speaking. "I didn't know Alejandro was so important to you. Why didn't you tell me? Who you love and the way you love is no big deal to me, you know."

Silently, Victor maneuvered the van to a parking space. He motioned several hungry carriers over to the vehicle and tipped them generously.

Dryly, he said, "Give me your ticket."

"I can do this by myself. I'd rather you talk to me. Look at me. Why didn't you tell me Alejandro was that important? It's no big deal."

"You're so predictable, Andrea." He followed the carriers to the baggage check-in.

Angrily, I called out to him, "Victor, don't walk away from me. You're sadistic."

He laughed softly. "You have a label for everything, don't you?"

I mistook his laughter for an opening and moved closer, put my hands on his chest. I looked up to his face, pale and beautiful.

With all the gentleness in me I murmured, "Victor, you can tell me anything. Don't you know that by now? Haven't I shared every detail of my life with you? Don't all these years mean something to you? I have my hands on you and I don't *feel* you. You've pulled away from me." Despairing, I begged, "Don't do this. I'm sorry about the singer. He was nothing. I

can't leave feeling that I've done you some terrible wrong. I know it's Alejandro. Has that been it all this time? All these years? Don't you know anything you do is all right with me?"

His jaw tightened. His entire body became rigid as I pressed closer to him. He looked down at me and smiled bitterly.

"Andrea, I've never cared for what you think. I love you, not your thoughts. Already I hear in your voice a generous tendency to forgive me."

"Are you ending things between us?"

"No. I'm not vindictive. I'll keep rooting for your singing. And of course, I'll keep sending you things for your boutique. I want you to do well."

*Mexico City*
*May 24, 1968*

*Dear Andrea,*

*Spare me your pity and your anger. Celebrate with me. Trust me to have done the right thing for myself.*

*The decision to do this was made long ago. Mother's early death last month liberated me to take this step. I could never have left her to suffer my loss.*

*This letter asks nothing from you, least of all forgiveness. I want to assure you that I am relieving years of pain, pain so constant a companion that at times we seemed lovers. Often I have begged God to send me another love, to let me hold the hand of joy. He never has.*

*You have often expressed admiration for my success. Now I should tell you that I have envied the facility with which you start over. I have never seen you defeated. From a silent distance I have coveted your ease with violence and love.*

*You were born to move at will, but I was cast, cast so solidly that the slightest breach tormented me. In my travels I pursued new rules. I tried to bend, but my soul censured my desires so savagely*

that I craved death. I have lived through many little deaths, Andrea. This is merely the formal act.

I am gambling that God will receive me in His arms earlier than He decreed. I laugh as I write this because I have never taken a gamble in my life. Truth is, I am exhausted with living a spiritual life on earth.

Earth and what it offers, and what I want from it, have never borne me anything but wretchedness. Perhaps others like me are able to exist spiritually on this temporal plane. For me, the compromise has not been possible, nor, to be truthful, desired.

Believe that this act is my hedonistic choice. Applaud and love me as you have always. My last words I send to you, the only person I allowed to love me, the only person I have truly loved.

Victor

I finally got his letter—fifteen days after Mother's call. Victor would have been annoyed that the letter took so long to reach me. Knowing him, he probably gave it five days at the most. He registered it. That may have delayed it some. It was also my fault. I paid no attention to the yellow slip of paper left by the postman.

For two weeks I tried to understand the why of it all. I relived every moment of our lives together. I closed my store. I didn't want to see the merchandise. His signature was everywhere—on the papier-mâché animals, the hand-stitched Indian blouses, the belts, the dresses.

I went to my closet, stood on a chair and threw everything down from the top shelf.

I found the albums. The soft black pages had separated from the string that was to serve as binding. Some of the deckle-edged photographs scattered around my feet. I lay on the floor and pressed those early pictures to my lips, to my breasts. I pressed them hard. I wanted them to enter me and never leave me. I read and reread his letters and postcards.

Sickened by all my unsaid words, I found myself yearning for a ritual, an act, a prayer outside myself. I had fought to keep myself whole and I was losing. I realized I needed to divorce, to cleanse myself completely from him.

Lying among those mementos was the straw hat Victor had bought for me in the plaza the day we stole Armida's money. I tore the hat to shreds and spread the brittle straw throughout my apartment.

I chanted, "*Madre Santa, Madre Purísima.*"

Then I swept it up and out my front door, where I regathered it and put it in a paper bag and set fire to it. It blazed for twenty seconds—at most.

Even exorcism had failed.

I looked down at the tiny pile of ashes and screamed, "This is a dirty trick, Victor, a dirty rotten trick!"

Blind with fury, I filled cardboard boxes, every large market bag, old suitcases with the albums, the postcards, letters, all the merchandise that was downstairs, all that Victor had prom-ised would sell, and crammed everything into my car and drove the two blocks to the beach.

It took over an hour for me to unload the car and haul everything to the seashore. I made a high neat pile—nothing was to get away. Then I doused it all with charcoal lighter and lit it.

Sunset had started, the tide was low, and I could hear the crackling fire. It was a warm evening but I sat close to the flames and listened as they devoured all I held most dear to me. Tearfully, bitterly, I howled at my burning past.

"Victor, you loved me. All these years you loved me—but with restraint. I spit on your control, on your fear of yourself. You abandoned me. I first saw life with you. You had no right to sever that tie. Had you asked me, I would have given you permission. I would have kissed you farewell. You denied me that. You left me nothing but your death."

Onlookers gathered and stared into the fire. Invaded, I gath-ered a fistful of sand and flung it at them. "Get away. Get the fuck away from here . . ."

"All right. Crazy bitch."

Burdened, crushed, sinking, I keened, "Victor, why didn't I give you my First Communion kiss? Dear love, it was you who truly needed it. How quick you were to judge Armida's fate in hell.

"Armida, my first view of woman was you. Your blood is on my hands. I threw the death stone. Can you hear me? It wasn't on purpose. Armida, do you know the number of nights I have shuddered in shame, buried my face in my pillow, as I recall how Don Pancho beat you? Your legs parted in front of our neighbors. My voice bears the brand of my unredeemed sin toward you.

"A rope held your treasure which we stole. You used a rope to save you from dishonor.

"Victor, I never told you that: I killed Armida. You may have thought I was right in doing what I did. I kept secrets from you, Victor. I protected you, spared you. I shouldn't have. You kept secrets too and your secrets killed you.

"How smug I was to think I was the only one who had a secret chamber. How cold and lonely your crypt must have been. Why did you accept those precut patterns? Why did you fear inventing new roads for yourself? It kept you from loving life. You enslaved yourself."

The beach was dark; the flames were nearly dying. Gentle breezes carried the ashes upward and away. Some fell on me, and as I brushed them off, I saw that I was truly alone.

The loneliness afforded me freedom I dared never take. I returned to my car and drove away. I searched for the pyre in my rearview mirror but I couldn't see it.

Unburdened, clean, I vowed to start over.

Victor was right—I'm not afraid of regeneration.

If it is madness to envy others' happiness, it is equal folly to follow another's anguish.

I will speak of that now. I will sing of it now.

To
Aida Gomez de Fontes

⸻

*You led me to the books
that asked the questions,
then pointed to
the typewriter.*